Folk Stories from the Hills of Puerto Rico / Cuentos folklóricos de las montañas de Puerto Rico

Folk Stories from the Hills of Puerto Rico / Cuentos folklóricos de las montañas de Puerto Rico

RAFAEL OCASIO

RUTGERS UNIVERSITY PRESS

NEW BRUNSWICK, CAMDEN, AND NEWARK,

NEW JERSEY, AND LONDON

Library of Congress Cataloging-in-Publication Data

Names: Ocasio, Rafael, editor.
Title: Folk stories from the hills of Puerto Rico = Cuentos folklóricos de las montañas de Puerto Rico / [edited by] Rafael Ocasio.
Other titles: Cuentos folklóricos de las montañas de Puerto Rico
Description: New Brunswick : Rutgers University Press, [2021] | Series: Critical Caribbean studies | Includes bibliographical references and index. | Stories in English and Spanish.
Identifiers: LCCN 2020034450 | ISBN 9781978822993 (hardcover) | ISBN 9781978822986 (paperback) | ISBN 9781978823006 (epub) | ISBN 9781978823013 (mobi) | ISBN 9781978823020 (pdf)
Subjects: LCSH: Folklore—Puerto Rico. | Folklore—Fieldwork. | Boas, Franz, 1858–1942—Travel—Puerto Rico.
Classification: LCC GR121.P8 F65 2021 | DDC 398.2097295—dc23
LC record available at https://lccn.loc.gov/2020034450

A British Cataloging-in-Publication record for this book is available from the British Library.

♾ The paper used in this publication meets the requirements of the American National Standard for Information Sciences—Permanence of Paper for Printed Library Materials, ANSI Z39.48-1992.

www.rutgersuniversitypress.org

Manufactured in the United States of America

In memoriam

In memory of Agnes Scott College Emerita Associate Professor of Spanish M. Eloise Herbert, whose friendship and mentorship guided my academic career for many years. Her gifted skills as a translator facilitated this project. I so much wish she could have seen this book published.

Contents

A Note on the Stories

The original texts were published without much editing in order to preserve the oral narrative devices of their cultural informants. In a few instances, I have edited the length of extremely long sentences and clarified subjects of restrictive clauses. Although the informal oral flavor is preserved, I have reduced the use of transitional conjunctions to facilitate a more dynamic reading. I also edited accents, punctuation, and capitalization to follow current practices, and all typographic mistakes were corrected. The format was redesigned to highlight dialogue, and long paragraphs were split up.

My English translations are based on the revised Spanish texts. Occasionally, multiclauses characteristic of oral Spanish are translated as independent sentences, given the preference in English for shorter sentences. In a handful of cases where a reference to a cultural artifact is integral to the understanding of the plotline, an effort was made to find an equivalent or the importance of the object is explained in the introduction.

Folk Stories from the Hills of Puerto Rico / Cuentos folklóricos de las montañas de Puerto Rico

Approaching Guayama from the interior, by the Military Road, Porto Rico

Introduction

A los antiguos cuentos legendarios siguen hoy otros del mismo carácter pero procedentes de regiones sajonas que van introduciendo nuevas ideas, nuevos mitos, y suplantando aquéllos que sirvieron para formar el ideal racial, por así decirlo, de las pasadas generaciones.

Following the old, legendary tales are today others of the same character but products of Saxon regions that are introducing new ideas, new myths, and supplanting those that served to form the racial idea, so to speak, of past generations.

—Rafael Ramírez de Arellano, *Folklore portorriqueño:
Cuentos y adivinanzas recogidos de la tradición oral*

A NOTE TO SPANISH-LANGUAGE READERS

Esta antología recoge cuentos orales representativos de la cultura rural del jíbaro o el campesino puertorriqueño, que fueron compilados durante La investigación científica de Porto Rico y las Islas Vírgenes (Scientific Survey of Porto Rico and the Virgin Islands). John Alden Mason y Franz Boas, destacados antropólogos y folkloristas norteamericanos, en visitas a la isla entre 1914 y 1915 documentaron cientos de historias protagonizadas por personajes populares: la simpática pareja de enamorados, Cucarachita Martina y Ratoncito Pérez; el valiente y generoso pirata, Roberto Cofresí; y el "tonto más listo del campo," Juan Bobo. Los cuentos de la abuela han pasado de generación a generación; hoy continúan enseñando a los niños sobre tradiciones populares mientras que deleitan a los adultos con sus ingeniosas adaptaciones de protagonistas de cuentos de hadas internacionales, tales

como la Cenizosa, una Cenicienta jíbara. Una más extensa introducción en español se encuentra disponible en el siguiente enlace: www
.rutgersuniversitypress.org/cuentos.

DOCUMENTING A PUERTO RICAN IDENTITY THROUGH ORAL FOLKLORE:
THE SCIENTIFIC SURVEY OF PORTO RICO AND THE VIRGIN ISLANDS

At the end of the Spanish American War in 1898, Puerto Rico was handed
over to the United States, and a U.S. military government was established to
administer the colony. American readers learned of this newly acquired
possession, if at all, through maps and scientific field research that encour-
aged the financial exploitation of the island's natural resources. Further,
knowledge of the island was available to Americans as eager readers of
popular scientific magazines like *National Geographic*, a publication that
was widely available at an affordable price. Most commonly, however,
knowledge of the island spread through descriptive travelogues written by
eager American travelers. They also photographed the island's breathtak-
ing tropical geographical features and produced photographic portraits
of certain types of inhabitants—among others, street vendors, fishermen,
and farmers proudly posing with their delicious and exotic produce.

American colleges and universities frequently made Puerto Rico the
site of large-scale research projects, as the island became a laboratory for
field studies in various scientific areas. In 1913, the New York Academy of
Sciences, hosted by the Puerto Rican government, started the Scientific
Survey of Porto Rico and the Virgin Islands, a sizeable, complex project
that has been described as "one of the most complete descriptions of the
natural history of any tropical area ever attempted" (Figueroa Colón viii).

Under the direction of Franz Boas (1858–1942), the Scientific Survey
also included the comprehensive cataloging of native archeological rem-
nants and the recording of the island's expansive oral folklore. Celebrated
as "the most important single force in shaping American anthropology
in the first part of the twentieth century," Boas led a team of archeolo-
gists who scouted the Puerto Rican rural landscape in search of physical

documentation of the native Taíno nation (Stocking 1). Their most significant finding was the "ancient village site at Capá," which had functioned as a ballpark with a strong religious significance to the indigenous Taíno. Boas himself arranged for the Puerto Rican government to survey the privately owned plot and recommended that it be purchased and preserved as an archaeological park. This action would have protected the area from illegal excavations that had already begun.

Boas's recommendation did not become reality until 1956, under the administration of Luis Muñoz Marín, the first Puerto Rican governor elected by popular vote. The eventual restoration of Capá, known today as Centro Ceremonial Caguana (Ceremonial Center Caguana), has directly impacted a community of Taíno descendants both in Puerto Rico and in the United States who have come to consider this site as their rightful ancestral home for the performance of religious and socioethnic indigenous celebrations.

In early December 1914, John Alden Mason (1885–1967), a young anthropologist and folklorist, arrived on the island to prepare the way for Boas's trip, which took place a few months later, beginning on an undetermined date in May 1915. During the month he was there, Boas continued his research, recording and analyzing the physical measurements and proportions of different kinds of people in Puerto Rico. On November 6, 1913, Boas wrote to Arthur Yager, the American-appointed governor of Puerto Rico at the time, reporting that he intended to explore "the effects of race-mixture with reference to form of heredity in man" and "the effect of tropical environment upon the development of man."[1] Although he had traveled to Puerto Rico shortly after having facial surgery that removed a potentially cancerous tumor, he kept a busy work schedule. Most of his stay in Puerto Rico was devoted to the anthropometric documentation of boys and men, data that sourced his only article written about the trip to the island, "The Anthropometry of Porto Rico."

Boas was also a pioneering folklore scholar (Zumwalt 69). His earlier work with the Inuit, which included both physical anthropology and linguistics, led to a career as "one of the most creative and prolific participants in the project of modern anthropology" (Jacobson 33). He also documented Native American oral folklore traditions from both the United States and Mexico.

Boas supervised Mason on a second extensive field research project in Puerto Rico. Mason was charged with documenting rural oral folklore through transcriptions of his conversations with peasants of varying ages and from a variety of geographical locations. From people well known in their communities as entertaining storytellers, Mason wrote down an out standing number of oral folklore samples: poetry, conundrums, sayings, tales, legends, and anecdotes. He also noted the striking rural traits of the Spanish spoken by the "jíbaro de la altura" (peasant of the highlands), who became his favorite performers of native forms of oral folklore.

Mason also recorded their rural musical performances. The musical repertoire of the Puerto Rican peasants was extensive and well known throughout the island. *Aguinaldos* (Christmas carols), which he must have enjoyed upon his arrival in the early days of December 1914, caught his attention, but he also recorded other popular metric poetic songs, such as *décimas*, *bombas*, and *versos*. The songs were recorded on wax rolls, to be played on a small Gem Edison phonograph. Proudly, he indicated to Boas on January 5, 1915, that he had located two "very good singers who are eager to sing (for a slight compensation)." These musical samples from the early part of the twentieth century are among the first such modern recordings produced in Puerto Rico for the purpose of linguistic investigation.

The authentication of the largest possible number of samples was Mason's goal, as part of an extensive process that had the support of the administrators of the Puerto Rican public school system. Through them, Mason gained access to numerous schoolchildren in rural areas who were asked to write down oral folklore pieces. Indeed, Mason traveled extensively throughout the island, visiting schools and training teachers in how to instruct children on documenting techniques. The instructions, as school superintendent Edward M. Bainter detailed to teachers on December 10, 1914, included having children interview older individuals known in their communities as reputed storytellers. The children were also instructed to write the stories down "from the verbatim dictation of a person who has lived many years in Porto Rico and is acquainted with some old legend or tradition."

The children wrote profusely. They produced a massive collection that Mason summarized as riddles, poetry, and "muchas canciones populares, romances, cuentos cantados y otro material musical" (many popular songs, ballads, sung stories, and other musical material; *Folklore puertorriqueño* 10).

Other cultural informants who served as writers included adult storytellers. Like the schoolchildren, they were rural people of varying ages and from a variety of geographical locations. These individuals worked hard for Mason. As he reported to Boas on January 12, 1915, they took great pride in "making a real effort not to duplicate material." Mason was ultimately satisfied with the work done: "The material on the whole is very well written, both as regards style and orthography."

By asking rural individuals to write down oral folklore samples, however, Mason did not realize that both the children and the adults were acting as formal "authors" of the pieces—indeed, for these stories, it was the first time in Puerto Rican literary history that they had been written down. Unfortunately, the stories appeared in publication without an indication of the type of transcription method used or any information about the identity of the informant, such as geographical location or name.

Mason's collection was earmarked for publication in the *Journal of American Folklore*, the official publication of the American Folklore Society, of which Boas served as an editor. At the time, this reputable journal was seeking to expand its geographical focus to include coverage of Latin American oral folklore. Beginning in 1916, the *Journal of American Folklore* began the publication of Mason's compiled folk material, edited by Aurelio Espinosa (1880–1958). A folklorist and Spanish professor at Stanford University, Espinosa cofounded the American Association of Teachers of Spanish and Portuguese (AATSP) in 1917 and served as the editor of its journal, *Hispania*. As he often referred to himself, Espinosa was a Nuevo Mexicano, well versed in New Mexican oral folklore after having conducted his own field research in the southwestern United States.

Espinosa edited all the story samples gathered by Mason to conform to traditional Spanish grammatical structures—or, as he insisted to Boas on October 9, 1916, "in [as] correct Castilian as possible." He also standardized the vocabulary of the agrarian practices of Jíbaro storytellers while providing alternative terms that were easily understood by international Spanish speakers.[2] As the only native Spanish speaker involved in the editing project, Espinosa frequently highlighted "my intimate knowledge of Spanish & the dialects," as he proudly proclaimed in his letter to Boas dated April 24, 1917. Regrettably, the original texts did not survive; today there is no way to perform a comparative analysis of Espinosa's editing processes—turning the Jíbaros' grammatical structures into "correct Castilian"—or to review his methodology of sanitizing the colorful vocabulary of the Puerto Rican countryside, transforming the peculiarities of colloquial phrases into standard Spanish.

Folktales dominate the oral folklore project, which celebrated local characters experiencing rural traditions. As a whole, Mason described the stories as of "traditional Spanish origin, although often changed or distorted" ("Introductory Remarks" 143). He also collected oral stories of Black folklore, which he vaguely categorized as of "African origin" (143). Unfortunately, these so-called African stories did not appear in a published form, nor do any transcriptions of them exist. Surviving field notes indicate, however, that Mason documented the island's rich culture of African descendants in Loíza, a fishing village on the northeastern coast.

Mason carefully recorded his numerous activities while in Puerto Rico. He collected a significant number of folk stories in Utuado, a rural town at the heart of an agrarian-based society. Located at the Cordillera Central, on a mountainous range, Utuado served Mason as an outstanding site for the exploration of Jíbaro culture. Boas came to know Utuado well, as home to the archeological ruins of Capá.

While Mason and Boas were engaged in their research, local literary writers, political analysts, and politicians were simultaneously engaged with a pronationalist project. Jíbaros, depicted as White people of Spanish descent, became identified as representatives of a well-developed Puerto Rican identity. Their close attachment to ancestral Spanish traditions that had adapted to the island's rural setting created a vibrant hybrid culture that even today is seen as the "heart" of the Puerto Rican identity. In the early part of the twentieth century, when U.S. federal laws started imposing political control over the island, compilations of local folktales that established a national identity in literary form started appearing in Puerto Rico. Historian Cayetano Coll y Toste's *Tradiciones y leyendas puertorriqueñas* (*Puerto Rican Traditions and Folk Legends*), although published in book form between 1924 and 1925, had already been featured in newspapers throughout the 1910s. Coll y Toste (1850–1930), who was the official historian of the Puerto Rican government, also strove to preserve popular renditions of historical accounts as a testimonial documentation of a Puerto Rican identity.

Through his political and cultural connections, Mason was introduced to other scholars performing oral folklore research in the field. Mason met Coll y Toste upon his arrival in Puerto Rico. Local folklorist Rafael Ramírez de Arellano, who had been working on an oral folklore project for twenty years prior to Mason's arrival, in his *Folklore portorriqueño: Cuentos y adivinanzas recogidos de la tradición oral* (*Porto Rican Folklore: Tales and Riddles Collected from Oral Tradition*), fueled political discussions about the pronationalist values of native folklore as a basis for literary productions and as an ideological representation of Puerto Rican identity.

Mason was certainly interested in identifying colorful characters and local themes. His choice of the Jíbaro as the representative of a native Puerto Rican culture not only determined the type of stories collected but also shaped the ways that he uncovered the folk material. Mason clearly favored rural characters and stories that emphasized the customs of the

Puerto Rican *campo*, the countryside that was a setting of sentimental importance to the people he interviewed.

The folk stories were extremely popular with the tightly knit Jíbaro communities. Mason noted that storytelling was a favorite source of entertainment, often performed at *velorios* (wakes) held over the dead. A field note documented the popularity of storytellers: "The assembled company tell stories all night to keep awake and those with good reputations as storytellers take pain to increase their repertoire." His own writers had learned "muchos cuentos" (many stories) in "beladas [*sic*]" (all-night soirees), where stories were told "para quitar el sueño" (to keep people awake). In such communal gatherings, the stories were passed down from previous male storytellers.

Upon his return from Puerto Rico in early July 1915, Boas briefly described to the New York Scientific Board Mason's oral collection as "many hundreds of folk tales, riddles, rhymes, ballads, songs, [that] ... will give us a clear insight into the traditional literature of the island" (qtd. in Baatz 212). He was hopeful that the stories would have a utilitarian value. While referring to the role of the Puerto Rican Department of Education as an important agent in the actual collection of the oral folklore pieces, Boas revealed his expectation that this material could "furnish reading matter for the rural schools, attractive and interesting to the children" (Baatz 212).

Except for the riddles, published many years later in book format as *Folklore puertorriqueño: Adivinanzas* (*Puerto Rican Folklore: Riddles*), the work gathered from the oral folklore project remains unpublished in Puerto Rico. Significantly, most of Boas's biographers have either ignored his trip to Puerto Rico or treated it as an afterthought in his busy international and national travel schedule. The complex details behind Boas's and Mason's research trips to the island as part of the Scientific Survey of Puerto Rico and the Virgin Islands are the subject of my book *Race and Nation in Puerto Rican Folklore: Franz Boas and John Alden Mason in Porto Rico*, which serves as a critical guide to this anthology of selected folktales.

Indeed, in my use of the imposed renaming of the island as "Porto Rico," I highlight ways in which Puerto Ricans managed to oppose U.S. federal mandates imposed upon sociocultural traditions.

Jíbaros as Spokespersons of a Puerto Rican National and Cultural Identity

Mason frequently spoke to Jíbaros of the mountainous heartland, who loved to retell and reinterpret traditional folktales, native legends, and fables. They drew from local characters and subjects that spoke to them within the harsh socioeconomic environment of the Puerto Rican countryside. They also incorporated references to rural traditions as settings or plotlines that fully defined the characters as peasants.

Mason fell for the charms of the picturesque town of Utuado as he experienced daily agrarian traditions and festive celebrations. Founded in 1739, Utuado had an important role in the development of a type of Puerto Rican rural culture that since the nineteenth century has been described as a "símbolo de la criollidad y de la puertorriqueñidad" (symbol of Puerto Rican creole culture and Puerto Ricanness; Alicea Ortega 54). Fernando Miyares González (1749–1818), a Cuban native who served as a secretary to the Spanish governor of Puerto Rico beginning in 1769, highlighted Utuado's isolated geographical location as "tierra adentro" (inland; 68) with a "clima fresco" (cool climate; 69) in his travelogue *Noticias particulares de la Isla y Plaza de San Juan Bautista de Puerto Rico* (News about the Island of Puerto Rico and the city of San Juan). He was impressed by Utuado's "fértiles campos que producen con abundancia arroz, maíz y café" (fertile fields that produce in abundance rice, corn and coffee; 69) and its "muchos ganados" (many cattle; 69).

Whether Mason chose Utuado because he knew about these travelogues that underscored its developed rural culture is not a topic of discussion in his ample correspondence with Boas. However, his surviving field notes reveal that Mason was struck by the area's agrarian landscape. He also notated medicinal practices, such as his earliest entry in December 1914: "The bite of the poisonous spider is cured by soaking the same spider in rum and drinking it."[3] Scenes from rural daily life are often reflected in the oral folktales, whose settings are often either the local or a mythical countryside, while the characters themselves are clearly common peasants.

A missing piece of data from the published pieces is information about the narrators, including age, gender, and ethnicity. On March 19, 1915, Mason portrayed them as "the Gibaros [sic] in the hills." He continued, "[They] present greater variations as the negro blood is less, the white blood predominating with traces of Indian blood." Even though an important component of his field research included the anthropological exploration of surviving Taíno cultural practices, Mason failed to document the rich indigenous oral folklore—often religious myths— widely available in the island's mountainous areas. Luckily, today Taíno myths are available through the efforts of local indigenous associations grouped as Indian nations.

Mason did not display the common biased views toward Jíbaros, who since the colonial period and after the Spanish American War were often described as culturally backward. In fact, he preferred to work with "ordinary gíbaros," a qualifier he never explained to Boas. The references to his search for *muy bruto* (crude) Jíbaros implied, however, his desire to collect samples from illiterate peasants.

When Boas invited Espinosa, freshly arrived from Puerto Rico on July 12, 1915, to serve as the editor of Mason's Puerto Rican samples, Boas shared his pride in the fact that the material (left unquantified) had been "largely written by young Porto Ricans." Although rural children within the public school system wrote "hundreds" of the folktales, there was never any description of the methodology Mason used to prepare the children for this task. Mason did not record their ages, genders, or literacy skills (in terms of their schooling levels).

Telling folktales in Latin American societies is a popular activity that informally teaches and allows one to "make sense of the world people could not control, to reinforce traditions, and to pass along wisdoms" (Elswit 1). A year after his trip to Puerto Rico, in his critical article "The Development of Folk-Tales and Myths," Boas stressed the reflective nature of oral folklore: "The formulas of myths and folk-tales, if we disregard the particular incidents that form the substance with which the framework is filled in, are almost exclusively events that reflect the occurrences of human life, particularly those that stir the emotions of the people" (405). Folklore, according to Espinosa, had an intricate value as the "estudio de la vida de las gentes, de su modo de pensar, de su arte, de sus creencias y prácticas" (study of people's lives, about their ways of thinking, their art, beliefs and practices; "La ciencia" 9).

Boas had indirectly influenced Espinosa's own field research. Espinosa had also edited Paul Radin's oral folklore from Mexico. Radin, a former student of Boas at Columbia University, published a Mexican oral folklore collection in 1914 that thematically resembles not only Mason's Puerto Rican oral folklore but also Espinosa's own pioneering samples documented from Spanish-speaking communities in the U.S. Southwest.

Espinosa considered Mason's collection to be the "más abundante e importante de cuentos hispanoamericanos que hasta ahora se ha recogido" (most abundant and important of Spanish American stories ever gathered; *Cuentos populares* 18). The lengthy editing, which lasted from 1916 to 1929, was rather contentious, given that Espinosa often objected to Mason's transcription practices, including the quality of the written pieces produced by the rural children and adults. Espinosa frequently questioned the origin of the stories while pointing out the possibility that students copied versions from school textbooks or cheap commercial children's books. Boas remained marginal in these disputes, often to the detriment of the working relationship between Mason and Espinosa.

Espinosa was responsible for the initial thematic groupings of the folk stories as *Cuentos picarescos* (Picaresque stories), *Cuentos de fuerza y valor extraordinarios* (Tales of extraordinary force and courage), *Cuentos de encantamiento* (Stories of enchantment), *Cuentos del Diablo* (Stories of the devil), *Cuentos de brujería* (Stories of witchcraft), *Cuentos de animales* (Stories of animals), *Cuentos puertorriqueños* (Puerto Rican stories), and *Cuentitos, anécdotas y chistes* (Brief stories, anecdotes, and jokes). Animal stories reveal an obvious connection to Puerto Rican fauna, while Puerto Rican stories document legends about local heroes of historical significance. Anecdotes incorporate native characters as they go about their daily routines while performing rural tasks underscored as cultural traditions. Some of them are also jokes with heavy gender and racial biases. Traditional fairy tales comprise the largest portion of the collection and are the most complex of the stories, formally and aesthetically.

Puerto Rican Folk Stories: Tales of Princesses and Tricksters from the Hills of Puerto Rico

The present anthology gathers Puerto Rican folktales that underscore two types of oral folk stories. First, there are readaptations of well-known international fairy tales, ingenious examples of redeveloped plotlines and adaptations of characters to fit the needs of a rural Puerto Rican audience. Tales of adventure also follow the same pattern of introducing children or young people as protagonists, whose situations, although perhaps foreign to rural Puerto Rican children, appeal to them because of their similar plights in growth and development.

The folktales chosen for this anthology are solidly grounded in rural cultural practices; often they provide the background for exciting plotlines and popular Jíbaro characters. The stories also draw on two types of local protagonists. First, there is Juan Bobo, fully established in a long Hispanic picaresque literary tradition, who has become synonymous with the ingenuity needed to survive harsh socioeconomic conditions. Juan Bobo's stories are most frequently published in English translations in the United States as representative of a strong Puerto Rican cultural identity.[4]

The *campo*, the lush countryside at the heart of native Puerto Rican traditions, is often the stage of many of the folk stories. The hinterlands, also referred to as *el monte* (the wilderness), can be a dangerous place, as the second type of a daring local protagonist fully reflects. Anecdotes about feared bandits, such as the infamous historic pirate Roberto Cofresí, were at the time of Mason's visit widely known throughout the island. Cofresí's adventures are *leyendas* (legends), which even today highlight a Robin Hood–like hero with a strong popular appeal among children and adults alike.

Chapter 1, "Jíbaro Readaptations of Fairy Tales: Snow White and la Cenizosa (Cinderella)," groups rural adaptations of two popular international fairy tales: Snow White and Cinderella. Whether schoolchildren actually wrote these stories is not as important as the deviations from the original tales. Some of the new components celebrate rural traditions common to the Puerto Rican countryside. The stories also incorporate local religious customs and key supernatural characters such as fairy godmothers and evil and good witches.

Puerto Rican traditional fairy tales often warn listeners about dangers lurking in the countryside. The first version of Snow White highlights the classic evil stepmother figure. Although she is described as a witch, her attempts to kill Snow White are not of a supernatural nature. Three times she hires help to poison Snow White, whose flaw is precisely that she ignores the many previous warnings by the wise dwarfs to avoid coming into contact with strangers. In the second version, the differences in the plot and character development are more evident. The dwarfs become characters with importance. Although nameless, they have a slightly more active role. In this version, for instance, one of them substitutes for the iconic figure of the prince, becoming Snow White's happy, everlasting husband.

A native version of Snow White, "Blanca Flor" (White Flower), brings a different type of warning that is common in themed "stories about the family." Blanca Flor's mother, who is jealous of her daughter's outstanding beauty, attempts to kill her three times. The evil mother's impersonation of a *quincallera* (female traveling merchant) reflected a popular figure in the countryside. Quincalleras' exotic objects, such as those that the evil mother sells to Blanca Flor, like brooches and ornamental *peinetas* (Spanish combs), were highly sought out. Their merchandise was often the only purchasing option, other than traveling to the *pueblo* (downtown) or shopping at plantation stores owned by the landowners. The latter forced workers to purchase articles at high prices, often replacing salaries with vouchers to be used only in their stores. Thus in disguising herself as a traveling merchant, Blanca Flor's mother was assured that she would be seen not as a threat but as a welcomed opportunity to view an exotic world, as represented by the apple, a U.S. import so far removed from the rustic countryside environment that served as Blanca Flor's prison.

There are significant changes in the Cinderella stories.[5] Renamed Cenizosa, a more descriptive nickname for a pitiful orphan girl covered in ashes, she is a kindhearted Jíbara girl whose name also appears as María or Rosa.[6] The plotline is very similar to the original story, which is widely known throughout the world. Cenizosa, in spite of her father's warnings, seals her own fate when she convinces her father to marry an old woman who is well known as an evil individual. The stepmother commands Cenizosa to perform the dirtiest house chores; however, this is a rural household. Cleaning tripe beside the river as the first step in cooking *mondongo* (tripe stew) leads Cenizosa into a cave where four fairy godmothers live in a messy house. They are, however, *encantadas*, or humans who have fallen under the spells of evil characters. In appreciation of Cenizosa's hard work of cleaning their soiled house, they gift Cenizosa *la varita de la virtud*, a magical wand that appears in other supernatural stories as a way to escape impossible problems. Other fantastical gifts are diamonds and pearls that drop from Cenizosa's hair anytime she combs her hair and gold nuggets that appear every time she speaks.

The Puerto Rican versions give the stepsister a more prominent place in the story, though she remains an antagonist. There is a lesson to be learned, even for the evil stepsister, who after attempting to fool the encantadas is cursed by spells that radically change her outlook on life. Failing to trick the fairy godmothers, the evil stepsister is gifted with rather peculiar curses. She will grow horns and one foot until they drag her down, and whenever she speaks, frogs and snakes will come out of her mouth incessantly. That was indeed a hard lesson learned! Another curious deviation from the traditional Cinderella plot is Cenizosa's handling of her predicaments without the intervention of an iconic prince.

Puerto Rican fairy tales often feature rather unusual spells. Chapter 2, "Rescuing Encantados," gathers stories that explain the circumstances surrounding people who have been turned into animals or plants through a spell uttered by a mean-spirited individual, often a witch or a disappointed parent. Although the length of the curses varies, they can only be lifted through the intervention of kindhearted individuals. It is not an easy task, though; in the stories, the rescuer must go on a quest through dangerous rural settings or unknown supernatural geographies. Only after proving their unconditional love (mostly in the case of girl or young women protagonists) or performing brave acts (enduring physical or emotional pain) do they successfully break a terrible spell. As in the traditional fairy tale, their reward is a handsome prince or a beautiful princess who, in return, bestows upon them immeasurable riches.

Three stories, "El príncipe clavel" (The Carnation Price), "El príncipe becerro" (The Calf Prince), and "Las tres rosas de Alejandría" (The Three Roses of Alexandria), celebrate kindhearted young women who bravely free enchanted princes from their spells. In "The Carnation Prince," an enchanted prince reveals himself as a jumping flower, a carnation, to three beautiful sisters, allowing only one of them to grab him. He then reveals himself as a handsome prince, and one of the sisters falls in love. In spite of the prince's warning, an accident provoked by his lover's carelessness while handling a candle forces him to go into hiding, and the repentant girl must now find him if they are to remain together. But the task is not that simple: she must wear a heavy dress of lead, a pair of shoes, and a hat and walk until they wear out. The young woman willingly takes on the challenge; she enters into a fantastic world and overcomes many physical obstacles, even at the cost of losing body parts to a hungry bird that is serving her as a means of transportation.

There are certainly plenty of brave young women in these stories willing to embark on impossible quests that combine exciting love and action plots. "The Calf Prince" has a young woman protagonist falling in love with the voice of a prince, whose face she has been warned not to look at—a warning she, of course, foolishly ignores. A jealous character tricks her into lighting a candle to discover the identity of her mysterious lover. Once the warning is ignored and the image of a prince as a calf is revealed, the girl must go out on a whimsical journey. At the core of this more complex story, she comes into contact with strangers who facilitate (or prevent) her rather fantastic quest for her enchanted prince.

Simple, random acts of kindness can also lead to profitable rewards. With a more extensive plotline, the young woman protagonist of "The Three Roses of Alexandria" is visited by an enchanted bird. She is, however, a rather absent-minded listener, as it takes the bird three times before it manages to catch her attention. After that, she speaks to the bird at once and ends the prince's curse.

A special kind of unfortunate enchantment is the subject of "Los siete cuervos" (The Seven Crows). Seven brothers are turned into crows after their own father curses them. In this much longer adventure story, the reader learns about the menial reason for the father's action and how their youngest sister, who indirectly causes her father to wish that his children would be turned into crows, becomes their rescuer. She is a brave little girl who willingly embarks upon yet another voyage into a fantastic world, aided by supernatural means. The story ends with a warning to adults about the power of "bad words."

Lastly, four rural-based stories feature horses as enchanted princes. Horses commonly appear in these stories either as a colorful component of an agrarian culture or as a source of entertainment, particularly competitions of fanciful horse tricks. Three stories, "El caballo misterioso" (The Mysterious Horse), "El caballito negro" (The Little Black Horse), and

"El padre y los tres hijos" (The Father and the Three Sons), have young rural Jíbaros as protagonists in a world that it is often confusing and dangerous. "The Little Black Horse" and "The Father and the Three Sons" dwell on a frequently explored theme of fraternal rivalry, as two older brothers gang up on their kindhearted little brother in order to gain their father's attention. The stories bring to the forefront how the horses come into the lives of the protagonists, serving them well as their advisors in overcoming adversity, aided by magical means or supernatural warnings.

Horses continuously warn overly kind protagonists to beware of mean people—even one's own brothers. This is the subject of "El caballo de siete colores" (The Horse of Seven Colors), which introduces Juan Bobo, the most popular child character in Puerto Rican folklore. Juan Bobo manages to overcome his brothers' jealousy with the help of not only his fantastic horse of seven colors but, most importantly, his own natural instincts as a trickster.[7] The story is an outstanding example of the merging of plotlines from other fanciful stories, perhaps as a result of the children entertaining themselves while writing.

Chapter 3, "Fantastic and Impossible Quests," features stories whose protagonists bravely overcome the perils of voyages into the unknown, either through their instinctive alertness or by supernatural means that favor their cause. "La flor del olivar" (The Flower of the Olive Grove) begins with three young brothers on a trip in search of that mythical bloom. As in other stories of enchantment, only the one character who follows a simple piece of advice is triumphant—but not without experiencing the wrath of his jealous siblings. Similarly, "La joven y la serpiente" (The Maiden and the Serpent) has three peasant boys testing their luck, carrying with them a magical object; only one of them asked for his mother's blessing, while the others wanted money. This story highlights young protagonists willing to face supernatural elements; only one brother is triumphant because he trusted the blessing and could use his magic object effectively.

A third, more complex quest story with adult sexual content is "Los tres trajes" (The Three Dresses). The plot involves a father in search of impossible objects. He must find three dresses: one "the color of the stars," one "the color of the fish in the sea," and one "the color of all the flowers in the world." These requests are his daughter's desperate attempts to stop him from marrying her. Once he brings her these fantastic objects, she escapes with them into the wilderness. Her clever use of these unusual dresses lands her a prince—but not without the help of another magical object, the *varita de virtud*, the magic wand that connects this story with the Cenizosa series.

The clever ways in which international enchantment stories were adapted to appeal to a Puerto Rican audience was frequently a topic of discussion during the editing process. Espinosa strongly believed that some fairy tale versions were widely available on the island by means of commercial publications. In particular, the Spanish book publishing house known as Calleja produced an extensive number of cheaply made publications (Fernández de Córdoba y Calleja 26). Indeed, the Calleja children's materials had flooded the Spanish and Latin American markets with more than 3,000 titles, selling up to 3.5 million copies (Fermín Pérez 14). Their small size (easily handled by the small hands of young readers), their considerably low prices (some costing a mere *perra gorda* [pennies]), and the richly illustrated color drawings by over 140 illustrators (Fernández de Córdoba y Calleja 91, 92) made the books extremely popular (Fermín Pérez 13). However, Espinosa never cited specific examples on which to base his theory of children copying tales from such popular publications.

A considerable number of Puerto Rican folktales illustrate the importance of the survival techniques that cunning Jíbaro protagonists deployed to protect themselves in a menacing countryside. Chapter 4, "Juan Bobo: A Deceiving Trickster," presents picaresque stories of the well-known mischievous child who frequently finds himself in trouble with his mother, neighbors, or strangers. Although his adventures often bring him into borderline criminal situations from which he successfully escapes—sometimes unscathed—he is also frequently physically punished. His name has a double connotation: a witty boy or an adolescent who, while pretending

to be a simpleton, emerges triumphantly from adventures, many of them
with a comical ending. But he is also a *bobo* (dummy), a rural nickname
for a mental disability that makes him the butt of numerous cruel jokes. In
either case, Juan Bobo finds himself involved in events that end badly for
those unfortunate characters with whom he comes in contact in a number
of comical anecdotes that are still frequently reproduced in Puerto Rico as
prime readers for schoolchildren or as inspiration for fiction writers.

Mason left no comments about the reasons behind the Jíbaros' strong
attraction to Juan Bobo. However, it seems that Mason might have considered these stories as a tribal type of oral tradition of which Juan Bobo was
a popular character for listeners of all ages. He recognized the importance
of Juan Bobo as a folk character immediately upon his arrival to the island.
On December 8, 1914, he reported to Boas that he had already started col-
lecting Juan Bobo stories in Utuado. He eventually documented numerous
versions of Juan Bobo stories throughout the island.

In their introduction to "Cuentos picarescos," Mason and Espinosa
pointed out that the Puerto Rican versions of picaresque stories reflected
European influences. The "main elements" of the Puerto Rican stories were
cataloged as "traditional," an indirect reference to their connection with
"many versions of European folk-tales" (143). Thus Juan Bobo was equated
to other *pícaros* in the Hispanic tradition, such as Juan Sin Miedo, Juan
Tonto, Pedro Urdemalas, and even Mano Fashico, a popular picaresque
character in New Mexico, where a "practically identical" version of Juan
Bobo survived (143–144). The Puerto Rican Juan Bobo offered, however,
a unique angle on the trickster, with "many new and important develop-
ments" (143). Another popular rascal in Puerto Rico was Pedro Urdemalas,
also a mischievous young man, whose origins were similar to those of Juan
Bobo, as the story reproduced in this volume clearly suggests.

The stories selected here underscore different aspects of Juan Bobo as a
notable trickster. "Juan Bobo manda la cerda a misa" (Juan Bobo Sends the
Pig to Mass) presents him as a "dunce" in his handling his mother's simple
request: "Be careful that the sun doesn't hit the pig." He decides to dress

the sow in his mother's clothes and expensive jewels and sends the animal off to meet its owner at church. The fact that the mother is wealthy and Juan Bobo dresses up her sow stands out as a social commentary criticizing her extravagance amid the extreme poverty of the countryside.

Whether Juan Bobo is truly a dunce or fakes it either to play a joke on the innocent bystander or for his financial advantage is the subject of "Juan mata la vaca" (Juan Kills the Cow). Having accidentally killed his family's cow, the main sustenance of the household, Juan Bobo sets out to sell the meat. On his way to the market, he comes across some unusual buyers, "the young ladies of the shawl"—in reality, a swarm of flies—and a one-eyed dog, to whom he sells the meat on credit. Two weeks later, at the comical conclusion of the story, the wife of a one-eyed man has to deal with Juan Bobo's rather violent demands of payment for the meat that his "one-eyed one" had bought from him.

There are stories that attempt to make Juan Bobo the butt of the joke, but they are turned into "the joke is on you" anecdotes. "Juan Bobo se muere cuando el burro se tire tres pedos" (Juan Bobo Dies When the Donkey Farts Three Times) plays on Juan Bobo's childlike innocence when he takes at face value the warning of a mean-spirited man that he will die the moment Juan Bobo hears a donkey passing gas three times. Once it happens, Juan Bobo fakes his death as a playful ploy to chastise those who abuse his naïveté. But Juan Bobo can also physically punish those who abuse him. He violently retaliates against those who attempt to steal from him in "Juan y los objetos mágicos" (Juan and the Magical Objects). Although he is seemingly easily robbed of two of his magical objects, he cleverly uses the third magical object, a self-propelled stick, to mercilessly beat the surprised thieves.

Juan Bobo has allies that join him in well-organized and successfully performed scams. Three stories, "La olla que calienta agua sin fuego" (The Pot That Heats Water without Fire), "El conejo que llama a su amo" (The Rabbit That Calls His Master), and "El pito que resucita" (The Whistle That Brings People Back to Life), feature Juan and his mother working together to execute their rather simple schemes. The anecdotes feature a pot that heats up without fire (avoiding the time-consuming gathering of wood), a trained rabbit that eases housewives' chore of fetching their husbands working deep in planting fields, and—the most "magical" of the objects—a whistle that brings the dead back to life. The scammed people pay dearly, and Juan Bobo and his mother escape the wrath of those who have been cheated.

The thirst for fast money is a common theme in Juan Bobo's folktales. "Juan y los ladrones" (Juan and the Thieves), a much longer and more complex story, underlines an episodic plot that is grounded in a rather scatological anecdote. When a gang of thieves appears at the door of Juan Bobo's house requesting permission to spend the night, he immediately plans a ruse to keep all of the stolen money they carry. Although he presents himself as a welcoming host, he also fakes an air of craziness, leading to his unusual admonition: he would physically castigate those who soil the bedsheets. The graphic details of his ploy to make this happen constitute most of the plotline, a crude example of Juan Bobo's cunning abilities as an adult.

Danger to children, including physical abuse from their parents, is yet another important subject of folktales. Chapter 5, "Beware of Strangers," groups three versions of reinterpretations of the iconic child characters Hansel and Gretel. There are some notable deviations from the original fairy tale. In "Los niños perdidos" (The Lost Children), protagonists Mariquita and Juanito get lost while trying to fetch water from a river to ease the heavy burden of their old father. Suddenly they stumble upon an old witch. Although they keep away from her, she successfully lures them into her home, tempting them not with delicious sweets but with fried meat and white rice and kidney beans, a staple of Puerto Rican rural cuisine. The ending is also significant. It adds a new character, an old man who warns the children about the woman's evil intentions. He also suggests a picaresque trick to lead the witch to her iconic death by fire.

"Los niños huérfanos" (The Orphaned Children) displays more connections to the classic Hansel and Gretel story, but the digressions are still striking examples of cultural adaptations to fit the taste of a rural audience. The first version features an evil stepmother who convinces her husband to send his children deep into the forest to avoid feeding them. The trail to find their way back is also different. The children use coal ashes from the kitchen's hearth to create the trail, which disappears after a hard downpour. The ending is happy, though, and includes their return home to their recently widowed father. The second version also makes the stepmother responsible for the father's decision to abandon his children in "the world's most remote forests." They manage to come back home thanks to white pebbles that the smart Pepito had "thrown along the way [and which] shone like gold coins."

A consistent message in the stories with children as protagonists is that adults can indeed be foes. Orphans such as Cinderella, Snow White, and the local versions of Hansel and Gretel are abused at the hands of their stepmothers, who are presented as strangers and thus potential enemies. Biological mothers can also inflict pain, however, as seen in the Juan Bobo stories. More tragically, they can even kill their children. One such warning story, "La mata de ají" (The Pepper Plant), highlights a mother who kills her daughter because of three missing figs. Although the innocent girl falls for her mother's dirty trick, she manages to come back to life as a pepper plant. Once the crime is revealed, the mother is violently punished, and peace returns to the household.

Chapter 6, "El Pirata Cofresí: A National Hero and Other Notable Bandits," gathers leyendas (legends) of the most dreaded of thieves, the infamous Puerto Rican–born pirate Roberto Cofresí y Ramírez de Arellano (1791–1825), whose Robin Hood–like deeds make him a popular protagonist of adventure stories. He was infamously known for daring robberies at sea that took him from his operational base on Cabo Rojo's western coast to nearby ports in the Dominican Republic and the surrounding islands of the Lesser Antilles—even as far as Lima, Peru. The four stories reproduced here follow his life story as a literary character of highly emotive anecdotes. "El niño Cofresí" (The Boy Cofresí) serves as an introduction to this popular pirate. It was perhaps the work of a mature storyteller, an adult who produced an exciting psychological profile of Cofresí as a boy. The child, after witnessing his father being abused by a foreign captain, swears that he will become the captain of a twenty-four-man crew that many years later restores his father's honor.

Cofresí's stories praise his personal honor and his pride in his Puerto Rican identity. "Cofresí defiende su honor" (Cofresí Defends His Honor), a much longer and more complex piece that reveals the skill of a learned writer, dwells on details leading to Cofresí's duel with a local gentleman of Spanish descent, whose snarky comment about Cofresí's short height terribly offended him. The story ends with a *promesa de honor* (a gentlemen's promise) that neither one will ever fight the other as they swear while a priest holds the holy host in front of them. These were the old good old days when one could trust a gentleman's word!

A third story, "Cofresí en el palacio misterioso" (Cofresí in the Mysterious Palace) is a fantastic anecdote that ponders Cofresí's uncanny ability to identify burial grounds that, through supernatural means, effectively hide his allegedly immense booties. A fourth story, "Recordando a Cofresí" (Remembering Cofresí), dwells on Cofresí's image as a folk hero, a reputation that, as the admirer protagonist remembers, endured after his capture and subsequent military execution in 1825.

A final piece, "Contreras"—a short legend, perhaps written by a schoolchild as a class assignment—is dedicated to another notable thief. This text reinforces the attraction of storytellers to benevolent robbers, whose criminal stunts benefited the poor, particularly older people who they often protected and financially supported.

The last chapter, "Brief Stories and Anecdotes," gathers a variety of pedagogical, brief short stories and funny anecdotes that draw heavily from rural settings, popular characters, and plotlines that were well known among Jíbaros. Together, the stories reflect strong survival lessons and stress best practices for surviving life in the countryside, including stories that warn individuals about acting selfishly against the well-being of their community. The lesson is, however, always the same: the kindhearted person who faces a bully with quick and smart thinking, and sometimes magical interventions, defeats the villain's wicked ways while improving their own destitute lives.

The stories "Dios, el rico y el pobre" (God, the Rich Man, and the Poor Man) and "El carbonero" (The Charcoal Maker) stress the useful advice of not judging people by their physical appearance. "God, the Rich Man, and the Poor Man" is about characters deceived by God himself, who appears to them as a poor, wandering pilgrim. Only the poor man, who sees beyond the ugly image of a destitute pilgrim seeking refuge (who strongly resembles the biblical figure of Lazarus, a popular saint in Puerto Rican religious lore), is eventually handsomely rewarded. The same lesson is expressed in "The Charcoal Maker," where the supernatural apparitions are Luck and Death, and the poor charcoal maker must choose between the two. His smart decision to be kind to Death because death comes for both the poor and the rich is the salient lesson of this pedagogical story.

The dangers of greed and, better yet, the punishments that await greedy individuals are the subjects of "La vieja miserable" (The Miserable Old Woman) and "La mala esposa" (The Bad Wife), together with two picaresque stories that are part of the Juanito series: "Juan sabe más que el rey" (Juan Knows More Than the King) and "Juanito, el Hijo de la Burra" (Juanito, the Son of the Donkey). In "The Miserable Old Woman," a greedy old woman, egotistical to the point of not wanting to share orange pits, receives a well-deserved punishment through the magic awarded to the kindhearted individual to whom she had denied the pits. "The Bad Wife" has as its central protagonist a conniving woman whose tricks, designed to keep food for herself, are discovered by her more astute husband. The characterization of the wife as untrustworthy also reflects the highly patriarchal social system operating in the Puerto Rican countryside.

Two stories, "Juan Knows More Than the King" and "Juanito, the Son of the Donkey," feature tricksters who set out to explore the world, a trope that often takes these smart protagonists out of abject poverty. "Juan Knows More Than the King" centers on a cunning scheme to derail a deceitful king's plans to kill Juan out of jealousy for the youngster's wisdom. "Juanito, the Son of the Donkey," although a fantastic story, suggests that the foundation of Ponce, Puerto Rico's second largest city, is the direct result of the smart deed of a brave, picaresque character.

Finally, no anthology of Puerto Rican folktales can be complete without Cucarachita Martina. A beautiful and smart cockroach, Martina, marries a friendly mouse, Ratoncito Pérez, who provides food for his dear wife. Cucarachita Martina laments Ratoncito Pérez's untimely death through a song that even today is a popular couplet, and there are multiple versions of Martina heard throughout the island: "Ratoncito Pérez cayó en la olla / Cucarachita Martina lo canta y lo llora" (Ratoncito Pérez fell into the pot / Cucarachita Martina sings to him and cries for him). The second story chosen here depicts Martina as a spider whose love for Ratoncito Pérez is still as strong as that of Martina, the friendly cockroach.

The Value of Oral Folktales in Puerto Rico Today

This anthology documents rural oral folk stories as integral components of Puerto Rican social practices and as reflections of a cultural identity that is deeply rooted in a trans-Atlantic and Caribbean postcolonial history. Indeed, as I trace in *Race and Nation in Puerto Rican Folklore*, which describes Boas's and Mason's historical trips to Puerto Rico and serves as a critical study of their oral folklore collection, a notable characteristic of these early twentieth-century folk stories is their configuration of ongoing socioeconomic issues into popular literary formats. Most importantly, for the first time in literary history, the Jíbaros, the iconic inhabitants of the Puerto Rican *campos*, became the writers of their own stories. The ingenuity they used to transform well-known international folktales and fairy tales into stories that appealed to a rural imagination was certainly outstanding. Additionally, the Jíbaros adapted legends and historic anecdotes to serve their own needs, whether as a source of entertainment or as a formal means of literary expression.

The reader of this book is in for a treat. I hope you enjoy these stories as much as I did as a schoolchild who learned about literary analysis through my reading of such classical stories. These are tales for all ages and will cross over national boundaries. Whether fairy tales, stories of adventure and fantasy, accounts of supernatural happenings, or legends that highlight local historical figures are your favorite narrative genre, I assure you that you will laugh at the many daring sensual and sociopolitical innuendos in these tales. Above all, you are invited to enjoy them as much as Mason's writers and storytellers did. Remember, they were popular forms of entertainment, narrated often during the long hours of a wake, or perhaps in the midst of a lunch break in the heat of the day. A testimony of their appeal is reflected in the continued printing of versions by writers in both Puerto Rico and the United States who still make these characters repositories of a vibrant, distinctive Puerto Rican cultural identity.[8]

This is also my humble testimony as the child of two proud *jíbaros* whose memories of growing up in the *tierra adentro* (hinterland) shaped my liking—and also disliking—of native Puerto Rican traditions, whether it is *música jíbara* (country music), my father's favorite pastime on Saturday afternoons, or my mother's comida criolla (creole cooking). No one can make *pasteles* like her! To my parents, I owe my love and passion for the native culture of la isla de Puerto Rico, the island of my dreams even after having lived for so many years *afuera*. "Living outside" is a Puerto Rican's polite but also political euphemism for refusing to refer to the United States as the "mainland."

In keeping with the historical significance of the scientific exploration of John Alden Mason and Franz Boas throughout Puerto Rico beginning in late 1914 through 1915, each chapter highlights a photograph taken on the island around this time period. Through the camera lens, modern readers will experience the expansive, lush, and green landscape of the interior mountain ranges of Puerto Rico that so much enchanted Mason and, for that matter, the first U.S. travelers exploring the island after the Spanish American War of 1898. The majority of the photos in their collections highlight a Jíbaro way of life, with numerous images of the iconic straw-roofed huts and rural peons (men and women) proudly posing with fruitful crops, an exotic view of a newly discovered commercial enterprise for U.S. import companies. It was not an idyllic existence, as the subjects of several stories in this anthology reflect upon. There was terrible hunger and economic want, menacing bandits on the rural roads, high rates of illiteracy, tropical diseases, and violence against women and children. Against such a dire background, the stories in this anthology celebrate the Jíbaros' emotional strength in the face of adversity, a trait that still characterizes Puerto Ricans on the island and in the United States today.

Amid the charms of Porto Rico; delicious pineapples in the fields of Mayagüez

CHAPTER 1

Jíbaro Readaptations
of Fairy Tales

SNOW WHITE AND LA CENIZOSA (CINDERELLA)

BLANCA NIEVES / SNOW WHITE

Blanca Nieves (1)[1]

Había un matrimonio que nunca había tenido familia. Un día estando la esposa lavándose las manos se cortó una mano y, cayendo algunas gotas sobre la nieve, se formó un color muy bonito. Ella se dijo a sí misma que desearía tener una hija de aquel color para ponerle Blanca Nieves. Al poco tiempo, dio a luz a una niñita y le pusieron Blanca Nieves.

Había en otra provincia una señora muy bonita llamada Sol y Luna. Le preguntó a un espejo que estaba colgado a la pared:

"Espejito mío, ¿habrá otra mujer más linda que yo?"

El espejo le contestó:

"Más bonita que tú no la había, pero ha nacido una llamada Blanca Nieves, que es más bonita."

Entonces, Sol y Luna alquiló a un peón para que le llevara el corazón y los ojos de Blanca Nieves en un cofre; a la sazón cuando venía ese peón, la encontró en el jardín entretenida cogiendo flores y se la llevó al bosque. Ella tenía una perrita que se fue con ella. Al llegar a la montaña, no pudo sacarle los ojos a la niña de lástima que le dio. Mató la perrita. Le sacó los ojos y el corazón y se los llevó a Sol y Luna en el cofre.

Blanca Nieves se fue a la montaña y caminó hasta que llegó a una casa donde habitaban siete enanos. Entró a ella y halló siete platillos de comida y siete pocillos de champán; de todos probó. Después se fue por la casa y encontró siete cuartos y siete camitas; en la última se acostó y durmió. Cuando los enanos vinieron, dijeron:

"Han probado mi comida."

Fueron a ver si quien había sido y encontraron a la niña dormida.

La despertaron y le preguntaron qué le pasaba. Ella les dijo que un hombre se la había traído a una montaña porque Sol y Luna le había mandado a buscar para matarla, ordenando que le llevaran los ojos y el corazón. Pero el peón, teniendo lástima de ella, le sacó los ojos a una perrita y el corazón llevándoselos a la mujer. Entonces, los enanos le dijeron que ellos no tenían mujer; le pidieron que se quedara y que la considerarían como hermana. Le advirtieron que no le abriera la puerta a nadie.

Por aquel tiempo la mujer, Sol y Luna, le preguntó al espejo:

"Espejito mío, ¿habrá otra mujer más bonita que yo?"

El espejo le contestó:

"¡Tú eres bonita, pero Blanca Nieves es más bonita que tú. Todavía esa niña vive en la montaña, en la casa de los siete enanos!"

Sol y Luna alquiló a una vieja bruja para que matara a Blanca Nieves; le daría una moneda grande. La vieja dijo que sí y se puso a preparar aros. Se fue disfrazada de quincallera a la casa de los enanos. Al llegar, le pidió a la niña que le abriera la puerta. Blanca Nieves le dijo que los enanos le habían dicho que no le abriera las puertas a nadie porque a ella la habían mandado a matar. Para que no volviera a pasar, debía hacer eso con todo el mundo.

Pero la vieja, como bruja al fin, le respondió que ella no lo haría; solo lo hacía la gente que no tenía conciencia. Tanto insistió hasta que Blanca Nieves abrió la puerta. Enseguida, la vieja bruja le hizo ponerse un aro en el dedo chiquito y, fulminantemente, Blanca Nieves cayó muerta. La bruja la cogió y la acostó en la cama y se fue enseguida.

Cuando los enanos vinieron, encontraron muerta a Blanca Nieves; le buscaron en las manos y le encontraron el aro. Se lo quitaron y revivió. Le preguntaron qué había pasado; Blanca Nieves les dijo que una vieja bruja le había puesto un aro y se había muerto. Entonces, los enanos le dijeron que no le volviera abrir la puerta a nadie.

Pero por ese tiempo volvió Sol y Luna al espejo, diciéndole que si había otra mujer más bonita que ella. El espejo le contestó:

"¡Sí, la hay! ¡Blanca Nieves!"

"Y, ¿todavía existe?"

"¡Sí!"

"¡Yo la he mandado a matar!"

El espejo le respondió:

"Sí, la mataron, pero los enanos la revivieron."

Sol y Luna volvió a alquilar a la vieja bruja para que matara a Blanca Nieves. Esta vez preparó unos corseletes, pero hizo uno especial para ella. La bruja llegó a la puerta y le dijo:

"Blanca Nieves, ábreme la puerta. Traigo corseletes de diferentes clases."

Tanto insistió hasta que Blanca Nieves abrió la puerta y la vieja se puso a medirle un corselete. Cuando se lo puso, Blanca Nieves cayó muerta; la bruja la llevó a la cama y la vistió.

Los enanos llegaron a la casa y no encontraron el almuerzo preparado.

"¡Con seguridad que la han matado!"

Fueron a buscar a Blanca Nieves y la hallaron muerta. Se pusieron a buscarla para ver si le encontraban lo que era; ya por la tarde le encontraron el corselete. Se lo quitaron y quedó viva; inmediatamente, Blanca Nieves les contó lo que había pasado. Ellos la regañaron, ¿por qué no hacía lo que le decían?

En ese tiempo Sol y Luna le dijo al espejo:

"Espejito mío, ¿habrá otra más bonita que yo?"

El espejo le contestó:

"¡Los siete enanos la reviven!"

Entonces, Sol y Luna le dijo a la vieja bruja que si la mataba le daba doble cantidad de la que le había dado primero. Enseguida, se fue la vieja y preparó unas manzanas. Hizo una con veneno y, cuando llegó a la casa donde Blanca Nieves estaba, le dijo:

"Blanca Nieves, ábreme la puerta."

"No te la abro. Ha venido una vieja que me ha matado; ya no me fío. Mis hermanos me han dicho que no le abra la puerta a nadie."

"¡No! Eso hace alguien que no te quiera, pero yo desde que te oí nombrar me has gustado."

Tanto le insistió que, al fin, Blanca Nieves abrió la puerta.

La vieja le dio la manzana; Blanca Nieves la probó y cayó muerta. La vieja abrió las puertas y la acostó en la cama. Se fue enseguida. Cuando los enanos vinieron y vieron la mesa sin almuerzo, se dijeron:

"¡Está muerta Blanca Nieves!"

Fueron al cuarto de ella y la encontraron muerta. Le buscaron y no le encontraron nada; muy tristes mandaron a hacer una vidriera y la pusieron en ella. Cuando se fueron a cazar, dos la velaban y los otros se iban por la montaña.

Un día llegó un príncipe de otra provincia hasta donde estaba esa niña en la vidriera. Les preguntó cuál imagen era aquélla que allí tenían. Ellos le contaron lo que les había pasado con ella desde el principio hasta el fin. El príncipe les dijo:

"Yo me llevo esa imagen a mi palacio."

Ellos le dijeron que no podía ser porque era su entretenimiento; no sabrían qué hacer si se la daban. El contestó que se la llevaba y que se fueran ellos también; serían bien recibidos en palacio.

Así lo hicieron. Se la llevó y los enanitos se fueron también. Cuando la llevaban, en el camino según iba moviéndose, se le salió un pedacito de manzana que había comido. El príncipe la vio y le sacó el otro pedacito de manzana. Enseguida, Blanca Nieves se movió y abrió los ojos, pero como hacía tantos días que no comía, le dio un accidente y, a fuerza de darle vino y bebidas sustanciosas, le revivieron.

Llegaron al palacio y el príncipe mandó a buscar al cura. Siguieron nueve días de fiestas reales, al cumplirse, se casaron.

Los enanitos se quedaron acompañando al príncipe y a Blanca Nieves, siendo considerados como si fueran hermanitos suyos y sin olvidarse nunca los unos a los otros.

~

Snow White (1)

Once upon a time, there was a married couple who had never had children. One day the wife cut one of her hands while she was washing them. Some drops of blood fell on the snow, forming a very pretty color. She told herself that she would love to have a little girl of that color, to be named Snow White. A little while later, the woman gave birth to a little girl, who she named Snow White.

In another province, there was a very pretty lady named Sun and Moon. She asked a mirror on the wall:

"My little mirror, is there possibly another woman prettier than I?"

The mirror answered her:

"There wasn't one prettier than you, but one named Snow White has been born. She is prettier than you!"

At once Sun and Moon hired a farmworker to bring her the heart and the eyes of Snow White in a jewel case. In due time, the laborer found the girl in the garden busily picking flowers. At once, the man carried her off to the forest. She had a little dog who went with her. When they arrived at the mountain, the laborer could not bear to take out the girl's eyes. He killed her dog and took out its eyes and its heart. He carried them to Sun and Moon in the jewel case.

Snow White left the mountain and traveled until she arrived at a house where seven dwarfs lived. She went in. There she found seven plates of food and seven little cups of champagne. She tasted from each one. Later she walked through the house and found seven bedrooms and seven little beds. In the last room, she went to bed and slept. When the dwarfs came home, they said:

"Somebody has been eating from my dinner."

They went to search for that person; immediately they found the girl sleeping.

They woke her up and asked her what had happened to her. She told them that a man had brought her to the mountain because Sun and Moon had sent him to find her and kill her, ordering him to bring her the girl's eyes and her heart. The laborer took pity on her, so he took out the eyes and the heart of her little dog to carry them to the woman, and he set Snow White free. The dwarfs told her that they had no women in the house; they invited her to stay and said they would consider her their sister. But they warned her not to open the door to anybody when they were not in the house.

About that time, the woman Sun and Moon asked her mirror:

"My little mirror, is there possibly another woman prettier than I?"

The mirror answered her:

"You are pretty, but Snow White is prettier than you, and that girl is still alive; she lives on the mountain in the house of the seven dwarfs!"

Sun and Moon hired an old witch to kill Snow White, saying she would give her a lot of money. The old woman agreed to do it and began to prepare rings. Disguised as an old peddler, she went to the dwarfs' house and asked the girl to open the door. Snow White said that the dwarfs had told her not to open the door to anybody because someone had been sent to kill her. To keep that from happening again, she should keep everybody away from the house.

But the old woman—who was a witch, after all—told her that she wouldn't do such a thing; that was the work of people without a conscience. She insisted so much that Snow White opened the door, and at once the witch pushed a ring onto the girl's little finger. Snow White died right away. The witch picked her up and placed her on a bed. She left immediately.

When the dwarfs came home and found her dead, they looked at her hands and found the ring. They took it from her hand, and she came back to life. The dwarfs asked her what happened to her. Snow White told them that an old witch had put a ring on her and she had died. The dwarfs told her again never to open the door to anybody.

But about that time, Sun and Moon again asked her mirror whether there was another woman who was prettier than she. The mirror answered her:

"Yes, there is! Snow White!"

"And she is still alive?" she asked.

"Yes," was the answer.

"I ordered her to be killed!"

The mirror replied:

"Yes, she was killed, but the dwarfs revived her."

Sun and Moon again hired the old witch to kill Snow White. The witch prepared some corsets, but she made a special one for Snow White. She went to Snow White's door and said to her:

"Snow White, open the door for me. I am bringing several kinds of corsets."

She insisted so much that Snow White opened the door. The old woman began to fit the corset, and when she put it on her, the girl fell dead. The witch carried her to the bed and dressed her.

When the dwarfs came in, they found no meal prepared. They said:

"Surely, they have killed Snow White!"

They started searching for her and found her dead. They began trying to find the cause of her death. They found the corset and took it off. She came alive and told them what was going on. The dwarfs asked her why she didn't do what they had told her to do.

About that time, Sun and Moon said to the mirror:

"My mirror, can there be another prettier than I?"

It answered her:

"Yes, there is. Snow White is much prettier!"

"But I've ordered her killed more than once, and still they have not killed her!"

The mirror replied:

"The seven dwarfs revived her!"

Sun and Moon told the old witch that if she killed the girl, she would give her twice the earlier payment. At once the old witch went off and fixed some apples. Into one apple she put poison. When she arrived at the house where the girl lived, she said:

"Snow White, open the door for me."

Snow White replied:

"I am not going to open it for you. An old woman came and killed me. I no longer trust people. My brothers have told me many times not to open the door for anybody."

The witch said to Snow White:

"No! That is what a person does who doesn't love you, but I have cared for you since the first time I heard your name."

She said this so many times that finally, Snow White finally opened the door.

The old witch gave her the poised apple. Snow White bit into it and fell dead. The old woman opened the door and put her into the bed. Then she left at once. When the dwarfs came and saw the table without lunch, they said:

"Snow White is dead!"

They went to her room and found Snow White dead. They searched her and found no cause, and, very sad, they ordered a glass vault and put her into it. When they went out to hunt, two of them watched over her while the others went out to the mountain.

One day a prince from another province saw Snow White in the glass vault; he asked the dwarfs what image they had there. They told him what had happened to Snow White from beginning to end. The prince said to them:

"I'll take that image to my palace!"

The dwarfs told him that he couldn't take Snow White; she was their only distraction. Without her, they would not know what to do. The prince replied that he was indeed taking her with him, but they could come too; they would be well received at the royal palace.

That's what they did. The prince carried Snow White off, and the seven dwarfs went along too. When they were carrying her, the coffin was jolted on the road, and a tiny piece of the apple that Snow White had eaten fell out. The prince saw what happened, and he took another piece of apple from her mouth. At once Snow White moved her body and opened her eyes, but because she had not eaten for so many days, she fainted. They revived her with some wine and nourishing drinks.

As soon as they arrived at the palace, the prince sent for the priest. After nine days of royal balls, they were married.

The seven dwarfs continued to accompany Snow White and the prince. They were treated as their little brothers. They never forgot to take care of each other.

Blanca Nieves (2)[2]

Había un matrimonio que tenía una hija, la cual era tan linda y tan blanca que le pusieron sus padres Blanca Nieves. A los pocos años, Blanca Nieves quedó huérfana de madre. Por el barrio había una joven que tenía envidia de las joyas de Blanca Nieves, y decidió casarse con el padre de ella, haciéndole brillantes proposiciones a la niña. Halagada por sus lindas palabras, Blanca Nieves se lo hizo saber a su padre. Como dote pensaba casarse, aceptó las proposiciones que le hacía su hija; a los pocos meses, se casó con la joven vecina.

A los dos o tres meses tuvo él que hacer un viaje; les preguntó qué deseaban les trajese. La esposa le pidió un espejito mágico y la hija le pidió un corte de traje de los más lindos que él encontrara.

Mientras él estaba en su viaje, la madrastra trataba muy mal a la niña y hasta la ponía a comer amarrada por una pierna junto con los gatos y los perros. Un día le pegó tan fuerte que le hizo un cardenal en la cara. Cuando más desesperada estaba la niña, llegó su padre del viaje; así fue como pudo descansar un poco del mal trato que su madrastra le daba.

Rosa, que así se llamaba la esposa del padre de Blanca Nieves, sacó enseguida el espejo mágico; mirándose en él, le preguntó:

"¿Quién es más bonita, Blanca Nieves o yo?"

El espejo le contestó:

"Tú eres bonita, pero Blanca Nieves te gana."

Con tal respuesta se indignó la mujer. Cuando su esposo salió, mandó a los criados que cogieran a la niña y se la llevaran al monte; ordenó que la mataran y le llevaran los ojos. Obedecieron ellos el mandato, pero fue tanta la pena que les dio que no la mataron. La dejaron en casa de unos enanos encantados que vivían en el bosque. Luego cogieron un perrito, le sacaron los ojos y se los llevaron, quedando la cruel Rosa muy satisfecha.

Al cabo de muchos días Rosa volvió a consultar el espejo, quedando más indignada; la respuesta fue que en verdad ella era bonita, pero Blanca Nieves, la que estaba en la casa de los enanos, lo era más. Entonces, se

vistió de una mujer cualquiera; salió vendiendo manzanas, habiendo partido primero una por la mitad para envenenarla.

Se fue vendiendo sus manzanas, pero como a Blanca Nieves le habían
dicho que no bájese a comprar nada, no quiso bajar al principio; inducida
por la mujer y por el olor de las manzanas, decidió bajar. La vieja le dio de
la manzana que tenía veneno.

No bien hubo probado el primer bocado, Blanca Nieves quedó envenenada. Cuando regresaron los enanos, la encontraron muerta. La cogieron y
se la llevaron a un médico, quien le extrajo el pedazo de manzana que tenía
en la garganta. Blanca Nieves quedó viva otra vez.

Uno de los enanos estaba loco enamorado de Blanca Nieves. A los pocos
días se casó con ella, haciéndola feliz por el resto de su vida, y no dando la
madrastra con ella ni encontrando medios de poder matarla.

~

Snow White (2)

Once upon a time, a married couple had a daughter so pretty and so white
that they named her Snow White. A few years later, her mother died. In
their neighborhood there was a young woman who coveted Snow White's
jewels. She had decided to marry Snow White's father by making brilliant
promises to the girl. Flattered by these beautiful words, Snow White told
her father about the woman. Since he was thinking about finding a wife,
he accepted at once the proposition that his daughter conveyed. A few
months later, Snow White's father married their young neighbor.

Two or three months later, Snow White's father had to take a trip. He
asked what they wanted him to bring them. His wife asked for a little
magic mirror. Snow White asked him for a length from one of the prettiest
cloths that he found.

While he was traveling, the stepmother treated the girl very badly. She
even tied her legs and forced her to eat with the cats and the dogs. One
day her stepmother beat her so badly that it left a big bruise on the girl's

face. When the girl was most in despair, her father returned from the trip, and finally she could rest a little from the abuse that her stepmother was giving her.

Rosa, as Snow White's father's wife was named, at once took out the magic mirror. Looking at herself in it, she asked:

"Who is prettier, Snow White or I?"

The mirror answered,

"You are pretty, but Snow White wins over you!"

The woman was indignant about the answer. When her husband was away, she ordered the servants to seize the girl and carry her to the wilderness. She commanded them to kill her and carry her eyes back to Rosa. The servants obeyed her orders, but they were so distressed that they could not kill Snow White. They left her in the house of some dwarf sorcerers who lived in the forest. Before they left, they trapped a little dog and took out its eyes. They carried the eyes to cruel Rosa. She was then well satisfied.

After many days Rosa consulted the magic mirror again. She was most vexed, since the answer was that she was truly pretty, but Snow White, who was living at the dwarfs' house, was more so. At once Rosa dressed like an ordinary woman and went out selling apples. She cut one into halves, but it was poisoned. Immediately, she went around selling her apples.

The dwarfs told Snow White not to leave her room to open the door to any stranger. Initially, she refused to speak to the woman peddler, but the witch persuaded her, and the apples smelled so good. Snow White finally left her room, and the old woman then gave her the poisoned apple.

As soon as she took the first bite, she was poisoned. When the dwarfs came back, they found her dead. They picked her up and carried her to a physician, who took out the piece of apple that she had in her throat. She was alive again.

One of the dwarfs was madly in love with Snow White. A few days later he married her, making her happy for the rest of her life and not letting her stepmother find ways to kill her.

Blanca Flor[3]

Había una vez un rey casado con una reina que tenía una hija que se llamaba Blanca Flor. La reina quería ser más bonita que Blanca Flor, pero no lo era. Blanca Flor, aunque sucia y mal vestida, era más bonita que la reina.

Un día la reina se vistió con un traje muy bonito, compró un espejo mágico y le preguntó:

"Espejito mío, ¿quién es más bonita, Blanca Flor o yo?"

El espejito le contestó:

"¡Blanca Flor!"

Entonces, ella cogió el espejo y lo rompió. Enseguida mandó a buscar a un criado y le dijo:

"Irá usted a lo más espeso del bosque y matará a esta niña, trayéndome el corazón y los ojos de ella."

El criado se llevó a la niña al bosque con una perrita que se fue en su seguimiento. Al llegar al bosque al criado le dio pena matar a la niña; le dijo que no podía, mataría la perrita. Blanca Nieves dijo que sí.

Entonces, él mató la perrita; le sacó el corazón y los ojos y se los llevó a la reina. Blanca Flor se fue por el bosque y llegó a la casa de unos enanos. Ella hizo comida, puso la mesa y les limpió la casa. Después se metió debajo de la mesa.

Cuando llegaron los enanos, se preguntaron unos a otros, diciendo:

"¿Quién sería quien nos hizo este favor?"

Entonces, Blanca Flor salió de debajo de la mesa; les dijo que había sido ella. Ellos le dijeron:

"Te quedarás aquí como hermana de nosotros."

Al otro día se fueron los enanos a trabajar; le dijeron que no le abriera la puerta a nadie. La niña así lo prometió.

Mientras tanto la reina compró otro espejo. Le preguntó quién era la más bonita, ella o Blanca Flor. El espejo le contestó:

"¡Blanca Flor!"

La reina dijo:

"¿Blanca Flor existe?"

El espejo le dijo:

"¡Sí!"

Entonces, ella rompió el espejo.

Se disfrazó de quincallera y se fue a la casa de los enanos a vender prendedores. Cuando llegó estaba Blanca Flor en la puerta y le dijo:

"¿Quién compra un bonito prendedor?"

La niña le dijo que ella no porque sus hermanos le habían dicho que no abriera la puerta a nadie. La quincallera le dijo que el prendedor era muy bonito, que lo viniera a ver. Blanca Flor bajó; la reina, al ponérselo en el pecho, se lo enterró. La niña cayó muerta.

La reina se fue. Cuando los enanos encontraron muerta a Blanca Flor, empezaron a llorar; la registraron y encontraron el prendedor. Se lo sacaron y quedó viva otra vez la niña. Ellos le dijeron:

"Hermanita, nosotros te hemos dicho que no le abras la puerta a nadie."

Cuando la reina llegó a su casa, se vistió otra vez, compró otro espejo.

Le preguntó:

"Espejito mío, ¿quién es más bonita de Blanca Flor o yo?"

El espejito le contestó:

"¡Blanca Flor!"

La reina dijo:

"Blanca Flor, ¿existe todavía?"

El espejo le dijo:

"Sí, todavía."

A los pocos días, se vistió de quincallera otra vez y se fue a vender peinetas. Cuando llegó a la casa de los enanos, le preguntó a Blanca Flor si quería comprar una peineta muy bonita. Ella le contestó que sus hermanos le habían dicho que no le abriera la puerta a nadie.

La reina le dijo:

"Es una peineta muy buena para el pelo, mídasela."

Al ponérsela se la clavó en la cabeza; Blanca Nieves cayó muerta.

Cuando llegaron los enanos, la encontraron muerta y empezaron a llorar; le buscaron y le encontraron la peineta. Se la sacaron y le dijeron: "Nosotros ya te hemos dicho que no le abrieras la puerta a nadie."

Cuando la reina llegó a su casa se vistió, compró otro espejo, y le preguntó: "¿Cuál es más bonita de Blanca Flor y yo?"

Le contestó:

"¡Blanca Flor!"

"¿Y todavía Blanca Flor existe?"

"¡Todavía!"

Entonces, la reina rompió el espejo, se vistió de quincallera otra vez, y se fue a vender manzanas, entre ellas iba una envenenada.

Cuando llegó a la casa de los enanos, gritó:

"¿Quién compra manzanas? Están muy dulces."

Blanca Flor se asomó a la ventana, y le dijo:

"No, porque mis hermanos me han dicho que no le abra la puerta a nadie."

La reina le dijo:

"Mire, están dulces."

Y probó una de las que no estaban envenenadas.

Blanca Flor compró una y la quincallera le vendió la que estaba envenenada. Al probarla, el primer bocado se le quedó en la garganta; Blanca Flor se ahogó y cayó muerta. Cuando llegaron los enanos, la encontraron muerta y empezaron a llorar. La registraron y no le encontraron nada.

La reina en su casa le preguntó a otro espejo quién era más bonita. ¿Ella o Blanca Flor? El espejo no le contestó nada. La reina se quedó contenta, creyéndose la más bonita de la tierra.

Los enanos pusieron a Blanca Flor en una caja. Al colocarla sobre la mesa tropezaron, ella devolvió el bocado de manzana, quedando viva.

El hermano mayor le escribió al rey que si le daba a su hija para casarse con ella porque su esposa había tratado muchas veces de matarla. El rey le concedió su permiso, además, le regaló un palacio. El enano se casó y se fueron a vivir en él.

El rey les preguntó a los enanos qué harían con la reina que era tan mala. Los enanos le contestaron que la mandara a matar. Así lo hizo el rey.

Los enanos quedaron contentos y felices, viviendo todos al lado de Blanca Flor.

~

White Flower

Once upon a time, there was a king who had a daughter named White Flower. His queen wanted to be prettier than White Flower, but she wasn't. Even dirty and in rags, White Flower was prettier than the queen.

One day the queen put on a very pretty gown and bought a magic mirror. She asked the mirror:

"My little mirror, who is prettier, White Flower or I?"

The little mirror answered her:

"White Flower!"

She picked up the mirror and broke it. At once she sent for a servant. She told him:

"You will go into the depths of the forest and kill this girl. Bring me her heart and her eyes."

The servant took the girl into the forest with a little dog following them. In the forest, the servant couldn't bear to kill the child; instead, he could kill the little dog. White Flower agreed.

The man killed the little dog, took out its heart and its eyes, and carried them to the queen. White Flower went deeper into the forest; soon she arrived at the home of some dwarfs. She made dinner, set the table, and cleaned the house. Afterward she crawled under the table.

When the dwarfs arrived, they asked each other:

"Who could have done us this kindness?"

White Flower came out from under the table and told them that she had done it. The dwarfs said to her:

"You will stay here as our sister."

The next day the dwarfs went off to work. They told White Flower not to open the door for anybody. The girl promised not to.

Meanwhile, the queen bought another mirror and asked it who was prettier, she or White Flower. The mirror answered:

"White Flower!"

The queen asked:

"Is White Flower alive?"

The mirror said:

"Yes!"

Then she broke the mirror.

She disguised herself as a peddler and went off to the dwarfs' house to sell brooches. When she arrived, White Flower was in the doorway. She said to the girl:

"Will you buy a pretty brooch?"

White Flower said she wouldn't. Her brothers had forbidden her to open the door for anybody. The evil woman insisted; she asked White Flower to come closer to see how pretty the brooch was. White Flower went out, and the queen buried the brooch into her breast. The girl fell dead.

Happily, the queen went away. When the dwarfs found White Flower dead, they started crying. They examined her and found the brooch. They pulled it out, and the girl lived again. They told her:

"Little sister, have we not warned you not to open the door for anybody?"

As soon as the queen got home, she changed into her regal clothes. She bought another mirror. She asked it:

"My little mirror, who is prettier, White Flower or I?"

The little mirror answered:

"White Flower!"

The queen said:

"Is White Flower still alive?"

The mirror told her:

"Yes, still."

A few days later, the queen, dressed again as a peddler, left the palace to sell ornamental combs. When she arrived at the dwarfs' home, she asked White Flower if she would buy a very pretty comb. The girl told her that the dwarfs warned her not to open the door for anybody. The queen said to her:

"This comb will look good with your beautiful hair. Try it on."

When the girl tried it on, the queen buried it deep into the girl's head. White Flower fell dead.

When the dwarfs came home, they found White Flower dead. They started crying, but while searching her body, they found the comb. At once, they pulled it out. They scolded her:

"We had told you not to open the door for anybody."

When the queen got home, she dressed up in regal clothes, bought another mirror, and asked:

"Who is prettier, White Flower or I?"

It answered:

"White Flower!"

"Is she still alive?"

"Still!" it replied.

The queen broke the mirror, dressed again as a peddler, and left to sell apples; one of which was poisoned.

When she arrived at the dwarfs' house, she shouted:

"Who will buy my apples? They are very sweet."

White Flower came to the window. She told her:

"No, I can't buy your apples. My brothers have told me not to open the door for anybody."

The queen said:

"Look! They are very sweet."

And the queen tried one that was not poisoned.

White Flower bought one, and the queen gave her one that was poisoned. When she tasted it, the first bite stuck in her throat; shocked, White Flower fell dead. When the dwarfs came home, they found her dead. They started crying and searched her body. But this time, they found nothing.

The queen, back at home, asked another mirror who was prettier—she or White Flower? The mirror said nothing. Finally, the queen was content, believing that she was the prettiest woman in the land.

The dwarfs put White Flower into a box, but as they were about to place it on a table, they stumbled. The bite of apple fell out of her mouth, and White Flower lived.

The oldest dwarf wrote to the king, asking for him for his daughter's hand in marriage. The dwarf also told the king that the queen had tried many times to kill White Flower. The king granted his permission. Furthermore, the king gave the dwarf and White Flower a palace. They got married and went to live there.

The king asked the dwarfs what should be done to such a wicked queen. The dwarfs immediately answered that he should order her to be killed. The king did just that.

The dwarfs lived contented and happy ever after with White Flower.

La Cenizosa / Cinderella

María, la Ceninoza[4]

Había una vez un matrimonio que tenía una hija, pero al poco tiempo murió la madre, dejando viudo al esposo. Había otra vieja que tenía otra hija llamada Cenicienta. La muchacha del padre tenía una chivita; cada vez que ella iba a mudar su chivita, la vieja le decía:

"Si obligas a tu padre a que se case conmigo te doy sopas de miel."

Cuando la muchacha se lo decía al padre, él contestaba:

"Hoy te las da de miel y mañana de hiel."

Pero la niña estuvo insistiendo tanto hasta que el padre se casó.

La vieja le compró una chivita a Cenicienta; desde el segundo día, María, que así se llamaba la hija del padre viudo, era la Cenicienta, y la Cenicienta fue llamada María.

Un día a María se le antojó que mataran la chivita de Cenicienta; por más que la muchacha lloró para que no se la mataran, no hubo remedio. La vieja le dio de golpes a la muchacha y siempre le mató la chivita. La mandó a limpiar el mondongo al río. Le contó las tripas, diciéndole que si perdía una tripa, la iba a pasar muy mal.

Como la muchacha le tenía tanto miedo a su madrastra, se puso a limpiar el mondongo con mucho cuidado. Cuando ya iba a venirse se le cayó una tripa al río. La muchacha se tiró al río, diciendo:

"Río, río, río abajo, ¡dame mi tripita, que si no me la das, mi madre me mata!"

Y seguía diciendo:

"Río, río, río abajo, ¡dame mi tripita!"

Cuando estaba en tan grande afán salió a un palacio que estaba muy sucio. Allí vivían unas encantadas. Las mujeres habían salido para misa y la perrita se quedó en la casa, que también estaba sucia. La muchacha desde que llegó allí, en seguida empezó a limpiar el palacio, echó la basura en el basurero, bañó también la perrita. Inmediatamente, se escondió detrás de la puerta.

Cuando las encantadas llegaron, las mujeres empezaron a gritar:

"¿Quién sería el que nos hizo este trabajo?"

Y la perrita gritaba:

"Jua, jau, jau, ¡detrás de la puerta está!"

Pero como la muchacha no salía, una de las encantadas dijo:

"¡Yo le doy, que cada vez que hable, eche rubíes y diamantes por la boca!"

La siguiente encantada dijo:

"¡Yo le doy que cada vez que se peine, eche perlas y oro!"

Otra encantada dijo:

"¡Yo le doy la estrella del oriente, que le salga en la frente!"

Y la última le dijo:

"¡Yo le doy la varita de virtud!"

Le dieron la tripita y la muchacha se fue.

Cuando llegó a su casa, cada vez que iba a hablar, hacía "¡Blu, blu, blu!"—y echaba rubíes y diamantes. La vieja recogía los diamantes y rubíes; estaba muy contenta.

Como al otro día, le dijo a su hija que matara su chivita. Le cortó las tripas y la muchacha se fue. Echó la tripa al río y empezaba a gritar:

"¡Río, río, río abajo!" porque su hermanastra le había contado que así había dicho ella.

Cuando llegó al palacio estaba muy limpio. Entonces, ella echó la basura en el palacio e hizo muchas porquerías. Cuando las encantadas vinieron, muy enojadas dijeron:

"¿Quién me haría esta maldad? ¡La otra vez me hicieron un favor y ahora una maldad!"

Una de las encantadas dijo:

"¡Yo le doy que le salga el chino del burro en la frente!"

La otra dijo:

"¡Yo le doy que cada vez que hable, eche porquerías de caballo por la boca!"

Otra dijo:

"¡Yo le doy que cada vez que se peine, eche canánganas y piojos!"

Inmediatamente, la muchacha se fue.

Cuando llegó a su casa, cada vez que hablaba, echaba porquerías de caballo por la boca. Si se peinaba, echaba canánganas y piojos y siempre el chino del burro le salía más grande cada vez que la madre se lo cortaba.

Un día vinieron a convidar para un baile de un príncipe. Cenicienta dijo: "¡Ay, yo voy!"

Ella le dieron de patadas, y entonces, ella se quedó callada.

La noche del baile la madrastra y su hija se vistieron y se fueron. Dejaron a Cenicienta atrancada en el fogón. Como a las diez de la noche, hora en que estaba anunciado el baile, Cenicienta dijo:

"Varita de virtud, por la virtud que tú tienes y la que Dios te ha dado, quiero que me pongas con el traje que yo sola alumbre y no haya necesidad de luces. Quiero que me pongas allá con un coche que tenga las ruedas de oro y un caballo tan hermoso que no se encuentre en ninguna parte."

Cuando abrió los ojos estaba allá. El príncipe, desde que la vio, enseguida se enamoró de ella y la empezó a sacar a bailar. Como ya eran como las cuatro de la mañana, ella le estaba diciendo que se iba, porque ya era tarde. El príncipe le preguntaba:

"¿Usted es María, la Cenicienta?"

Ella le contestaba:

"¡La misma!"

Entonces, el príncipe le dijo que le iba a buscar un refresco antes que se fuera. Cuando el hombre salió, Cenicienta se tiró, se montó en el coche y se fue.

El príncipe no encontró a Cenicienta. Se volvió loco; empezó a darles de palos a los músicos y a los que los acompañaban. Se acabó el baile.

~

María, Cinderella

Once upon a time, a married couple had a daughter, but shortly afterward the mother died, leaving her husband a widower. There was another old woman who had a daughter called Cinderella. The widower's daughter had a little goat, and every time the girl set out to move her little goat to another pasture, the woman would say to her:

"If you persuade your father to marry me, I'll give you honey soup."

But every time María told her father, he would always answer:

"Today she gives you honey and tomorrow, bile."

The daughter kept on insisting so much that the father married the woman.

The old woman bought a nanny goat for Cinderella, but the very next day, María, the widower's daughter, became Cinderella, and Cinderella was known as María.

One day the stepdaughter had a whim to have Cinderella's little goat killed. No matter how much Cinderella wept to keep them from killing it, there was no way out. The woman beat up her stepdaughter and killed the nanny goat. She sent Cinderella to the river to wash its entrails, but she counted the tripe, telling her stepdaughter that if even one bit of it was missing, she would be punished.

Since Cinderella greatly feared the woman, she began to clean the tripe with much care. When the girl was turning to leave, one piece of the tripe fell into the river. She threw herself forward, saying:

"River, river, downriver, give me my little tripe; if you don't give it to me, my stepmother will kill me!"

She kept running while saying:

"River, river, downriver, give me my little tripe!"

While she was searching in such great anxiety, she came upon a very dirty palace. Some enchanted women lived there. They had gone out for Mass, leaving behind a very dirty little dog. As soon as the girl arrived, she began to clean the palace; she threw the garbage into the trash can, and she also bathed the little dog. Later, she hid behind the door.

When the enchanted women arrived, they shouted:

"Who could it be that did this work for us?"

The little dog started barking:

"Bow, wow, wow, she is behind the door!"

But since the girl did not come out, one of the enchanted women said:

"My gift to you is that each time you speak, rubies and diamonds will fall from your lips."

Another of the enchanted women said:

"My gift to you is that every time you comb your hair, you will sprinkle pearls and gold!"

And yet another said:

"I give you the eastern star upon your forehead."

The last of the enchanted women said:

"I give you a magic wand!"

They gave her the tripe, and the girl left.

When Cinderella got home, each time that she was going to speak, she made the sounds "Blu, blu, blu!"—but she spat out rubies and diamonds. The mean stepmother immediately gathered the diamonds and the rubies. She was now well pleased with her stepdaughter.

Just as before, the old woman told her daughter to kill her little goat, which was done at once. Then her daughter gathered the tripe, and she left the house. The mean girl dropped the piece of tripe into the river, and while jumping into the river, she began to shout, "River, river, downriver!" She was doing as her stepsister had told her she had done.

When she arrived at the palace, it was quite clean. The evil stepdaughter started trashing the palace until she made a huge mess. When the enchanted women arrived, one of them said:

"Who could have done this evil deed to me? Once they did me a favor, but now they have played an ugly prank."

Another of the woman said:

"I make you the gift of the growth of frizzled donkey's hair on your forehead!"

The next woman said:

"My gift to you is that when you speak, you will spit out horse manure!"

Yet the last of the enchanted women said:

"My gift to you is that every time you comb your hair, you will fling out ticks and lice!"

Immediately, the mean girl left.

When she got home, every time she spoke, she spewed horse manure from her mouth. If she combed her hair, she hurled ticks and lice, and always the frizzled donkey's hair grew out thicker each time her mother cut it.

One day an invitation came to a dance that a prince was hosting. Cinderella said at once:

"Oh, I am going!"

The two women kicked her; soon Cinderella stopped talking.

The night of the dance, the old woman and her daughter got dressed and went to the ball. Cinderella was left alone, huddled by the fireplace. At about ten o'clock that evening, the time announced for the dance, Cinderella said:

"Little magic wand, by the virtue that you have and the virtue that God has given you, I want you to place me at the dance in a glowing gown that I can illuminate without the need of lights. I want you to take me there in a coach with wheels of gold and a horse handsome beyond comparison."

When Cinderella opened her eyes, she was there. As soon as the prince saw her, he fell in love with the beautiful woman. The charming prince asked Cinderella to dance. At four in the morning, Cinderella told him that she had to leave because it was so late. The prince asked her:

"Are you María, the Cinderella?"

She answered:

"Yes, I am."

The prince told María Cinderella that he was going to get her something to drink before she left. While he was gone, María dashed out, leaped into the coach, and vanished.

It was all over right then. The prince went mad; he began to beat the musicians and their companions with sticks. Just like that, the dance ended.

Rosa, la Cenizosa[5]

Una vez una vieja tenía dos hijas, una que era lo más maldita y la otra que era blanca y bonísima, la cual se llamaba Rosa y la otra Carmen. La mamá quería más a Carmen que a Rosa y ésta tenía que hacer todos los trabajos de la casa. Rosa siempre estaba en la calle haciendo mandados y en el río lavando.

Un día en que mataron un puerco en su casa, mandaron a Rosa a lavar las tripitas al río. Y mientras las estaba lavando, se le fue una con la corriente. Ella se fue, diciendo:

"¡Río abajo, río arriba, dame mi tripita!"

Finalmente, llegó a una casita donde vivían tres brujas con dos chiquitos y un perrito. Rosa entró en la casa. Lavó todo lo que había sucio, recogió la casa y la barrió. A los muchachitos y el perrito, los bañó y los puso aseados.

Cuando las brujas llegaron, encontraron la casa tan bien recogida y a los muchachos y el perro limpios. Se preguntaron unas a otras, quién sería la que les hizo aquel favor. El perro les ladraba:

"¡Jau, jau, jau, detrás de la puerta está!"

Ellas buscaron quien había sido; le preguntaron a Rosa si había sido verdad. Después de haberle hecho varias preguntas, una bruja le dijo:

"¡Pues, yo te deseo que cuando llores, llueva aguacero tieso y que cuando te laves las manos, no necesites coger jabón de ninguna clase para lavártelas!"

La segunda le dijo:

"¡Cuando hables, lo que ha de salir de tu boca serán diamantes y perlas y cuando te peines, lo que caiga de tu cabeza serán granos de oro!"

La última le regaló una vara de virtud, para que cuando necesitase algo, diera tres veces sobre una piedra con ella; lo que pidiera se le concediera.

Cuando llegó de regreso a su casa, su mamá regañó a Rosa. Le pegó, diciéndole por qué se había tardado tanto. Tan pronto como Rosa empezó a llorar, llovía un aguacero tieso y cuando le fue a contestar, empezaron a salir diamantes y perlas. Después Rosa se fue a peinar; mientras se peinaba, caían granos de oro sobre su falda. Al ver tanto oro, Carmen corrió a decírselo a su mamá. La madre le dijo:

"¡Granos de oro! ¡Canángalas serán!"

Carmen le dijo:

"¡Es verdad, mamá! ¿Quieres que te traiga unos pocos para que los veas?"

Cuando se los trajo, la madre se sorprendió mucho. Inmediatamente, corrió hacia Rosa para preguntarle quién le había dado esa gracia. Rosa le contó, pero en vez de contar lo mismo, contó lo contrario.

Entonces, la madre, que quería todo para Carmen, mató otro puerco y la mandó a lavar las tripas. Carmen dejó ir una tripita con el agua; se fue diciendo lo mismo que Rosa hasta que llegó a la misma casa. Hizo todo lo que Rosa le había dicho. Se escondió detrás de la puerta hasta que llegaron las amas de casa.

La encontraron, y después de haberla maltratado, le desearon que le saliera un mango de burro en la frente que cada día le creciera más y más largo hasta que le arrastrara. Le dijeron que el pie le creciera igual y que cada vez que hablara, fueran sapos y culebras lo que saliera de su boca. Carmen se entristeció muchísimo.

Al llegar a la casa, cuando su mamá vio a Carmen, le preguntó qué le había pasado. Al contárselo, se le llenó a Carmen la cara de sapos y culebras.

Esto les pasa a las niñas que son egoístas y envidiosas y a las madres que quieren más a un hijo que a otro, que todo lo quieren para él.

~

Rosa, Cinderella

Once upon a time, an old lady had two daughters, one exceedingly bad and the other fair and extremely good; one was Rosa and the other was Carmen. The mother loved Carmen more than she did Rosa, so Rosa had to do all the housework. She was always out running errands and at the river washing.

One day they killed a pig at their house. They sent Rosa to wash the tripe in the river. While she was washing it, one piece was swept away by the current; she started running along, crying:

"Down river, up river, give me back my little tripe!"

Finally, she reached a little house where three witches lived with two little children and a little dog. She entered the house and cleaned everything that was dirty; she tidied up the house and swept it. She bathed and tidied up the little children and the little dog.

When the witches arrived, they found the house very tidy, and the children and the dog were clean. They asked each other who could have done them that favor. The dog was following them, barking:

"Woof, woof, woof, she is behind the door!"

So they searched, found Rosa, and asked her if the dog was speaking the truth. Rosa answered yes; it had been her.

After questioning her more, one witch told her:

"Well, I grant you a hard downpour when you cry and no need for soap when you wash your hands!"

The second witch said:

"When you speak, diamonds and pearls will drop from your mouth, and when you comb your hair, what falls from your head will be grains of gold!"

The last one gave her a magic wand so that when she needed something, she could tap it three times on a stone and then receive whatever she asked for.

When Rosa got home, her mother scolded and beat her, demanding to know why she was so late. As soon as Rosa began to cry, her tears became a downpour of water. As she attempted to speak, diamonds and pearls fell from her mouth. Afterward Rosa went to brush her hair. While combing her hair, grains of gold fell on Rosa's skirt. Upon seeing so much gold, Carmen ran to tell her mother. The mother said:

"Grains of gold! They must be ticks!"

Carmen insisted:

"But it is true, Mama. Do you want me to bring you a few for you to see them?"

Carmen then brought them to her mother. The woman was surprised; she ran toward Rosa to ask her who had given her that grace. Rosa told her but told them the opposite instead of the truth.

The mother, who wanted Carmen to have everything Rosa had, killed another pig, ordering Carmen to wash the tripe. Carmen let a piece of tripe fall into the river. She went along saying what Rosa had said until she arrived at the same house. She trashed the house as Rosa had told her to do. She hid behind the door until the witches arrived.

Soon the witches found Carmen. They punished her instead with terrible gifts; they imposed upon her forehead frizzled donkey's hair that every day would grow longer and longer until it dragged on the ground. They told her that her feet would also grow huge and that each time she spoke, she would spew toads and snakes out of her mouth.

Carmen became extremely sad. As soon as she got home, her mother saw her terrible transformation. She asked Carmen what had happened. As the sad girl spoke to her mother, her face suddenly filled with toads and snakes.

This is what happens to girls who are selfish and envious and to those mothers who love one child more than another and want everything for that child.

Rosita, la Cenicienta[6]

Una vez había un viudo que se llamaba Simplicio. Este buen hombre tenía una niñita llamada Rosa, y cerca de la casa donde vivían, habitaba una viuda que también tenía una hija. La hija del viudo era muy bonita y la de la viuda era fea. Don Simplicio había encargado a su hija que no fuera a casa de la viuda Pepa, que así se llamaba la vecina.

Don Simplicio todos los días se iba a trabajar, dejando a Rosa haciendo el almuerzo; sucedió que un día se la apagó la candela, y Rosa fue a casa de la vieja a buscar con que encenderla. La vieja enseguida la lavó y la peinó, diciéndole que le dijera a su padre que se casara con ella. La muchachita se lo dijo a su papá y él se quedó espantado; se casaría con la vieja cuando se le acabaran unos zapatos muy fuertes que se compró, pero tenía que ser sin usarlos.

Como Rosita veía que la vieja era complaciente con ella, quiso que los zapatos se acabaran pronto, y todos los días trataba de romperlos. Al fin, los zapatos se acabaron y Simplicio se casó con la vieja.

Los primeros días, Pepa cuidaba muchísimo de Rosita, pero después acabó por maltratarla. La niña tenía una cabrita y Pepa la mató. Después la mandó a lavar las tripas, pero una se le fue río abajo; la pobre niña no consiguió cogerla. Se fue río abajo hasta que llegó a una casita de encantadas. Rosita entró en la casita, la limpió y la arregló todo lo que pudo. Después se escondió detrás de una puerta para ver lo que pasaba.

Tan pronto como llegaron, las encantadas vieron el bien que les habían hecho; empezaron a preguntarse quién sería la persona que les hizo tanto bien. Ellas tenían un perrito que decía:

"¡Jai, jai, detrás de la puerta está!"

Y las mujeres contestaban:

"¡Ay, perrito embustero, si tú dijeras la verdad!"

Pero al fin, encontraron a Rosita.

Las encantadas la colmaron de regalos; entre ellos, le dieron una varita de virtud y le desearon que le saliera el sol y la luna en la cara, a fin de que se pusiera muy bonita.

Cuando Rosita, la niña, fue a su casa, la madrastra tenía ya coraje y la estaba esperando con un fuete para darle, pero cuando la vio tan bonita, le preguntó la causa. Explicándole todo, la vieja mandó a matar una vaca y, a Juana, su hija, a lavar las tripas. Pero le pasó todo lo contrario que a Rosita, porque ésta, en vez de hacer bien, hizo mucho mal, rompiendo y ensuciando todo en la casa. Cuando vinieron las encantadas, la consumieron a maldiciones. Una de ellas le deseó que le saliera un chifle en la frente que, mientras más le cortaran, más le creciera.

Cuando Juana llegó a su casa, la madre ya estaba deshecha porque llegara y verla tan bonita como Rosita. Al verla tan fea, por poco queda loca del susto.

En la vecindad vivía un rey que tenía un hijo. El príncipe quería casarse e hizo una fiesta a fin de que fueran todas las jóvenes para elegir él una. La vieja Pepa se fue con Juana, su hija, a la fiesta; antes de irse derramó un quintal de mostaza y otro de semilla de tabaco para que lo juntara. Mató una res para que Rosita les preparara una comida que no estuviera ni fría ni caliente. Rosita tenía que tenerlo hecho, escoger y recoger las semillas para cuando ellas llegaran.

Como Rosita tenía la varita de virtud, consiguió hacerlo todo. Después le dijo a la varita:

"Varita de virtud, por la virtud que tú tienes y la que Dios te ha dado, quiero que me traigas el mejor vestido del mundo y un caballo que corra como el viento."

En seguida se le apareció un vestido color cielo y un caballo, tal como ella lo había pedido.

Rosita montó a caballo y emprendió el viaje. En muy poco tiempo llegó al lugar de la fiesta, que ya estaba muy bonita. Cuando Rosita entró, se alegró mucho más. Al entrar Rosita, Juana dijo a su mamá:

"Mira, Mamá, ¡ésa es Rosa!"

Su madre le contestó:

"¡Qué va a ser, muchacha! Si con el trabajo que yo le dejé es imposible que pueda venir, a menos que deje el trabajo y, si cuando yo llegue ha sucedido, hoy mismo le rompo los huesos. Si no le pegué cuando las tripas, ahora me la paga."

Como las encantadas le echaron tantas maldiciones a Juana, ésta cada vez que escupía dejaba un olor muy malo, y ya las iban a echar de la fiesta.

Rosita era tan bonita que el príncipe se enamoró de ella; no la dejaba sola ni un momento. Cuando ella vio que la fiesta se iba a terminar, le rogó al príncipe que le diera una copa de agua. El fue a buscársela, y en esto ella se fue.

Por tres veces se hizo una fiesta. A todas fue Rosita, pero en la última vez se le cayó un zapatito. Entonces, el príncipe mandó a un número de gente a buscar a la que le viniera el zapatito, pero a nadie le servía.

Por fin fueron a casa de la vieja Pepa y ésta escondió a Rosita en la cocina. Salió sola con su Juanita. Trataron de ponerle el zapato a Juana, pero no le sirvió. La vieja empezó a cortarle pedazos del pie, pero nunca le sirvió. La Cenizosa estaba en la cocina y la gente la veía por las hendiduras. Se oía una voz que decía:

"Quizás sí, quizás no, quizás sí sería yo."

La vieja mandó a callar a Rosita y la gente le preguntó a quién mandaba a callar. Ella contestó que a nadie, pero al fin hicieron salir a la Cenizosa. Le midieron el zapato y le sirvió.

Entonces, llevaron a Rosita donde estaba el príncipe y se casó con él. Juana se quedó con sus pies enfermos.

~

Rosita, Cinderella

Once there was a widower named Simplicio. This good man and his little girl, Rosa, affectively known as Rosita, lived near the house where a widow, Pepa, lived with her daughter. The widower's daughter was very pretty, but the widow's daughter was ugly. Simplicio had ordered his daughter not to go into Pepa's house.

Don Simplicio went to work every day, leaving Rosa alone to prepare lunch, but it happened that one day, the firepit went out, and Rosita went to the old woman's house looking for a flame. Immediately the widow bathed her and combed her hair. The wicked woman told Rosa to tell her father to marry Pepa. Rosita told her papa, and he, shocked, answered that he would marry the widow only after some very stout shoes that he had bought were worn out without ever having been worn.

Since Rosita saw that the old lady was indulgent toward her, she wanted the shoes to wear out fast, so every day she tried to tear them. Finally, the shoes were ruined. Simplicio married the old lady.

At first Pepa took excellent care of Rosita, but she ended up mistreating her stepdaughter. Rosita had a little goat. Pepa killed it and then ordered Rosita to wash its tripe, but one piece fell into the river, and the poor girl couldn't catch it. She went down the river until she arrived at a little house that belonged to witches. Rosita entered the house. She cleaned it and tidied it as much as she could. She then hid behind a door in order to see what happened.

Soon some enchanted women arrived. They saw the good deeds that someone had done for them; they began to ask themselves who could have done them this kindness. The women's little dog started barking:

"Uf, uf, she is behind the door!"

The women scolded the dog:

"You are fibbing, puppy. If only you could tell the truth!"

But they finally found Rosita.

The enchanted women showered Rosa with gifts, including a magic wand. They also wished the sun and the moon to shine upon her face. Rosita became extremely beautiful.

When Rosita got home, her stepmother was angry with her. She had been patiently waiting for her with a whip to beat her, but as soon as she saw how pretty Rosita looked, she started questioning her. After Rosita told her stepmother what had happened, the old woman ordered a cow to be killed. She then sent Juana, her daughter, to wash its tripe. What Juana did, however, was exactly the opposite of what Rosita had done. Juana did not do the enchanted women a favor; instead, she tore up and soiled the entire house. When the women arrived, they overwhelmed Juana with curses. One of the women wished upon her a horn on her forehead that would grow longer every time it was cut.

When Juana got home, her mother was waiting, eagerly expecting her. She wanted her daughter to look as pretty as Rosita. But upon seeing Juana so ugly, Pepa almost lost her mind.

In their neighborhood there was a king who had a son, a prince who wished to marry. The prince planned a dance for all young women to attend; he so much wanted to find a woman to marry her.

Pepa and her daughter, Juana, went to the ball. Before leaving, however, Pepa scattered a hundred pounds of mustard seeds plus an equal amount of tobacco seeds. She also killed a cow for Rosita to prepare a meal that was neither too cold nor too hot. Rosita also had to gather and separate the two kinds of seeds—all of these tasks before Pepa's and Juana's return from the party.

Since Rosita had the magic wand, she managed to complete the chores fast. She then said to the wand:

"Little magic wand, by your own virtue and by that given to you by God, I want you to bring me the best gown in the world and a horse that runs like the wind."

At once there appeared a heavenly blue dress and a horse exactly as she had asked for.

Rosita mounted the horse and began the trip. Soon she arrived at the place where the ball was already a beautiful sight. When Rosita entered the ballroom, she was delighted with the exquisite sight of the room. Upon seeing Rosita, Juana said to her mother:

"Look, Mom, it's Rosa!"

Her mother answered:

"How can that be, girl? All the work I left her made it impossible for her to be able to come—unless she just left the work undone. If, when I get home, that has happened, today I'll break her bones. If I did not beat her for losing the tripe, I'll make her pay for it now."

But since the enchanted women had placed so many curses on Juana, every time she spat, she released a foul odor. They were about to be thrown out of the ball.

Rosita was so pretty that the prince fell in love with her. The prince wouldn't leave her alone for even a moment. When Rosita saw that the ball was about to end, she asked the prince to get her a cup of water. To please her, he went to get it. She immediately left the ball.

There were three other parties, and Rosita attended all of them. At the third ball, she lost one of her little slippers. At once the prince ordered a lot of people to search for someone whose foot fit the slipper. But it did not fit anybody.

Finally, they went to the house of old Pepa, who hid Rosita in the kitchen. She went out of the house with Juana to meet the prince. They tried to put the slipper on Juana, but it did not fit. The old woman began to cut pieces from the girl's foot, but the shoe still did not fit. Rosita, Cinderella, who was in the kitchen, where the prince's servants could see her through the cracks, started singing:

"Maybe yes, maybe no, maybe I am the one."

The old woman ordered Rosita to be silent, but the prince's servants asked whom she had ordered to be silent. Pepa lied and said:

"Nobody."

The servants finally made Cinderella come out. They measured the shoe, and it fit her. Immediately, they carried Rosita to the prince.

Rosita, Cinderella, married the handsome prince. Juana was left in pain with a badly injured foot.

A Porto Rican orange vendor

CHAPTER 2

Rescuing Encantados

El príncipe clavel[1]

Una vez había tres hermanas, siendo la más pequeña la más bonita. Una mañana la más grande estaba barriendo el balcón cuando salió un clavel saltando, y entonces, ella quiso cogerlo, pero él no se dejó coger. Se fue a contarles a las otras dos hermanas lo que le había sucedido. Dijo la del medio:

"Pues, ¡yo voy y lo cojo!"

Las otras dos le dijeron que fuera. El clavel salió, pero ella no pudo cogerlo.

La segunda dijo:

"Pues, ¡yo voy y lo cojo!"

Se fue y cuando ella estaba barriendo, salió el clavel y lo cogió. Entonces, se fue y lo guardó. Esa noche, cuando fue a buscarlo, se encontró con que se había transformado en un príncipe encantado.

El príncipe empezó a enamorarla; después de muchos días, una noche ella estaba buscando más cosas y, sin darse cuenta, le cayeron tres gotas de esperma al príncipe encantado. El le dijo que lo había encantado más; ahora para desencantarlo tendría que pasar muchos trabajos. Necesitaba comprarse un vestido de plomo, un par de zapatos y un sombrero y empezar a andar hasta que se gastaran.

Un mes ella estaba andando cuando llegó al bohío donde vivía una vieja solitaria. Le preguntó si sabía donde vivía el príncipe clavel. La anciana le dijo que nunca lo había oído nombrar, pero que su hijo, que era el sol, andaba tanto y tanto, quizás lo habría oído mentar. Le dijo que él tenía muy mal genio, que se escondiera en un barril para que cuando él viniera no la viera.

Más tarde llegó el sol. Le dijo a la viejita:

"Fo, fo, a carne humana me huele aquí,

si no me la das,

¡te como a ti!"

La viejita le dijo:

"¡Ay hijo, si es que tú estás suda'o!"[2]

"¡No, no; sí es que aquí hay carne humana!" le contestó el sol.

La viejita le dijo que era una niña que andaba en busca de Príncipe Clavel. El sol le dijo que lo había oído nombrar; para encontrarlo tenía que andar como cinco meses. Entonces, la vieja le regaló a la niña una gallina de oro.

Habían transcurrido como dos meses cuando la niña llegó a casa de la luna. Le preguntó si no había oído nombrar a Príncipe Clavel. La luna le dijo que sí, pero todavía le faltaba mucho para llegar. Le dio una peineta de oro y la niña empezó a andar otra vez.

Después de tres meses, la niña llegó a la casa de la madre de todos los animales. Entonces, empezaron a llegar animales, pero ninguno le daba noticias.

Llegó luego el ave que más volaba. Le dijo que conocía al Príncipe Clavel; ese mismo día se celebrarían las bodas del príncipe. La niña se puso triste. Le dijo que si la quería llevar hasta allá. El ave le dijo que sí; la niña cogió cuatrocientos sacos de comestibles y él se fue con ella por en medio del mar.

Se terminó todo lo que había de comer. El ave le dijo a la niña:

"¡Dame de comer o te suelto!"

Entonces, ella le dijo que le comiera un brazo. Así el pájaro le comió los brazos y las dos piernas; cuando llegaron a un árbol, cerca de la casa del príncipe, ella estaba con su vestido de plomo.

El príncipe estaba listo para casarse. La niña le dijo a la novia del príncipe que si la dejaba entrar a ver al que iba a ser su esposo, le daba la
gallina de oro. Ella, como ya iba él a ser su marido, accedió. La niña fue
hasta donde estaba el príncipe y empezó a contarle cómo había pasado ese
tiempo. El príncipe le dijo:

"¡Pues, tú debes ser mi esposa!"

Entonces, le dio a la otra unos cantazos, casándose muy contento con
la niña.

La boda fue bonita y vivieron felices.

~

The Carnation Prince

Once upon a time, there were three sisters; the youngest was the prettiest. One morning the oldest sister was sweeping the porch when a carnation flew in. She tried to grab it, but it would not let her catch it. The girl
then went to tell her two sisters what had happened to her. The middle
sister said to her:

"Well, I'm going out there. I will catch it!"

The others told her to go on. The carnation came up; she could not
catch it either. The youngest sister said:

"Well, I'm off to catch it!"

She went, and while she was sweeping, the carnation came up. She
caught it. She put it away. That night she went to look for the carnation.
She found that it had been transformed into an enchanted prince.

The prince began to flirt with her. After many days, one night as she was
looking for something, without her noticing, three drops of candle wax
fell upon the enchanted prince. He told her that she had enchanted him
even more. Now in order to disenchant him, she would have to perform
many tasks. She had to buy herself a dress of lead, a pair of shoes, and a hat
and begin walking until they were worn out.

She had been walking for several months when she arrived at a hut
where a solitary old woman lived. The girl asked the woman whether she
knew where Prince Carnation lived. The old woman told her that she had
never heard of him, but her son, who was the sun, went around and around
so much that maybe he would have heard him mentioned. She warned the
girl about her son's bad disposition; she should hide in a barrel so that
when the sun came, he would not see her.

Later the sun finally came. He said to the little old lady:

"Sniff, sniff, I smell human flesh here,
and if you don't give it to me
I'll eat you!"

The little old lady said to the sun:
"Oh, dear son, that's just because you are sweaty!"
"Oh, no, it's that there is human flesh here," replied the sun.

The old woman told her son that it was a girl traveling in search of
Prince Carnation. The sun replied that he had heard the name, but
in order to find the prince, the girl had to walk for about five months.
The little old lady gave the girl a golden chicken. The girl left at once.

After walking about two months, the girl arrived at the house of the
moon. There she asked whether the moon had heard of Prince Carnation.
The moon told her yes, but it would be a long time before the girl reached
him. The moon gave her a small golden comb. The girl set out to walk
again.

After a total of three months, the girl arrived at the home of the mother
of all animals. There she inquired about the prince again. The animals
began to arrive, but none of them gave her any news.

Soon after came the bird that flies high and wide. The bird told her that
he knew Prince Carnation; in fact, that that very day they would celebrate
the prince's wedding. The girl became sad, and she asked whether the bird
would be willing to carry her there. He said yes. After the girl grabbed four
hundred bags of food, off they went over the middle of the sea.

The bird finished off all the food in the bags. He then said to the girl:

"Give me something to eat or I'll drop you!"

She told him to eat one of her arms. So he ate her arms and both her legs. When they reached a tree near the prince's house, she was in her dress of lead.

The prince was dressed for the wedding. The girl told the prince's bride that if she was allowed to see the groom, she would give her the golden chicken. The bride-to-be agreed. As soon as the girl reached the prince, the girl began to tell him what had happened to her. The prince told the tired the girl:

"Well, it's you who ought to be my wife!"

After giving his bride-to-be some beatings, the prince joyfully married the girl.

The wedding was pretty. They lived happily ever after.

El príncipe becerro[3]

Esta era una vez y dos son tres había una señora que tenía tres hijas, y cuando su padre salía de viaje le encargaban algo, todas ellas menos la más pequeña. Un día le dijo el padre a la niña:

"Hijita mía, ¿por qué cuando yo salgo no me encargas nada?"

Su hija dijo:

"Papá, tráeme una rosa."

El padre dijo:

"Por ser la primera vez que mi hija más pequeña me encarga algo, ni me encarga nada de valor, solamente una rosa. En fin, se la traeré."

El fue al pueblo y, al estar ya casi en su casa, se acordó de la rosa que se le había olvidado, pero siguió andando cuando vio un jardín. Se preguntó para sí:

"¿De quién serán estas flores?"

Como él a nadie veía, se metió en el jardín sin permiso y cogió una rosa. Por debajo de la tierra oyó una voz que le dijo:

"Coge la rosa, pero tienes que traerme a tu hijita el sábado próximo."

Él, al oír estas palabras, se sorprendió, pero se dijo:

"¡No ha de ser tanto problema!"

El sábado siguiente allí estaba el padre con su hija. Oyó una voz que le dijo que se fuera. Debía dejar a la niña allí.

Enseguida la niña vio una casa muy bonita. Escuchó una voz:

"Entre usted, señorita."

Era el príncipe becerro, quien estaba encantado, le faltaban muy pocos meses para salir del encantamiento. Pronto se iba a casar.

Le pusieron a la niña café, pero ella no vio a nadie; se lo tomó porque tenía mucha hambre. La voz le dijo que no alumbrara con vela porque se le caería una gota de esperma; entonces, no podría verlo nunca. Pero un día, ella fue a su casa a ver a su madre, se llevó una vela; por la noche, la encendió para ver al príncipe. Entonces, le cayeron tantas gotas de esperma en la cara del príncipe que le quemó las pestañas. El le dijo:

"Me has encantado más ahora. Para poder conseguirme necesitas vestirte de bronce."

Ella se vistió en bronce y se fue a andar. Aunque estaba rendida de cansancio, seguía caminando hasta que llegó a la casa de la luna. Allí comió.

Después llegó a casa del sol; le preguntó si él sabía dónde vivía el príncipe becerro. El sol le contestó que desde que era sol y había alumbrado tanto, no había sabido dónde vivía el príncipe becerro. No debía apurarse, añadió. Le ordenó que fuera a ver a las nubes; ellas tal vez sabrían. La niña se fue.

Cuando llegó a la casa de las nubes, les dijo:

"Buenos días."

"Buenos se los dé Dios. Entre."

"No, vengo solamente a ver si ustedes me pueden decir dónde vive el príncipe becerro."

Ellas le dijeron:

"Desde que vivimos en el mundo no hemos oído nombrar al Príncipe Becerro. Pero no se apure, espere que venga el ave coja. Ella siempre busca las cosas mejores; quizás ella sepa."

Después de un momento llegó el ave coja. Le preguntaron por el príncipe becerro.

"Ahora vengo de su casamiento," contestó inmediatamente.

La niña le dijo que la llevara hasta el príncipe, pero el ave le contestó que tenía que pagarle algo. Enseguida la montó en su cuello y se la llevó. Ella llevaba una peineta, un peine de oro y una gallina con quince pollitos también de oro.

La criada le dijo al Príncipe Becerro:

"Mi amo, si usted supiera, allí hay una señora que tiene una peineta, un peine y una gallina de oro."

El le dijo:

"Vete, pregúntale si me las vende."

La niña le dijo que si la dejaba dormir a los pies del príncipe becerro. La señora le dijo que sí. Como a la media noche, cuando ya estaba dormida

la esposa del príncipe, la niña le iba diciendo que si se acordaba de esto y
de esto otro.

El se acordó y, enseguida, la abrazó.

El príncipe mandó quemar a la otra mujer. Se casó con la mujer valiente.

Colorín colorado, este cuento está terminado.

The Calf Prince

Once upon a time, or twice, or thrice, there was a woman who had three
daughters. Often whenever their father traveled, all of them asked him
to bring them something back, except for the smallest one. One day her
father said to her:

"Daughter, why is it that when I go out, you don't ask me to bring you
something?"

The girl replied:

"Papa, bring me a rose!"

The father said:

"This is the first time that my youngest daughter has asked me to bring
her something. She desires nothing costly, just a single rose. All right, I will
bring it to her."

He went away. On the way home, the man realized that he had forgotten
the rose. He kept walking until he came upon a garden. He asked himself:

"Whose flowers can these be?"

Not seeing anyone, he entered the garden without permission, and he
picked one rose. From beneath the ground, he suddenly heard a voice say
to him:

"You may pluck the rose, but next Saturday you must bring your little
daughter to me." Although he was surprised when he heard these words,
he told himself:

"Oh, that was nothing!"

The next Saturday the father brought his daughter to the mysterious garden. He heard again the same voice. It told him to go away and leave his daughter there alone, which he did at once. As the girl saw a very pretty house, she heard a voice:

"Come in, miss."

It was Prince Calf, who had been enchanted. He was to be freed in just a few months to get married.

Coffee was put before the girl. She saw nobody, but she drank it anyway because she was very hungry. The voice told her not to light a candle because if even a drop of the wax hit the face of the enchanted prince, she would never be able to see him.

One day the girl went home to visit with her mother. She carried a candle back with her. That night the disobedient girl lit the candle—so much did she wish to see her enchanted prince. So many drops of wax fell on his face that the prince's eyelashes were burned. The angry man said to her:

"You have now enchanted me even more. In order to free me, you will have to dress yourself in bronze."

She got dressed in bronze and started walking on foot. She was exhausted, but she kept marching until she reached the house of the moon, where she ate. Later on, she reached the house of the sun. The girl asked the sun if he knew where Prince Calf lived. The sun replied that although he was sunlight and he shone so much, he did not know where Prince Calf lived. She should not worry, though; if she could reach the clouds, perhaps they would know.

She left at once. Upon arriving at the house of the clouds, she said:

"Good day."

The clouds replied:

"May God make it good for you. Come in."

"No, I am just coming to ask if you can tell me where Prince Calf lives."

They told her:

"Ever since we have lived in the world, we have not heard the name of Prince Calf. Don't worry, though; wait until the lame bird comes, since she always searches for the best things. For sure, she must know."

A moment later the lame bird came. The clouds asked her about the prince.

"I've just come from his wedding."

The girl asked the bird to carry her to the palace's house, but the bird replied that the girl would have to pay her something. At once the bird mounted the girl on her neck and carried her away. She took with her a golden ornamental Spanish comb and a hair comb along with a hen with fifteen chicks, also of gold.

The Prince Calf's maid announced the girl's arrival to the palace:

"Master, you should know that there is a young lady who has arrived holding a Spanish comb, a comb, and a hen. All of gold!"

He told her:

"Go back; ask her if she would sell them to me."

The girl said yes, but only if Prince Calf would let her sleep at his feet. His wife agreed, and about midnight, while the wife was asleep, the girl talked to him about whether he remembered certain things.

He remembered. At once, he embraced her.

He ordered his wife to be burned. Prince Calf married the brave girl.

Red blush, this tale is ended.

Las tres rosas de Alejandría[4]

Una vez había un señor que tenía una hija llamada Alejandrina. La madre de Alejandrina había muerto, y el padre se había casado en segundas nupcias con una viuda que tenía dos hijas. La madrastra no quería mucho a Alejandrina, a quien procuraba perderla por todos los medios que estaban a su alcance.

El padre de Alejandrina tuvo que hacer un viaje; preguntó a sus hijas qué querían que les trajese. Una de las hijastras le pidió un vestido y la otra encargó un sombrero. Alejandrina le pidió las tres rosas de Alejandría. El padre le dijo:

"Hija, tú quieres perderme. ¿Dónde voy yo a encontrar esas rosas? Pero haré todo lo posible por conseguirlas."

El señor emprendió su viaje. Antes de regresar compró los regalos para sus hijastras sin conseguir el encargo de su hija. Cuando regresaba a casa se extravió en un bosque; allí se le apareció una viejecita. Ella le preguntó:

"¿En qué andas, hijo?"

"Señora, estoy buscando las tres rosas de Alejandría para llevárselas a mi hija."

"Te diré donde se encuentran, pero tienes que hacer lo que te mande. En el jardín de aquel castillo están las rosas, pero antes de llegar te van a gritar, a hacerte burla y a tirarte piedras. Tú no puedes mirar para atrás, porque si miras te pierdes."

El padre de Alejandrina siguió las indicaciones de la viejecita; cogió las tres rosas y se las llevó a su hija. Alejandrina sembró las tres rosas en el jardín de su casa; cuando las estaba sembrando un pajarito se paró en la rama de un árbol y le dijo:

"Alejandrina, háblame."

Ella no le hizo caso al pajarito.

La madrastra, quien quería perder a Alejandrina, fue a palacio. Le dijo al rey:

"Majestad, Alejandrina dice que se atreve a preparar la ropa de todo el ejército en un día."

El rey mandó a llamar a la muchacha. Le dijo:

"Si no cumples lo prometido te quitaré la vida."

El rey mandó que llevasen la ropa para que la muchacha la preparase. Alejandrina se fue al río y se puso a llorar. El pajarito se paró en la rama de un árbol y le preguntó:

"Alejandrina, ¿por qué lloras? ¿Qué te pasa? Háblame, yo te ayudaré."

Alejandrina permaneció callada, pero el pajarito le preparó toda la ropa en un instante. La muchacha se puso muy contenta. Inmediatamente llevó la ropa a palacio.

A los pocos días, la madrastra volvió al palacio del rey. Le dijo:

"Majestad, Alejandrina dice que se atreve a presentarle los pañales en que a usted le envolvieron recién nacido."

El rey mandó a buscar a Alejandrina; le dijo que si no le traía los pañales le quitaría la vida.

Alejandrina se fue para su casa y se puso a llorar. Cuando el pajarito la vio, le dijo:

"Alejandrina, háblame, sé lo que te sucede y te puedo ayudar."

Alejandrina no contestó, pero el pajarito le trajo los pañales. Ella se los llevó al rey.

El rey había perdido una sortija que apreciaba mucho. La madrastra de la muchacha le dijo al rey que aquélla podía traérsela. El rey la mandó llamar; le prometió que si le traía la sortija la casaría con su hijo. Alejandrina volvió a su casa, se vistió toda de luto y se puso a llorar.

El pajarito se le acercó. Le dijo con mucha dulzura:

"Alejandrina, qué triste está mi corazoncito."

Ella le contestó:

"El mío está más triste, y por eso, estoy vestida de luto."

Aquel pajarito era un príncipe, quien tan solo esperaba que aquella muchacha le hablase para recuperar su forma antigua. Al momento se convirtió en un apuesto joven. El llevó a Alejandrina al palacio, le contó al rey lo sucedido y se casó con ella.

Alejandrina fue feliz todo el resto de su vida.

~

The Three Roses of Alexandria

Once there was a man who had a daughter named Alejandrina. Her mother had died, and her father married a widow with two daughters. The stepmother did not like Alejandrina; she used any means she could to get rid of her.

Alejandrina's father had to take a long trip. Before leaving, he asked his daughters what they wanted him to bring them. One stepdaughter asked him for a dress, and the other asked him for a hat. Alejandrina asked him for the Three Roses of Alexandria. The father said to her:

"Daughter, do you want to ruin me? Where am I going to find those roses? But I will do anything to get them."

The man left on his trip. Before returning, he bought the gifts for his stepdaughters without finding what his own daughter wanted. On the way home, he got lost in a forest. A little old lady appeared before him. She asked him:

"What are you up to, son?"

He replied:

"Lady, I am searching for the Three Roses of Alexandria to carry them to my daughter."

"I will tell you where to find them, but you have to do what I order you. The roses are in the garden of that castle, but before you can get to it, you will be yelled at and made fun of. Rocks will also be thrown at you. Whatever you do, you must not look behind you. If you do, you are lost."

Alejandrina's father followed the little old lady's instructions. He plucked three roses and happily carried them to his daughter. Alejandrina then planted the three roses in the garden of their house. As she was planting them, a little bird landed on the branch of a tree. It said to her:

"Alejandrina, speak to me."

She paid no attention to the little bird.

The stepmother, who still wanted to get rid of her, went to the palace to speak to the king. She said:

"Your Majesty, Alejandrina says that she dares to wash the clothing of all the army in one day."

The king sent at once for the girl. He commanded her:

"If you do not fulfill your promise, I shall take your life from you."

The king ordered the soldiers to carry the clothing for the girl to wash them.

Alejandrina went to the river and began to cry. The little bird, perched on a branch of a tree, again spoke to her:

"Alejandrina, why are you crying? What is happening to you? Tell me so that I can help you."

Alejandrina kept silent, but in an instant, the little bird washed the clothing. The girl happily carried the clothes to the palace.

A few days later, the stepmother went back to the king's palace. She now claimed:

"Your Majesty, Alejandrina says she dares to present you with the clothes in which they wrapped you at your birth."

The angry king sent for Alejandrina; he told her that if she did not bring him his baby clothes, he would have her killed.

Alejandrina set out to go home; she was sad and bitterly crying. When the little bird saw her, once again it addressed her:

"Alejandrina, talk to me. I know what is happening to you. I can help you."

Although Alejandrina did not answer, the little bird brought her the king's baby clothes. Happily, she carried them to the king.

Next, because the king had lost a ring that he was very fond of, the girl's stepmother told him that the girl could bring it to him. The king sent for Alejandrina. He told her that if she brought him the ring, he would marry her to his son. Alejandrina went back home, dressed in mourning clothes; she was crying bitterly. The little bird approached. Kindly it spoke to her:

"Alejandrina, how sad my little heart is."

She finally replied:

"My heart is even sadder. That is why I am wearing mourning clothes."

That little bird was a prince; he had just been waiting for that girl to speak to him in order to recover his original form. At once he changed into a handsome youth. He carried her to the palace, told the king what had happened, and married her.

Alejandrina was happy for the rest of her life.

Los siete cuervos[5]

Había una vez un matrimonio que tenía siete hijos. El marido y su esposa anhelaban tener una hija y, al fin, fueron satisfechos sus deseos. La mujer fue madre de una niña tan delgada y diminuta que sus padres temían que se les muriera de un momento a otro.

Como el cura del pueblo estaba de viaje y no podía darle el agua del bautismo, decidieron darle el agua del socorro. El padre envió a sus hijos en busca de un cántaro de agua a la fuente. Los siete hermanos se fueron corriendo a la fuente y llenaron el cántaro.

Entonces, se pusieron a disputar quien de los siete llegaba primero, pero al empezar a correr, se les cayó el cántaro y se les hizo mil pedazos. Los siete hermanos se quedaron muy asustados por el suceso; se miraban unos a los otros sin atreverse a volver a casa. El padre desesperado por la tardanza de sus hijos se asomaba de un lado a otro y no aparecían esos granujas de chiquillos. El hombre estaba tan desesperado que lanzó una terrible maldición:

"¡Permita Dios que esos granujas de chiquillos se conviertan en cuervos!"

El padre y la madre lloraron amargamente porque no hay poder humano que evite los efectos de una maldición una vez lanzada.

Por fortuna la recién nacida no murió; siendo cada día más notable su gracia y su belleza. La niña era el único gozo y el mayor consuelo de sus padres que la querían mucho, quienes trataban de ocultarle el suceso. Una vecina suya muy chismosa y habladora llamó un día a la niña para acariciarla y regalarle varios dulces, y al mismo tiempo, como quien no quiere la cosa al decir nada de particular, le preguntó a la niña por sus hermanos.

La niña contestó:

"Yo no tengo hermanos, ya lo sabe usted."

La señora contestó:

"Vaya que si los tienes, y por cierto, tú tienes la culpa de su desgracia."

La niña se fue para su casa muy triste y se puso a llorar. Les pidió explicación a sus padres. Ellos, quienes siempre trataron de ocultárselo, no tuvieron otro remedio que confesar la verdad.

Un día desapareció de casa la niña sin llevarse nada más que un calabazo de agua, un cuchillo y una sortija de plata. Sus padres lloraron amargamente llenos de desesperación, y por poco, se mueren de disgusto. La niña se encontró en el camino a un ángel, quien le preguntó para dónde iba. Ella le dijo que iba en busca de sus hermanos.

"Tus hermanos viven en la montaña de cristal de roca. Toma esta llave y con ella puedes abrir las puertas."

La niña iba loca de contento porque podría cumplir con su obligación, pero cuando metió la mano en el bolsillo, no encontró la llave. Perdió la esperanza y lloró sin consuelo, pero de pronto se le ocurrió una idea:

"¿Quién sabe si el dedo pequeño de mi mano derecha pueda servir de ayuda y abra la cerradura?"

Sin pensar en el dolor que podría sufrir, cogió el cuchillo y se cortó el dedo.

No bien había metido el hueso en la cerradura, la puerta se abrió de par en par. La niña entró; salió a su encuentro un anciano, a quien le dijo que iba en busca de siete hermanos que eran siete cuervos negros. El le respondió:

"Aquí viven y han salido; no tardarán en venir."

Entonces, la niña se fue a la mesa. De cada plato cogió un poquito y de cada copa un sorbito, y en la última copa echó la sortija. Inmediatamente, se escondió.

No tardaron mucho en llegar los siete cuervos a su casa. El más pequeño dijo:

"Han tocado mi plato y mi copa."

Todos dijeron a una misma voz lo mismo. Cuando el mayor se tomó la copa de vino encontró la sortija, la cogió en el pico, exclamando:

"¡Oh! ¿Cómo habrá venido esta sortija aquí? Es de nuestra madre; si hubiese sido nuestra hermana y nos estrechara a uno por uno contra su corazón, recobraríamos la forma humana."

Al decir esto, salió la niña de donde estaba y besó a sus hermanos uno por uno en el pico, quienes quedaron hechos siete hermanos jóvenes. No tardaron nada más que en recoger sus tesoros que habían recogido en la montaña, y se pusieron en camino. Cuando llegaron a casa sus padres, quienes estaban próximos a morir de tristeza y pesar, recibieron la alegría más grande del mundo. Fueron muy felices con sus queridos hijos y con su bella y cariñosa hija.

El padre jamás volvió a intentar lanzar una blasfemia porque había sido tan desgraciado por su propia causa.

Las buenas palabras son como las joyas, pero las malas nos hieren y nos causan pesar.

~

The Seven Crows

Once upon a time, there was a married couple who had seven sons. Both husband and wife longed to have a daughter, and at last, their desire was satisfied. The woman was the mother of a baby girl so tiny and delicate that her parents were afraid she would die at any moment.

The town's priest was away on a trip and could not give her the water of baptism; the baby girl's parents decided to give her some healing water. The father sent his sons off to fetch some water from the fountain. The seven sons went running to the fountain and filled the jug.

They began to argue about which of the seven would get home first, but as they began to run, their jug fell into a thousand pieces. The seven brothers were much frightened by the accident. They looked at each other, not daring to go home. The father, desperate because of his sons' delay, looked for them in every direction. None of the little rascals appeared. He was so desperate that he yelled a terrible curse:

"May God turn those little rascals into crows!"

The father and the mother wept bitterly. They knew there is no human power to avoid the effects of a curse once it is cast.

Fortunately, the newborn did not die, and each day her beauty and grace became more noticeable. The girl was the only joy and comfort of her parents, who loved her dearly. They had tried to hide from her the sad event of the curse, but a talkative, gossipy neighbor of theirs called the girl over one day to cuddle her and to give her candy. While acting as if it meant nothing in particular, she asked the girl about her brothers.

The girl answered her:

"I have no brothers, as you know."

The woman answered her:

"Oh, yes, you do. You must know that you are to blame for their misfortune."

The girl went home feeling very sad and began to weep. She asked her parents what the neighbor meant. They had always tried to hide it from her, but now they had to confess the truth.

One day the girl left her home carrying only a gourd of water, a knife, and a silver ring. Her parents, filled with despair, wept bitterly and almost died from distress.

On the road the girl met an angel, who asked her where she was going. She told him that she was searching for her brothers. He replied:

"Your brothers live in the mountain of crystal rock. Take this key; it will open the door for you."

The girl was incredibly happy because she was going to fulfill her obligation; when she arrived, she put her hand into her pocket but could not find the key. She lost hope and wept beyond consolation, but suddenly she had an idea:

"Who knows whether the little finger of my right hand can open the lock?"

With no thought of the pain that she could suffer, she took the knife and cut off the finger.

She had scarcely put the bone into the lock when the door opened wide. The girl went in, and an old man met her. She told him that she was searching for seven brothers who were black crows. He replied:

"They live here, but they are not here now. They should come back soon."

The girl headed to the dining table. From each plate she took a little bite and from each glass a little sip, and in the last glass she put the ring. She immediately hid herself.

They were not late in coming to their dining table. The youngest brother said:

"Someone has touched my plate and my glass."

And all of them said the same thing as with one voice. When the oldest one drank from his wineglass, he found the ring, catching it in his beak. He exclaimed:

"Oh, how do you suppose this ring came here? It belongs to our mother. If this had been brought by our sister and she had embraced us one by one against her heart, we would recover our human form."

Upon hearing this, the girl came out from where she was. She kissed her brothers one after the other on the beak, and they were transformed into seven young brothers. Delaying only to fetch the treasures that they had gathered in the mountain, at once they hit the road. Their parents, who were near death from grief and worry, welcomed them as the greatest joy in the world. They were happy with their beloved sons and with their beautiful and loving daughter.

The father never again uttered a curse because he had been so unfortunate by his own fault.

Good words are like jewels, but bad ones hurt and cause us to suffer.

El caballo misterioso[6]

Había una vez un padre que tenía tres hijos, los cuales se llamaban Pedro, Juan y Francisco. Estos muchachos se ocupaban de vender los productos de su pequeña finca, que se componía de higos.

Se dice que una vez, Don Pancho, el padre de estos muchachos, necesitó vender unos higos y mandó a Pedro a venderlos. El muchacho tomó el caballo viejo que había y le puso unas banastas grandes, las cuales llenó de higos. Por el camino, cerca del río, se encontró a una vieja, quien le preguntó qué llevaba. Pedro le contestó, diciéndole que llevaba piedras. La vieja le dijo:

"Piedras se te volverán."

Llegó Pedro a la próxima ciudad y empezó a pregonar sus higos. Como éstos eran escasos en aquella época, mucha gente se acercó a comprarle higos, pero al meter la mano en las banastas, Pedro se encontró con que se habían convertido en piedras. La gente le cayó a pedradas. Volvió Pedro a su casa y Don Pancho también le dio una paliza.

Al poco tiempo el viejo llamó a Juan, entregándole una bestia cargada de higos. Juan llegó al río, encontrándose con la vieja, quien le preguntó qué llevaba. Juan le dijo que llevaba cuernos. Ella le dijo:

"Cuernos se te vuelvan."

Llegó Juan a la ciudad y empezó a anunciar sus higos, pero a medida que la muchedumbre le rodeaba para comprarle, fue a sacar los higos que estaban convertidos en cuernos. Le dieron también una solemne paliza; se volvió a su casa donde le aguardaba su padre, Don Panchín, como le llamaban. Don Panchín le pegó con un palo que tenía en la mano.

A la semana siguiente, Don Panchín llamó al más pequeño de sus hijos. "Francisco," le dijo, "tú irás a vender higos hoy."

Le entregó un caballo cargado de higos. Tomó Francisco el camino; pronto llegó al río, donde se encontró a una vieja, quien le dijo:

"¿Qué vendes, Francisco?"

"Higos, señora, ¿quiere usted alguno para su niño?"

La mujer le dio las gracias, diciéndole:

"Higos vendas, hijo mío."

Pronto llegó Francisco a la ciudad y empezó a gritar:

"¡Hoy llevo los buenos higos!"

La gente se acercó a él con fuete en mano para darle una fuetiza, pero Francisco era el único que realmente traía higos, y mientras más vendía, más aparecían en las banastas.

Acabó Panchito de vender los higos y pronto tomó el camino con dirección a su casa. Al llegar al río encontró a la vieja, quien le dijo que tomara otro camino para llegar a su casa. Sus dos hermanos le aguardaban para matarle.

Panchito tomó un estrecho; pronto llegó a su casa, entregándole a su padre la suma de dinero que importaban los higos. Los dos hermanos, Pedro y Juan, llegaron después; Don Pachín los regañó tanto que éstos decidieron abandonar la casa e irse a correr fortuna.

Don Panchín les preguntó que si querían dinero o bendición. Ellos dijeron que con bendición no se iba a ninguna parte; entonces, el padre les dio dinero. Al poco tiempo Francisco deseó irse también. Don Panchín le preguntó qué quería, si dinero o bendición. Panchito le dijo que le diera la bendición.

Se fue Panchito, y cuando iba cerca de una ciudad, se encontró a una vieja que le dijo que sus dos hermanos habían comprado dos hermosos caballos. Añadió que si él iba a comprar alguno que fuera a la cuadra, comprara uno que estaba muy viejo y lleno de basura. Panchito se fue a la cuadra y compró el caballo que le había indicado. Montó en él; siguió con dirección a donde estaban sus dos hermanos, quienes lo amenazaron con matarlo si decía que eran hermanos. La hija del rey dijo que Panchito se parecía a Pedro; entonces, Pedro le contestó que Panchito era el peón de su casa.

Salió una mañana Panchito. En el camino vio una pluma de un pájaro desconocido y la cogió. El caballo lo reprendió, diciéndole que aquella pluma le iba a costar muchos trabajos. Panchito se la puso en el sombrero y se presentó ante la princesa, quien le dijo que si no traía el pájaro de la pluma lo mandaría a matar.

Panchito se fue a llorar a la cuadra; el caballo le recordó lo que él le había dicho. Siguió llorando hasta que el caballo le dijo que irían al bosque donde se hallaba el pájaro. El caballo brincaría tres veces donde estaba el pájaro, y si, a la tercera vez no cogía el pájaro, todo sería perdido. Se hizo todo tal como dijo el caballo. Muy pronto trajo Panchito el pájaro a palacio.

Se dio una buena fiesta que consistía en coger una cinta perteneciente a una muchacha para poder bailar con ella. Panchito preparó su flaco y resistente caballo y tomó parte en la fiesta. Después de salir todos los caballos, apareció el de Pachito al galope. Panchito acertó a coger la cinta perteneciente a la princesa.

Aquella noche Panchito bailó con la hija del rey, pero pronto tuvo que preparar sus costillas para recibir una paliza que le fue dada por Pedro y Juan, sus dos hermanos. Siguió Panchito viviendo allí y no tardó en que tuviera que sufrir otra pena por causa de sus hermanos.

Juan oyó decir que la hija del rey había perdido un brillante en los golfos del mar. Pronto fue hasta el rey, le dijo que Panchito había dicho que él mismo lo sacaría del mar. Panchito recibió otra amenaza si no lo hacía. El y el caballo sacaron el brillante. Panchito se casó con la hija del rey.

El caballo desapareció como por encanto. Los hermanos fueron desterrados.

~

The Mysterious Horse

Once upon a time, there was a father who had three sons named Pedro, Juan, and Francisco. These boys worked hard selling the products of their ranch, most of which were figs. It is said that once, Don Pancho, the father of these boys, needed to sell some figs. He sent Pedro to sell them.

Pedro took one of the family's old horses and put large baskets upon it, which he filled with figs. On the road near a river, Pedro met an old

woman, who asked him what he was carrying. He told her that he was carrying stones. The old woman told him:

"Stones they will become for you."

Pedro arrived at the next city and began to hawk his figs; since figs were
scarce at that time, many came to buy figs from him. When Pedro put his
hand into the baskets, he found that the figs had turned into stones, which
the buyers threw at him. Pedro went back home. Don Pancho gave him
a good beating.

A little later, the old man called his other son, Juan, and gave him a
horse loaded with figs to sell. Juan arrived at the river and met the old
woman, who asked him what he was carrying. Juan told her that he was
carrying horns. She said to him:

"Horns they will become for you."

Juan reached the city and began to hawk his figs. As the crowd surrounded him to buy them, he went to take out the figs, but they had turned
into horns. They gave him a sound beating, and he went back home. Don
Panchín, as people sometimes called the old man, was waiting for his son
with a stick in his hand.

The next week, Don Panchín called the smallest of his sons.

"Francisco," he said, "you will go to sell figs today."

He gave the boy a horse loaded with figs. Panchito, as his neighbors
often called him, hit the road. Soon he arrived at the river, where he met
an old woman. She said to him:

"What are you selling, Panchito?"

"Figs, ma'am. Do you want some for your boy?"

She thanked him, saying:

"You will sell a lot of figs, son."

Not too long after, Panchito reached the city and began to shout:

"Today I bring good figs!"

People gathered around him with whips in hand to give him a good
beating, but this brother was the only one who had really brought figs. The
more he sold, the more figs appeared in the baskets.

Panchito finished selling the figs, and soon he headed for home. Upon arriving at the river, he met the old woman, who told him to take another road to go home. His two brothers were waiting there to kill him.

Panchito took a shortcut, safely arriving home. Gladly he handed his father the money brought in by the figs. The two brothers, Pedro and Juan, arrived later. Don Panchín scolded them so much that they decided to leave their father's house. They went off to seek their fortune.

Don Panchín asked his children whether they wanted money or his blessing. They said that they would get nowhere with a blessing; the old man gave them money. Shortly afterward, Panchito also wanted to go away. Don Panchín asked his dear son what he wanted, either money or a blessing. Panchito told him to give him his blessing.

Panchito set out, arriving near a city where he met an old woman who told him that his two brothers had bought two fine horses from her. If he was going to buy one, he should go to the stable and buy one that was very old and filthy. Panchito went to the stable and bought the horse that the old woman had indicated. He mounted it and continued to head for the place where his two brothers were.

Pedro and Juan threatened to kill Panchito if he said that they were his brothers. They were working at a palace. The king's daughter remarked that Panchito looked so much like Pedro, but Pedro denied it. He told the princess that the boy was his family's ranch hand.

One morning Panchito left town. On the road, he saw a feather of an unknown bird. He immediately picked it up. The old horse scolded him, saying that the feather was going to cost him dearly. He put the feather on his hat. Panchito appeared before the princess, who told him that if he did not bring her the bird that had shed the feather, she would order his death.

Panchito went off to cry in the stable. The horse reminded him of what he had told the boy. Panchito kept on crying. The horse suggested that they would go to the forest where the bird was found. Once there, the horse would leap three times whenever the bird appeared. If on the third try Panchito did not catch it, then all would really be lost. All this happened, and soon Panchito carried the bird to the palace.

The royal family threw a nice party, which included the custom of catching a girl's ribbon from one's horse in order to be able to dance with her. Pedro and Juan had prepared their tough, skinny horses to take part in the party.

After all the other horses went out, Panchito's went out in a gallop, and he managed to catch the ribbon belonging to the princess. That night Panchito danced with the king's daughter, but afterward, Pedro and Juan, his two brothers, beat him up badly. But despite their animosity, Panchito continued to live in that town.

It wasn't long before Panchito suffered more pain because of his brothers. Juan heard that the king's daughter had lost a diamond in the sea. Soon he told the princess that Panchito had claimed he would get it out of the seawater. Panchito received yet another threat if he could not deliver the ring as he had claimed. But Panchito and his old horse managed to get the diamond out of the depths of the ocean.

Panchito married the king's daughter. Right then the horse disappeared as if by magic. The two brothers were forced into exile.

El caballito negro[7]

Había una vez un pescador que era casado, pero nunca había tenido familia. Después de mucho tiempo tuvieron un niño. La señora del pescador se enamoró de otro pescador, y como su marido estaba siempre pescando, no sabía nada. Durante algún tiempo el niño fue creciendo; el amante de ella le dijo que el niño estaba creciendo mucho. Quería que lo matara porque si no, los descubriría. Ella le dijo al amante que le trajera un poco de veneno para matar al niño.

El niño tenía un potrito negro que era virtuoso; un día cuando el niño venía de la escuela, el caballo le dijo que no comiera porque la comida tenía veneno para matarlo. Llegó el niño a la casa y no quiso almorzar. Después llegó el padre de pescar, le dijo al niño que almorzara; él no quiso porque el almuerzo tenía veneno. Enojado, el padre le dijo que no comiera, y entonces, el niño le pidió que si quería, probara la comida para ver si tenía veneno. Le dieron la comida al perro, el cual se la comió y murió a las pocas horas.

Cuando vino el amante a ver si había muerto el niño, la señora del pescador le dijo que trajera una pluma para echársela en un zapato; cuando el niño llegara de la escuela, al cambiarse de calzado, caería muerto. El caballito le dijo al niño que cuando llegara no se cambiara de calzado porque su mamá le había puesto una pluma envenenada en el calzado. El niño llegó a su casa y no se cambió de zapatos.

Cuando su papá llegó le dijo que se cambiara de zapatos, pero el niño le dijo que un zapato tenía una pluma envenenada para matarlo. El niño le dijo que si quería probar, se los pusiera a su gato. El hombre cogió los zapatos y se los puso al gato. El gato cayó muerto al momento.

Cuando llegó el amante, al otro día, le preguntó a la mujer si no había matado a su hijo. Ella le contestó que no había podido porque el caballo le contaba todo cuando el niño venía de la escuela. El amante de la mujer del pescador le dijo que se hiciera como si tuviera un dolor tan fuerte que no se le quitaría con ninguna clase de medicina. Solo tomando la sangre del caballito negro se le quitaría el dolor.

El caballito esperó al niño que saliera de la escuela. Le dijo:

"Juanito, tu mamá se ha hecho con un dolor, y para poder matarte a ti, me van a matar, diciendo que tomando la sangre de mi cuerpo se le quita el dolor."

El niño llegó a la casa y su papá le dijo:

"Hijo mío, tu madre tiene un dolor y no se le quita si no es con la sangre del caballito negro."

El muchacho respondió:

"Yo dejo que maten al caballito, pero permítame que lo monte y dé una vuelta en él."

El niño se vistió como un general, ensilló el caballo y montó en su potro favorito. Se despidió y le pidió la bendición a su padre, diciéndole:

"Quédese con mi señora madre."

Juanito emprendió su marcha por una montaña. Al llegar al interior de la montaña, salió un león que atacó al pequeño general y su caballo. Entre Juanito y el caballo mataron al león. El caballito le dijo:

"Llena siete botellas de sangre y las enterrarás donde mismo hemos matado el león."

Juanito caminó en su potro hasta que llegó al palacio de un rey quien tenía tres hijas. Cuando llegó fue a alquilarle al rey los bajos del palacio para habitarlos. El rey le dijo que no, que se quedara allí y no pagara nada. Entonces, el pequeño general les traía dulces a las tres hijas del rey y a la reina.

Sucedió varias noches. Una noche no le trajo nada a la reina, a quien le dio mucho coraje. La mujer le dijo:

"Pequeño general, le voy a decir al general grande que tú te atreves a traer la belleza del mundo aquí."

El se fue inmediatamente y le dijo al caballito:

"Caballito mío, me exigen que traiga la belleza del mundo aquí porque les traje dulces a las tres muchachas y a la reina no le traje."

El caballito le dijo:

"Móntate en mis lomos; corre mucho hasta que me sudes. Te vas andando hasta que llegues a la casa de la belleza del mundo."

La niña que le decían belleza del mundo estaba en su hermoso jardín. Entonces, la belleza del mundo le dijo que le prestara el caballito para dar una carrera. El le hincó las espuelas al caballito y le dijo a la belleza que éste respingaba mucho, mejor que se montara en ancas con él. La niña belleza montó en las ancas del caballo; Juanito la llevó a donde estaba el rey.

Volvió a llevarles dulces a las hijas y no le llevaba a la reina. La señora le dijo:

"Saliste con ésa, pero no saldrás con ésta que te voy a echar ahora."

La señora le dijo al general grande que el general pequeño se atrevía a bailar en un castillo prendido en fuego. Juanito fue presto a donde estaba su caballito favorito y le dijo:

"Me quieren hacer bailar en un castillo prendido en fuego."

El caballito le dijo:

"Súdame bien sudado, después te bañas tú y me bañas a mí con las siete botellas de sangre del león que matamos en las montañas."

Se fue Juanito a bailar en el castillo prendido. El fuego se apagó con el sudor y la sangre. El general grande le preguntó con qué se había bañado para bailar en el castillo. El general pequeño le contestó con gas y agua de azahar, y también había bañado al caballito negro con gas y agua de azahar. El general grande cogió su hermoso caballo, se bañó él y después bañó su caballo con agua de azahar y gas.

Entonces, se fue a entrar a bailar en el castillo prendido, cogió fuego y se ardió. Juanito cogió a la reina y la metió en el fuego. Dejó a las tres hijas del rey habitando el palacio solas.

~

The Little Black Horse

Once upon a time, there was a fisherman who was married but had no children. After a very long time, the couple had a son. The fisherman's wife fell in love with another fisherman, but since her husband was always fishing, he knew nothing about it. Over time the boy grew in size, and her lover told her that the child was growing a lot. He wanted her to kill him because if not, the boy would disclose their affair. The wife asked her lover to bring her a little bit of poison for killing the child.

The boy had a little black colt that was virtuous. One day as the boy was coming back from school, the horse told him not to eat anything at home. The food contained poison to kill him. The child did not eat his lunch; when the father came home from fishing, he ordered him to eat it. The boy refused because he knew there was poison in the food. The father finally told him not to eat it, and the boy asked him if he wanted to find out if the food was poisoned. They gave the food to the dog, which ate it up. The poor animal died that night.

The lover came back, wondering whether the boy had died, but the fisherman's wife already had another plan. She told her lover to bring her a poisoned feather to fasten in the child's shoe. As soon as the child came home from school and changed his shoes, he would fall dead.

Once again, the little horse warned the child. He told him not to change his shoes when he got home because his mother had put a poisoned feather in his shoe that would kill him. The child came home and did not change his shoes.

When his papa came home, he told the boy to change his shoes, but the child told him that there was a poisoned feather in a shoe to kill him. The child said that he could prove it; he would put the shoes on their cat. The man picked up the shoes and put them on the cat. The cat fell dead immediately.

When the lover came the next day, he asked the woman whether she had killed her son. She replied that she had not been able to do so because the horse kept telling the boy everything they spoke about as soon as he came back from school. This time the fisherman had a plan. He told his lover to pretend that she had a pain that no medicine relieved; she should say that only by drinking the blood from the little black horse would she be cured.

The little black horse waited for the child to leave the school. He told him:

"Juanito, your mama has pretended to be in pain in order to kill you. She is going to kill me, saying that only taking the blood from my body will relieve her pain."

The boy went home. His papa sadly said to him:

"My son, your mother has a pain that can be cured only by the blood of the little black horse."

The boy replied:

"I'll let them kill the little horse as soon as I mount it and take a ride on it."

The boy dressed up as a general, saddled the horse, mounted his favorite colt, and waved goodbye. He asked for his father's blessings, saying:

"You stay with my lady mother."

Juanito set out on a trip through the wilderness. When he reached a mountain, a lion came out and attacked him and his horse. Together Juanito and his horse killed the lion. The little horse said to him:

"Fill seven bottles with the lion's blood and bury them in the same spot where we killed the lion."

Juanito rode the pony until he arrived at the palace of a king who had three daughters. He went there to rent the first floor of the palace; he wanted badly to live there. The king said that he could not rent the first floor but that he could stay there without paying anything. The little general took sweets to the king's daughters and to the queen.

This he did several nights in a row until one night, he brought no sweets to the queen, who got extremely mad at him. She challenged Juanito:

"Little general, I am going tell the big general that you had dared to bring here the beauty of the world."

Juanito went away at once. He said to his little horse:

"My little horse, they demand that I bring here the beauty of the world because I took sweets to the three princesses and none to the queen."

The little horse said to him:

"Get on my back, and we will run fast and far until you make me sweat, then continue walking until you reach the home of the beauty of the world."

The girl whom they call the beauty of the world was in her beautiful garden. The beauty of the world asked him to lend her the little horse so that she could ride it. As he pressed the spurs into the little horse, he told the beauty that his horse was bucking and that she should climb up on his hindquarters. The beauty of the world mounted the horse's hindquarters. Juanito immediately took her to the king.

Again Juanito took sweets to the king's daughters but none to the queen. The angry lady told him:

"You won out the first time, but you won't be so lucky with the situation that I am going to throw you into now."

The queen told the general of the king's army that the little general had dared to dance in a burning castle. Juanito went to his favorite little horse and told him:

"They want to make me dance in a burning castle."

The little horse said to him:

"Make me sweat freely and afterward bathe yourself and me with the seven bottles of the blood of the lion that we killed in the mountain."

Juanito went off to dance in the burning castle, and the fire was extinguished by the sweat and the blood. The big general asked him what he had bathed in for dancing in the castle. The little general answered that he had bathed himself in gas and he had bathed the little horse in gas and in orange blossom water. The big general grasped his handsome horse, then bathed himself and his horse with gas and orange blossom water. Then he left to enter the burning castle.

As the big general started dancing, he caught fire, and he was burned up. Juanito captured the queen and threw her into the fire. He left, leaving the king's three daughters living alone in the palace.

El padre y los tres hijos[8]

Había un padre que tenía tres hijos. El vivía en el campo ocupándose en la agricultura con ellos.

Sucedió que una vez, habiendo sembrado su finca de maíz fue comida por masantiques, aves que hay en el campo. Entonces, él fue con sus tres hijos, Juan, Pedro y Pío, y sembró maíz de nuevo. El maíz nació lo más bonito con la ayuda del agua hasta que llegó a mazorcarse.

Una tarde, habiendo visitado el viejo su finca, la encontró muy adelantada. Se dijo para sí:

"De aquí a un poco de tiempo cogeré todo mi maíz y estaré rico con un gran número de quintales que me servirán para pagar varias deudas que tengo."

Una mañana, habiéndose dirigido el viejo a su finca para ver cómo estaba, encontró gran parte de ésta destrozada por un animal cuadrúpedo. Supo que era así porque dejó marcadas las huellas en el terreno blando. El viejo regresó a su casa muy sombrío, contándoles a sus hijos lo que le pasaba. Tan pronto como llegó la noche, el viejo tomó una hamaca que tenía para pasar su siesta después de las comidas, se llegó hasta la finca y guindó su hamaca de dos árboles muy corpulentos que allí se encontraban.

A la media noche ya el sueño lo vencía, pero él siempre fuerte porque quería coger el animal que le estaba quitando la manutención. En la madrugada se quedó dormido. El animal dañino llegó y destrozó una cantidad como la anterior. No habiendo terminado de abastecerse, despertó el celador y oyó el ruido, pero cuando el viejo llegó al sitio donde se sentía, no encontró ya a nadie. Solo vio el daño hecho.

Regresó a la casa muy desconsolado. Se lo contó a su hijo más viejo, quien le contestó:

"Esta noche voy yo, Papá."

Llegó la noche y Juan le dijo a su padre:

"Padre, usted me dará una hamaca y una buena guitarra."

El padre accedió a lo que su hijo pedía, y en el momento, se lo buscó.

El muchacho se fue a su trabajo y colgó la hamaca del mismo sitio. Empezó a tocar la guitarra; a medida que las horas transcurrían, las notas del instrumento se sentían más melodiosas en el silencio de la noche. Le sucedió lo mismo que el padre. En la hora más pesada de la noche, se quedó dormido sin despertar hasta el amanecer. Se levantó muy de prisa; muy asustado se dirigió inmediatamente hasta el sitio donde se había redoblado el daño. Regresando a su casa muy desconsolado, le confesó a su padre que no había podido coger el animal.

A la otra noche fue el segundo hermano. Pedro le pidió a su padre los mismos efectos que los de su hermano mayor, pero después de haber estado en pie por un largo tiempo, le sucedió lo mismo que al mayor.

El más pequeño, Pío, un niño como siete años de edad, habló:

"Papá, si usted y mis dos hermanos mayores no han podido coger ese animal, yo estoy en la completa seguridad que lo cogeré."

A la tercera noche, o sea, la última, el muchacho dijo:

"Papá, usted me buscará una hamaca, un violín y cientos de alfileres."

El padre inmediatamente le trajo todos los encargos a su hijo, diciéndole:

"Todo lo que hagas es en vano."

Llegó la noche. El muchacho se dirigió a la finca; después de haberla observado por algún tiempo, colgó su hamaca de los árboles y empezó a poner los alfileres por todos sus agujeros. Eran para que, cuando se quedara dormido, los alfileres lo despertaran.

Pío tomó el violín y empezó a tocar. Como a las dos horas soltó el violín porque ya el sueño lo vencía, pero no se quedaba dormido porque los alfileres se lo impedían. A las tres de la madrugada oyó un ruido muy fuerte. Se dirigió al sitio donde se sentía, para su sorpresa, se encontró un caballo grande, color colorado y con manchas blancas en el espinazo.

El caballo cesó de comer, parándose casi en las dos patas traseras, le dijo:

"No pretendas hacerme daño. Soy una persona que anda por el mundo pagando una deuda. Me dispensarás y te quedaré agradecido; en cambio, conseguirás mucho de mí. Adiós."

Desapareció el caballo, pero el muchacho quedó atónito porque no supo cuál dirección tomó. No sintió miedo tampoco.

Por fin, regresó a su casa muy contento y le dijo a su padre que había cogido al pícaro.

"Y, ¿quién era?"

"Una yunta de bueyes, Papá."

"Y, ¿cómo lo supiste?"

"Porque la he cogido y me prometió que jamás volvería."

A los dos años murió el padre y quedaron los tres hijos en la casa. Los mayores maltrataban mucho al menor—tanto que teniendo cocinera en la casa, la echaron y lo pusieron a él en este oficio.

A los seis meses hubo una fiesta en un pueblo donde había un hombre muy rico. El rico anunció que el hombre, quien montado a caballo, tirara una bola de goma y cayera en la falda de su hija, Leonor, se casaría con ella. Recibiría, además, la mitad de su capital.

Llegó el día de la fiesta y todo el mundo se dirigió a tomar parte en este jurado. Los dos hermanos alistaron sus caballos y se fueron. Tiraban las bolas y todas pasaban por los contornos, pero ninguna caía en la falda de la joven. Era una empresa muy difícil porque era una distancia algo regular y también los saltos de los caballos lo impedían.

Como a las dos horas de haber salido los dos hermanos, Pío llamó su caballo, apareció en el momento, diciéndole:

"Estoy dispuesto a servirte lo que quieras."

El muchacho le dijo:

"Me traerás un traje de plata y también una bola. Tú irás adornado con el mismo metal."

A la media hora apareció aquel caballo como lo había pedido. Montó en él y se dirigió a la ciudad. Antes de llegar el muchacho al jurado, cogió la bola en sus manos, alargó el paso a su caballo, tiró la bola y fue a ponerse en la falda de la muchacha. El no se detuvo y regresó al momento a su casa. Hizo la comida; cuando llegaron los dos hermanos, empezaron a comer.

Cuando estaban ya por terminar, dijeron los hermanos:

"Mira, Pío, llegó un joven en su caballo muy hermoso, vestido con un traje de plata, quien tiró una bola de plata y cayó en la falda de Leonor."

El muchacho dijo:

"Quizás sí, quizás no, quizás sí sería yo."

Los hermanos se pusieron muy enojados y lo mandaron para la cocina a hacer sus quehaceres.

Al otro día se fueron los hermanos al jurado otra vez para ver si pescaban la paloma. Pío salió a la hora señalada con un traje de oro y la bola también de oro. Ya el padre de la muchacha tenía varias guardias para detenerlo. Llegó y tiró la bola; no erró el tiro. Enseguida, los guardias trataron de detenerlo, pero no pudieron. El caballo dio tres saltos y desapareció.

Los hermanos llegaron a la casa y le refirieron lo que pasaba a su hermano, quien ya los esperaba con la comida caliente. Pío dijo:

"Quizás sí, quizás no, quizás sí sería yo."

Le hicieron el mismo reproche y lo mandaron para la cocina.

Al otro día volvieron los dos hermanos. Pío llamó su caballo, que en el momento se le apareció como lo pedía su dueño. Montó, se fue, tiró la bola por tercera vez, y cayó en la falda de la joven. Antes de que la policía lo hiciera, se detuvo y, apeándose del caballo, lo soltó y fue a pararse en medio de los caballos de los dos hermanos. El subió y tomó por esposa a Leonor; tomó también la mitad del capital, como lo había prometido el padre. Los dos hermanos regresaron a su hogar de lo más desconsolados porque su hermano cocinero había hecho más que ellos.

Pío se quedó viviendo en la casa, donde puso su caballo en un pesebre que había allí, sosteniéndolo con abundantes hierbas, maíz y avena. Transcurridos dos años, estando Pío peinando su caballo, el animal dio un salto y cayó muerto. Pío no hallaba qué hacer porque aquella era la prenda que más quería, pero no tenía otro remedio más que conformarse.

Este caballo era un hombre que estaba encantado, y de esta manera, estaba cumpliendo su misión. Aquel día se le llegaba su término, y por eso, murió.

~

The Father and the Three Sons

Once upon a time, there was a father who had three sons. They lived in the countryside where they all shared tasks on a farm.

As it happened, one time, after having sowed the farm with corn, masantiques, hungry birds that live in the fields, ate of all the seed. The old man with his three sons—Juan, Pedro, and Pío—sowed the field again. The corn came up very pretty, and in time, with the help of water, it produced many ears of corn.

One afternoon, the old man, after visiting his farm, found it at the peak of production. He told himself:

"Very soon I shall reap all my corn. I shall be rich with all these hundreds of pounds that will let me pay off several of my debts."

One morning, the old man headed to his farm, where to his horror he found a great part of it destroyed by a four-legged animal. He figured this out because the animal had left tracks in the soft earth there. The old man went home very gloomy and told his sons what had happened. As soon as night fell, the old man took a hammock that he had around for taking naps after meals. He left for the field and hung his hammock from two thick trees.

At midnight, sleep was overcoming him, but he kept awake. He wanted badly to catch the animal that was taking away his livelihood. But in the early morning, he fell soundly asleep. The animal that was causing the damage arrived and destroyed an amount like the one before. Certainly, it had not completely satisfied the creature's hunger. Hearing a noise, the old man woke up, but upon reaching the source of the noise, he could not find anything. He saw only the damage done.

The old man went home disconsolate. He related his bad experience to his oldest son. Juan proudly said:

"Tonight I am going, Papa."

Night came and Juan said:

"Father, give me a hammock and a good guitar."

His father agreed, and he went at once to get them.

Juan went off to his task; he hung the hammock at the same place as his father had done before. He began to play his guitar, and as the hours passed, the notes from the instrument sounded more and more melodious in the silence of the night. As it had happened to his father, the same thing happened to Juan. In the heaviest hours of the night, Juan fell asleep and did not wake up until dawn. He got up hastily. Very alarmed, he headed immediately for the spot where the damage had doubled. Going home heartbroken, Juan told his father that unfortunately, he had failed to catch the mysterious animal.

The next night Pedro, the second son, went to the field carrying the same objects that his older brother had requested. But after a long time waiting, even while standing, the same thing happened to Pedro as had happened to his older brother and to his father.

The youngest brother, named Pío, a boy about seven years old, said to the old man:

"Papa, you and my two older brothers have not been able to catch that animal. I am confident that I will catch it."

On the third night, or rather the last night, Pío said to his father:

"Papa, will you find me a hammock, a violin, and a hundred pins?"

Immediately the father brought him all the things requested. Nonetheless, he said to his son:

"Whatever you do will be in vain."

Night fell, and Pío headed for the fields. After observing his surroundings for some time, he hung his hammock from some trees. Next he put pins through all the hammock's holes. The pins would awaken him if he fell asleep.

Pío picked up the violin and began to play. After about two hours, he put down the violin because sleep was overcoming him, but he did not fall asleep because the pins prevented it. At three in the morning, he heard a loud noise. He headed for the place where it sounded. To his surprise, Pío found a large horse, red with white spots on its backbone.

The horse stopped eating. Standing almost on its two back legs, it said to Pío:

"Don't try to hurt me. I am a person who walks through the world in repayment of a debt. If you treat me kindly, I shall be very grateful to you. In exchange, you will find this deal to your advantage. Farewell."

The horse disappeared fast. Pío was left astonished, since he could not tell what direction the horse took. He was not afraid, though.

Pío went home quite content. He told his father that he had caught the rogue.

"And what was it?"

"A team of oxen, Papa."

"And how did you find out?"

"Because I caught them, and they promised me that they would never return."

Two years later, the father died. The three sons were left alone in the house. The older sons greatly abused the youngest—so much so that they discharged the cook and made Pío take over her chores.

Six months later, there was a party in a town, where there was a very rich man. The rich man announced that the man who, while mounted on a horse, was able to throw a rubber ball into the skirt of his daughter, Leonor, would marry her. Furthermore, he would receive half of his capital.

The day of the party came; everybody headed out to take part in the sworn challenge. The two older brothers got their horses ready and left. They threw the balls, but though the balls landed near Leonor, none fell into the young woman's skirt. It was indeed a difficult undertaking. Not only was it done from a somewhat considerable distance, but the horses' leaps were a challenging interference.

About two hours after the older two brothers left, Pío called his red horse, which appeared at once. As the horse had promised, he said to Pío:

"I am ready to serve you in whatever you wish."

The boy told it:

"Bring me a suit of silver and also a ball. You will be decorated with the same metal as well."

After half an hour, the horse brought what the boy had asked for. Pío mounted the red horse and headed quickly toward the fairgrounds. Before Pío even reached the target, he grasped the ball in his hands and lengthened the horse's stride. He threw the ball, which came to rest on the young woman's skirt. He did not stop to claim his prize; he went home at once. He cooked dinner. His two brothers arrived and began to eat in silence.

When the brothers were about to finish eating, they said to their younger brother:

"Look, Pío, a youngster dressed in a silver suit riding a very handsome horse arrived to the challenge game today. He threw a silver ball, which fell on Leonor's lap."

The boy said:

"Maybe yes, maybe no, maybe it was I."

The brothers became very angry at Pío. They sent him back to the kitchen to do his chores.

The next day, the two brothers went off again to the contest to see whether they could win the prize. Pío left in a suit of gold, holding a ball that was also made of gold. The girl's father had already placed several guards to detain the mysterious man. Pío arrived at once; he threw the ball, and the toss did not miss the target. At once the guards tried to stop him, but they could not. The horse jumped three times and disappeared.

The brothers came home and told their brother what had happened. Pío was waiting for them with a hot meal. He said again to them:

"Maybe yes, maybe no, maybe it was I."

They scolded him again and sent him into the kitchen.

The next day, the two brothers left again. Pío called his horse, which at once appeared to him as his master asked. He mounted the horse, left for the contest, and threw the ball for the third time. It fell into the young woman's lap. Before the guards could detain him, he stopped, and dismounting from the horse, he let it go.

Pío claimed Leonor for his wife. He also took half of the estate, as her father had promised. The two brothers went back home, among the unhappiest of men. Their cook-brother had done better than they.

Pío stayed living in his house, where he kept his red horse in a stable, feeding him abundant grasses, corn, and oats. Two years later, as Pío was grooming the horse, it fell dead. Pío felt helpless. The red horse was the possession he loved most, but he knew he had no choice but to accept it.

This horse was a man who had been bewitched; he was fulfilling his mission. That day the spell ended, and therefore, he died.

El caballo de siete colores[9]

Esta era una vez que había un rey que tenía tres hijos. El tenía una tala de trigo muy hermosa, pero todas las noches venía un animal que le demolía la tala.

Un día, el hijo mayor le dijo al rey que él se iba a ir toda la noche a la tala para ver si él podía coger el animal que venía a hacer daño. Por la noche se llevó una hamaca y una guitarra para que no quedarse dormido. Ya tarde en la noche lo venció el sueño y se quedó dormido. Llegó el animal. El daño que se hizo aquella noche fue más grande que las anteriores.

Por la mañana se fue el muchacho y le contó al padre lo que le había pasado. El rey lo cogió, lo ató a un árbol y le dio una fuetiza hasta que lo dejó casi medio muerto. El otro hijo se ofreció al rey a ir aquella noche y coger el animal. Al llegar, hizo lo mismo que su hermano mayor hasta que lo venció el sueño, y entonces, vino el animal haciendo el mismo daño.

Cuando el rey fue a la tala y vio el daño que había hecho el animal aquella noche, le dio otra fuetiza más grande que la que le había dado al hijo mayor el día anterior.

Entonces, el hijo más chiquito, que era Juan Bobo, le dijo:

"Papá, yo voy esta noche y verá como yo cojo el animal."

El rey le dijo:

"¡Qué vas tú a coger! Si los otros que son más listos no lo han cogido, ¿cómo vas tú a cogerlo, siendo como eres un bobo?"

Juan Bobo dijo:

"Ya verás, Papá, como voy y lo traigo, y si no, me mata."

El rey no le hizo caso, pero Juan Bobo, por la tarde, se llevó una hamaca y un paquete de alfileres. Cuando llegó, guindó la hamaca y le puso caíllos y alfileres por todas partes, dejando solamente la parte donde se iba a sentar.

Después se sentó y se puso a cantar; cuando lo vencía el sueño se caía sobre los alfileres y los caíllos que le hincaban y se le espantaba el sueño.

Entonces, llegó el animal y el muchacho se levantó enseguida a cogerlo. El animal era un caballo precioso de siete colores; era un príncipe encantado en un caballo. Cuando Juan Bobo cogió el caballo, le dijo que si lo soltaba le prometía no volver más a la tala. Le daría de muestra un pelo de cada color para que se los llevara al rey. En el futuro, en los trabajos que se viera, clamara por él.

Juan Bobo se fue. Cuando llegó a la casa los dos hermanos se reían de él, diciéndole bobo y cuanto más se les antojaba. Pero Juan Bobo se fue hasta el rey; le entregó los siete pelos de colores para que viera lo que había cogido. Desde entonces no hubo más daños en la tala de trigo.

A los pocos días, otro rey, compañero del padre de Juan Bobo, determinó casar a su hija, pero quería que fuera de su gusto. Así fue que decidió hacer una reunión y dijo:

"El que me traiga la flor del olivar se casa con mi hija."

Todos los príncipes salieron a diferentes partes en busca de la flor.

Juan Bobo también quiso ir, pero en vez de coger por los caminos buenos, cogió por una vereda, y al llegar a una montaña, se sentó a llorar. Entonces, se le presentó el caballo de los siete colores y le preguntó por qué lloraba. El le contó todo su trabajo. El caballo le proporcionó un caballo y un traje muy bonito. El caballo le dijo que se fuera; cuando llegara a un palacio muy bonito que era encantado, se detuviera. Allí se encontraba esa flor. Le advirtió que, por muchas cosas que viera, no se acobardara. Al llegar al palacio se le presentarían dos grandes leones, pero que no les cogiera miedo.

El se fue e hizo todo lo que el caballo de siete colores le explicó. Cuando llegó, le pasó todo cuanto el caballo le había dicho. Entonces, el muchacho entró al palacio. A la hora de comer, le sirvieron una mesa muy bien servida. Lo único que veía era una mano blanca y oía una voz muy dulce.

Cuando concluyó de comer, le dijo la voz:

"Ahora vente, vamos al jardín. Esta es la flor del olivar. Métela dentro de esta botella; cuando se llegue el momento de presentarla dices tres veces, 'Manita blanca, sal.' Entonces, se abre. Todo el mundo quedará asombrado."

El muchacho se fue otra vez para su casa. Ya todos los otros hombres habían llegado. Todos llevaban flores de todas clases muy bonitas, y al ver que Juan Bobo llegó sin ninguna, se burlaron de él.

Al otro día fue la presentación de las flores, y a cada toque de un timbre, salía un príncipe a presentar sus flores, pero a pesar de ser todas muy bonitas, ninguna era la flor del olivar.

El último en salir fue Juan Bobo; cuando salió, en el momento se abrió la botella. Salió una flor abierta, tan bonita, que todo el mundo se quedó admirado. La princesa dijo que era la flor del olivar. Aquel hombre tenía que ser su esposo.

Juan Bobo y la princesa se casaron. Fueron, desde entonces, muy felices.

~

The Horse of Seven Colors

Once upon a time, there was a king who had three sons. He had a very fine field of wheat, but every night an animal came and demolished the plantings.

One day the oldest son told the king that he was going to spend all night in the field. He intended to catch the animal that was causing so much damage. That night he carried a hammock and a guitar to keep himself awake, but late in the night as sleep overcame him, the oldest son fell asleep. The animal arrived, causing greater damage than on earlier nights.

In the morning, the older son told his father what had happened to him. The king grabbed him, tied him to a tree, and gave him a lashing that left him half dead. Next the second son offered to go that night to catch the animal for the king, but upon arriving, the same thing happened to him as had happened to his older brother. Sleep overwhelmed him, and the animal came, doing greater damage.

When the king went to the field, he saw the damage that the animal had done that night. He gave the second boy a worse beating than the one that he had given to the older son the previous day.

Then the youngest son, who was named Juan Bobo, said to his father:

"Papa, I am going tonight. You will see that I will catch the animal."

The king said to him:

"What do you mean that you are going to catch it? If your brothers, who are smart, haven't caught it, how are you going to do it, being a fool?"

Juan Bobo said:

"You'll see, Papa; I am going to catch it. You can kill me if I fail."

The king paid him no attention, but that afternoon, Juan Bobo carried off a hammock, a package of pins, and some prickly seeds. He hung the hammock and placed the thorny seeds and sharp pins everywhere on it, leaving bare only the area where he was going to sit down.

Afterward, Juan Bobo sat down on the hammock and he began to sing. When sleep overcame him, although he would fall on his back, the sharp pins and spiny seeds would stick into him, and sleep was driven away. The mysterious animal finally arrived. Juan Bobo got up at once to catch him.

The animal was a beautiful horse of seven colors. An enchantment had turned a prince into a magnificent horse. As Juan Bobo grabbed the horse, it told him that he should let him go. The horse promised never to return to the field. As a token of this promise, the horse would give Juan Bobo a hair of each of his colors to carry to the king. The horse also added that if Juan Bobo ever got into any trouble, the boy should cry out for his help.

Juan Bobo left. When he got home, his two brothers laughed at him, calling him a fool and whatever other insults they could think of. But Juan Bobo went to the king; he handed him the hairs of seven colors. From that day on, there was no damage in the wheat field.

A few days later, another king, a close friend of Juan Bobo's father, decided to arrange a marriage for his daughter, but he wanted it to be with her consent.

It was then decided to call a royal gathering. The king proclaimed:

"He who brings me the flower from the olive grove shall marry my daughter."

All the princes went off to different places to look for the flower.

Juan Bobo wanted to go, but instead of taking good roads, he chose a trail. Upon arriving in the wilderness, he sat down to cry. Right then the horse of seven colors appeared to him; he asked the boy why he was crying. Juan Bobo told him what the king had proclaimed. The horse provided Juan Bobo with his own horse and a very good-looking suit. It told Juan Bobo to go away, but whenever he arrived at a very pretty enchanted palace, he should stop. The flower from the olive grove would be found there. No matter what he saw, Juan Bobo should not be afraid. As he arrived, he would meet two great lions, but Juan Bobo should not fear them.

Juan Bobo went off and did exactly as the horse of seven colors had explained to him. He arrived at the enchanted palace. The boy went inside. It was dinner time, so Juan Bobo was served a fine meal. He did not see people; there was only a mysterious white hand, and he also heard a very sweet voice.

When he finished eating, that voice said to Juan Bobo:

"Now come, let's go to the garden. This is the flower from the olive grove. Put it into this little bottle; when the moment for presenting it to the king comes, you must say three times, 'White hand, come out.' The bottle will open to everyone's astonishment."

Juan Bobo left for the king's palace at once. All the other men had already arrived, every one of them carrying very pretty flowers of all kinds. Upon seeing that Juan Bobo arrived without any, the men made fun of him.

The next day was the presentation of the flowers. At each stroke of the bell, a prince came out to present his flower, but although all of them were very pretty, none was the flower from the olive grove.

The last to come out was Juan Bobo. He uttered the chant, and at that very moment, the bottle opened, to everyone's surprise. The full flower that came out left everybody amazed. The princess exclaimed that, indeed, that was the flower from the olive grove. She decided at once that Juan Bobo had to be her husband.

They immediately got married. From that day on, they lived happily ever after.

A native Porto Rican thatched hut

CHAPTER 3

Fantastic and Impossible Quests

La flor del olivar[1]

Había una vez unos esposos quienes tenían tres hijos. El mayor se llamaba Juan, el del medio, Felipe, y el más pequeño, Carlos. Al cabo de varios años el papá perdió la vista, quedando esta familia sin amparo porque él era quien trabajaba para mantener a su familia. Hacía ya algún tiempo que este hombre no veía cuando se le presentó un anciano. Le dijo que si se lavaba los ojos con el agua hervida con la flor del olivar, volvería a ver, pero era muy difícil de conseguir.

Tan pronto como el hijo mayor oyó, estuvo andando y andando para ver si conseguía lo que deseaba. Dejó un arbolito sembrado, y les dijo a sus otros dos hermanitos que cuando vieran el arbolito marchito, él se encontraba en trabajos.

Juan se fue andando, andando, andando, y al pasar un río, vio a una viejita lavando y a un niñito llorando muchísimo. Juan le dijo:

"Viejita, mire a ese niño que está llorando."

Ella le contestó:

"Está llorando de hambre. ¿No tiene usted un pedazo de pan?"

Juan, aunque llevaba consigo un bollo, le dijo que no tenía. La viejita le deseó que pasara malos caminos y muchos trabajos.

Pasaron tres semanas. Felipe, el hermano del medio, viendo que su hermano no regresaba, vio el arbolito muerto. Resolvió salir a buscar a Juan. Cuando hubo caminado muchas horas, se encontró con la misma viejita y el chiquito que se estaba ahogando. Al verlo, le dijo:

"Mire, viejita, que se ahoga ese chiquito."

La mujer le contestó:

"¡Ay, sáquelo! Está muy hondo y yo no puedo."

Felipe, en vez de sacarlo, lo metió más para adentro para que se acabara de ahogar.

La viejita le repitió las mismas palabras que antes le había dicho a Juan. Felipe estuvo como un mes andando. No encontró ni a su hermano ni la flor.

En vista de que ninguno de los dos regresaba, determinó el más pequeño de los hermanos irse tras ellos. Aunque tanto la madre como el padre le rogaron que no fuera porque era al quien más querían y quien mejores sentimientos tenía, Carlos siempre se fue.

Al pasar por el río, vio a la viejita y al niño llorando. Le dijo:

"Viejita, mire a ese niño llorando, cójalo para ver si se calla."

Ella le dijo que el niño tenía hambre, pero no tenía nada que darle. Carlos sacó del bolsillo un bollo de pan y le dio la mitad al niñito. La viejita dijo:

"Por ser tan bondadoso y por tener un alma noble, voy a decirte dónde están tus hermanos y dónde se encuentra la flor del olivar para que le devuelva la vista a tu padre. Ten cuidado; tus hermanos te matarán cuando sepan que tú has encontrado esa flor. Cuando la tengas, póntela en la planta del pie izquierdo."

Así le sucedió. No bien llegó junto a Juan y Felipe, supieron que Carlos tenía la flor apetecida. Después de registrarlo, le quitaron los zapatos y se la encontraron. Enseguida lo mataron y lo enterraron. Después se fueron a su casa, le devolvieron la vista al ciego. Le dijeron al padre que a su hermanito ni lo habían visto.

Cierto día el padre mandó a Juan a talar un terreno para sembrar caña, y al empezar, se oyó una voz:

"Hermanito, no me toques,
ni me dejes de tocar,
que tú mismo me mataste
por la flor del olivar."

Juan se fue corriendo a su casa y dijo que mandaran al otro hermano.

Se fue Felipe y oyó enseguida una voz que le decía:

"Hermanito, no me toques,
ni me dejes de tocar,
que tú no me mataste
pero ayudaste a enterrar."

Se fue Felipe y se lo dijo a sus papás, quienes fueron al lugar indicado. Oyeron una voz que les decía:

"Mis padrecitos queridos,
no me dejen de tocar.
Mis hermanos me han matado
por la flor del olivar."

Entonces, los padres empezaron a escarbar; encontraron a Carlos intacto y según era.

Lo abrazaron, lo besaron y le preguntaron qué castigo quería que recibieran sus hermanos.

Carlos le contestó que les perdonaba. Así fue y vivieron felices.

~

The Flower of the Olive Grove

Once upon a time, a married couple had three sons. The oldest was named Juan, the middle one was Felipe, and the youngest was Carlos. After several years, the father lost his sight, leaving the poor family destitute because he was the one who worked to provide for his family. This good man was blind for some time when an old man appeared to him. The old man said the father would see again if he washed his eyes in water boiled with the flower of the olive grove, but the flower was very hard to get.

As soon as Juan, the oldest son, heard about this advice, he left the house in search of the flower of the olive grove. Before departing, he said to his two youngest brothers that whenever they saw a little withered tree, he had found himself in trouble.

Juan went alone walking, walking, walking until, while passing a river, he saw an old woman washing clothes and a little boy weeping hard. Juan said:

"Old woman, look at that child who is weeping."

She answered him:

"He is crying from hunger. Don't you have a piece of bread?"

Although he was carrying a bread bun, Juan told her that he had none. The old lady wished him a bumpy road and many problems.

Three weeks passed. Felipe, the middle brother, seeing that his brother was not returning, noticed the little tree was dead. Right then Felipe decided to go out to look for Juan. When he had traveled many hours, Felipe came upon the same old woman and the little boy, who was drowning. Felipe exclaimed:

"Look, old woman, that little boy is drowning!"

She said to him:

"Oh, get him out! The river is very deep, and I can't help him."

Instead of taking him out, Felipe brought him into deeper water to finish the drowning.

The old woman repeated to him the same words that she had said earlier to Juan. Felipe kept walking for about one month; he found neither his brother nor the flower of the olive grove.

Since neither of the two had returned, Carlos, the youngest brother, decided to go out after them. His mother and his father begged him not to go because he was the son they loved most. He was such a kind son. Even so, Carlos left.

As he passed by the river, Carlos saw the old woman and the crying child. He said:

"Old woman, take a look at that weeping little child. Pick him up to see whether he quiets down."

She explained that the child was hungry; she had nothing to give him. Carlos took a bread roll from his pocket and gave half of it to the child. The old woman said:

"Because you are so kind and because you have a noble soul, I am going to tell you where your brothers are and where the flower of the olive grove is so that it may restore your father's sight. But be careful. Your brothers will kill you as soon as they find out that you have found that flower. When you find it, put it on the sole of your left foot."

That's exactly what happened. As soon as Carlos got close to Juan and Felipe, they realized that he had found the much-desired flower. After searching him, they took off his shoes and found the bloom. At once they killed him and buried him. Afterward, they went home and restored the blind father's sight. They told their parents that they had not seen their little brother.

One day, the father ordered Juan to clear the grass from a plot of land in order to plant sugar cane. As Juan began his chore, he heard a voice saying to him:

"Dear brother, touch me not,
nor stop touching me,
since you yourself killed me
for the flower of the olive grove."

Juan went running home. He asked his father to send the other son; he could not do the work.

Felipe went instead. At once he heard a voice that said to him:

"Dear brother, touch me not,
nor stop touching me,
you did not kill me,
but you helped bury me."

Felipe also went home in a hurry. He told his parents, who decided to check out that place. They too heard a voice that said to them:

"My beloved parents,
don't stop touching me.
My brothers have killed me
for the flower of the olive grove."

The parents began to die immediately; they found Carlos intact, just as he was in life.

They embraced and kissed Carlos. They asked him what punishment he wanted his brothers to receive. Carlos answered that he was forgiving his brothers.

They all lived happily ever after.

La joven y la serpiente[2]

Una vez había unos padres que tenían tres hijos, tres perros y tres caballos. Un día el padre no tenía dinero para comprar comida. Como él era pescador se fue a pescar, pero solamente pudo pescar un solo pescadito. Le dijo que no lo comiera; que dijera a la familia que el pescadito estaba enfermo y tenía tres espinas. Debía sembrar las tres espinitas en el patio.

Al cabo de un mes, se murió el pescador. Entonces, la mujer fue al patio donde estaban sembradas las espinas, allí encontró tres espadas. Le dio una a cada uno de sus hijos.

El hijo mayor le dijo a la madre que él se iba a correr fortuna. La madre le dijo que le daría un perro y un caballo. Le preguntó:

"¿Qué quería? ¿La bendición o dinero?"

El le dijo que le diera dinero; con la bendición no hacía nada.

El muchacho se fue y llegó a un hotel. Cuando se acostó, oyó un ruido que lo levantó. Le preguntó a la dueña qué era aquel escándalo. Ella le dijo que era un culebrón que se comía todos los días a una persona. El cogió miedo y se fue.

Al otro día, el hijo segundo le dijo a la madre que se iba a correr fortuna. La madre le dijo igual que al primero. El muchacho se fue. Cuando llegó al mismo hotel, la dueña le informó lo del culebrón que se comía todas las noches a una persona. Si no se la daban, los mataba a todos. Entonces, este hermano se fue también para su casa.

Al poco tiempo, el hijo menor le dijo a la madre que se quería ir a correr fortuna. La madre le preguntó qué quería, si la bendición o dinero. El le pidió la bendición; con dinero él no hacía nada. La madre le dio la bendición y dinero. El hijo se fue.

Llegó al mismo hotel que sus otros dos hermanos y oyó el mismo ruido. Le dijeron que era un culebrón que todos los días se comía a una persona. Aquella noche le tocaba a la hija del rey. El rey se la daba en matrimonio a quien la salvase de la fiera y le trajera las siete lenguas del culebrón.

El muchacho cogió su espada y se fue al lado de la cueva. Allí encontró a la hija del rey. Cuando el culebrón estaba saliendo, el hombre cogió la espada, picó la serpiente y le tiró el perro. La hija del rey le dio un pañuelo y una sortija. El hombre le sacó las siete lenguas; se las dio al perro para que se las guardara y también la sortija.

Entonces, la hija del rey se fue a su casa; ya estaba cerrada y todo el pueblo con luto. Por fin le abrieron la puerta. Inmediatamente, le hizo al padre la historia de lo que le había pasado.

Al poco tiempo vino un carbonero con las siete cabezas de la fiera. Como se iba a casar con la princesa, esa tarde se fue a comer a casa del rey. El otro hombre mandó al perro para que cuando el carbonero se fuera a echar un bocado de comida, le echara mano al hocico con el tenedor.

Así lo hizo el perro. El rey mandó a dos criados a buscar al dueño del perro. El dueño del perro le contestó que igual distancia había desde donde él estaba a la casa del rey. Ordenó que el rey fuera allá.

El rey tomó un coche. Le dijo al joven:

"Móntese en el coche."

El hombre le dijo que si no dejaba montar al perro, no iría. El rey contestó que lo montara.

Cuando llegaron a la casa del rey, el hombre le dijo al rey que le mandara a llamar a su hija. Debía pedirle una sortija y un pañuelo que la princesa tenía. El hombre dijo también que le buscaran las siete lenguas en las siete cabezas. Ninguna tendría lengua.

Entonces, el hombre le dijo al perro que echara las siete lenguas y la sortija. El perro las echó. El otro hombre se tiró por la ventana.

La hija del rey y el hombre se casaron. Fueron muy felices.

~

The Maiden and the Serpent

Once upon a time, there were some parents who had three sons, three dogs, and three horses. One day the father had no money to buy food, and since he was a fisherman, he went out to fish, but he caught only one little fish. The little fish told him that the man shouldn't wish to eat it. He should say to his family that the fish was ill, that it only had three bones. The man should then plant the three bones in the patio.

A month later, the fisherman died. His wife went to the patio where the fish bones were planted. She found three swords. She gave one to each of her sons.

The oldest son told his mother that he was going to seek his fortune. The mother told him that she would give him a dog, a horse, and his choice of either a blessing or money. He asked her to give him money, claiming he could do nothing with a blessing.

He went off. He arrived at a hotel, and when he went to bed, he heard a noise. He asked the innkeeper what that racket was all about. She told him that it was a huge snake that ate one person every day. He took fright and left for home.

The next day, the second son told his mother that he was going to seek his fortune. The mother told him just what she had told the first son; he chose the money too. He left at once. When he arrived at that same hotel, the innkeeper told him about the huge snake that ate up one person every night, and if it was not fed, the snake would kill everybody. Right then this son went back home too.

Shortly afterward, the youngest son told his mother that he wanted to seek his fortune. The mother asked him what he wanted, a blessing or money. He told her to give him her blessing because he had no use for money. The mother gave him both her blessing and money. Immediately, the son left.

He came to the same hotel as had his two brothers, and he heard the same noise. He asked about it. He was told that it was a huge snake that ate one person every day. That night, it was the king's daughter's turn to be eaten. The king had proclaimed that he would give her hand in marriage to the man who could save her from the beast. The man should bring to him the huge serpent's seven heads.

The young man grabbed his sword and went near the cave where the snake lived. There he found the king's daughter. When the serpent was coming out, he drew his sword, jabbed it, and the dog attacked it. The king's daughter gave the brave man a kerchief and a ring. He cut out the seven tongues and fed them to the dog so that it could guard them and the ring.

The king's daughter went back to the palace, which was already closed up; everyone was already mourning. Finally, they opened the door for her, and the princess told her father what had happened to her.

Shortly afterward, a coal peddler came to the castle with the beast's seven heads, claiming to have killed the beast. The impostor and the king's daughter were about to marry that afternoon. As soon as the coal peddler went off to eat in the king's house, the young man told his dog that when the impostor was about to take a bite of food, the dog should hit the fork with its muzzle.

The dog did so. The king then sent two servants to fetch the dog's owner. The boy answered him badly; he said that the distance was the same between him and the palace. The king should come to him.

The king took a coach, went to the third son's house, and told him: "Get into the coach."

But the man told him that he wouldn't go if the dog was not allowed to go. The king said that the dog could ride in the coach with them.

When they arrived at the king's house, the young man demanded that the king send for his daughter. The king should look for a ring and a kerchief that she had. The man also demanded that the king and his people search for the seven tongues in the seven heads, none of which, of course, had a tongue.

Then the man told the dog to produce the seven tongues and the ring, and the dog at once spat them out. The peddler jumped out of a window.

The king's daughter and the young man married. They were happy ever after.

Los tres trajes[3]

Había una vez un señor que tenía una señora y tuvieron una hija llamada Rosa. La madre de Rosa tenía una sortija. Un día le dijo al marido:

"Toma esta sortija, así que yo me muera, a la que le sirva esta sortija, tú te casarás con ella."

Pues pasó que ella murió, y a los pocos días, pasaron voces y fama que a la que le sirviera la sortija se casaba con él. Venían señoritas de todos puntos a medirse la sortija. A unas le quedaba grande y a otras les quedaba chica. Ya de eso transcurrieron muchos días.

Estaba la hija señorita cuando se perdió la sortija, perdida como por un año. Barriendo un día, Rosita la encontró, se la midió y le quedó muy bien.

El padre vino de su embarcación y le encantó ver que la sortija le quedaba. Le dijo a Rosita:

"Te tienes que casar conmigo porque mi mujer así me lo dijo."

Ella le dijo:

"¡Ay Papá! ¿Cómo puede ser casarme yo con mi padre?"

El le contestó:

"De cualquier manera te tienes que casar conmigo."

"Sí, Papá, yo me caso con usted, pero me tiene que traer un vestido color de las estrellas."

El le dijo:

"¡Cómo no!"

Pronto se fue a buscarle el vestido.

A los dos o tres días vino con el traje. Rosita se puso lo más triste.

"Bueno, Papá, yo necesito otro vestido color de los peces del mar."

Enseguida salió el padre; a los tres días vino con el traje. Rosita, al verlo, se echó a llorar. Ella le dijo:

"Papá, yo con los dos trajes no me encuentro contenta, pues necesito tres para casarme. Necesito otro color de las flores del mundo."

Como la quería tanto se fue a buscarlo; al otro día vino con él. El padre se fue de inmediato para el pueblo a buscar los gastos para el casamiento.

Rápido que salió él, ella lió su ropa y una varita de virtud que tenía. Se fue montaña adentro. Hacía dos o tres días que estaba en la montaña cuando se encontró una leoncita. La mató, le sacó el cuero y se metió dentro de él; se mantenía viva pidiéndole a la varita.

En un reinado había un príncipe, llamado Juanito, quien se vino a cazar a la montaña. Allí se encontró una paloma y le tiró. La paloma volaba de gancho en gancho y él detrás de ella; tanto corrió que llegó a donde estaba la leoncita. El dijo:

"Me la voy a llevar para que Mamá se entretenga."

La cogió y se la llevó para su casa.

"Mamá, mire lo que le traigo aquí—una leoncita para que usted se entretenga."

Ella la cogió y la amarró debajo del fogón. Allí le ponían la comida.

El sábado siguiente Juanito tenía un baile. Se arregló y se fue. Enseguida que oscureció, le dijo la leoncita a la señora:

"Déjeme ir a ver el baile."

Ella le dijo:

"Mira que si Juanito te ve allá, te mata."

La leoncita le dijo:

"Déjeme ir. El no me hace nada."

"Pues, vete."

Enseguida, le pidió a la varita de virtud un caballo aparejado con oro reluciente; ella se puso el traje color de las estrellas. Montó el caballo y se fue.

Cuando llegó al baile, toda la gente salió a recibirla a la puerta para ver a aquella princesa reluciendo en oro. Juanito, quien tenía allí a su novia, no hizo ni cuenta de ella. Se entusiasmó de la princesa; comenzaron a bailar y él empezó a enamorarla hasta que ella le dio el compromiso. Dijo la princesa, ya amaneciendo, que se venía y él le regaló un aro cifrado con el nombre de él. Ella le regaló otro aro y, rápido, montó en su caballo. Se vino y entró en el cuerito.

Al poco rato llegó el príncipe Juanito, contándole a la madre sobre la princesa que había visto. La leoncita le contestaba:

"Quizás sí, quizás no, quizás sí sería yo."

Le dieron un macetazo. El dijo:

"Mamá, yo voy a hacer otro baile el sábado."

A la semana hizo la fiesta. Si bueno estuvo aquel baile, éste estaba mejor. La leoncita le pidió permiso a la madre para que la dejara ir. La mujer le dijo:

"¡Dios te libre que te vayas!"

La leoncita le dijo:

"Yo voy."

Enseguida, le dijo a la varita de virtud:

"Varita de virtud, por la virtud que tú tienes y la que Dios te ha dado, que si bonita me pusiste la otra vez, que me pongas más bonita y dame el caballo más precioso que haya en el mundo."

Ella se puso el vestido de los peces del mar, montó su caballo y se fue.

Cuando llegó al baile la gente loca con ella. Empezó a bailar con el príncipe Juanito y él loco con ella. Ya al amanecer, le dijo a Juanito:

"Me voy porque se me está haciendo tarde."

Juanito le regaló una leontina; ella le regaló otra prenda. La leoncita en su caballo y desapareció.

Cuando la gente vino a ver, ya la leoncita venía muy lejos. Juanito se quedó llorando con mal de amores.

La leoncita se metió en el cuerito, y al poco rato, llegó Juanito. Le dijo a su madre:

"¡Ay Mamá! ¡Me muero! Si bonita estuvo la princesa la primera vez, ahora estaba más preciosa."

La leoncita le contestó:

"Quizás sí, quizás no, quizás sí sería yo."

Le dieron con la paleta. El príncipe dijo:

"Más no es tanto, el sábado voy a hacer otro baile."

A los ocho días se hizo el baile, y si buenos estuvieron los primeros, mejor va a estar éste. Juanito ese día no quiso comer; se fue bien temprano a esperar a la princesa. La leoncita a las seis de la tarde le pidió permiso a la señora para que la dejara ir. Por ser tan majadera, la mujer le dijo que cogiera el camino y se fuera. ¡Ojalá que la mataran!

La leoncita enseguida se fue a vestir; si bonita estaba las otras dos veces, hoy estaba mucho más bonita. Se puso el traje color de las flores del mundo, montó en el caballo reluciendo en oro y plata y se fue para el baile.

Juanito se tiró y la cogió del brazo, la subió al salón y se pusieron a bailar. Enseguida puso guardias dobles para que ella no se fuera, pero a ella nada de eso le molestaba para irse. Al poquito rato él le dio una prenda y ella le dio otra. Inmediatamente, desapareció.

La leoncita vino a su casa. Se metió en el cuerito. Cuando llegó Juanito cogió la cama con mal de amores, tan mal estaba que ni pasaba el agua. La mamá sentía muchísimo sentimiento porque era su único hijo. Como a los quince días, la leoncita le preguntó a la dueña de la casa si Juanito quería comer unos pastelitos. Le preguntaron si los quería. El dijo que no quería comer nada.

La leoncita pidió como favor que ella quería hacer los pastelitos para ver si Juanito los comía. La viejita le dijo que no, porque si él sabía que ella los había hecho no los querría. La leoncita respondió que él no lo sabría.

Se puso la leoncita a hacerlos; hizo tres pastelitos. En uno le echó la leontina, en otro le puso un aro y en el otro le puso una sortija.

"Aunque no los coma, pero que los parta," se dijo.

Se los llevó a Juanito. Partió el primero y le encontró la leontina; en el segundo halló el aro; en el otro la sortija. El preguntó:

"Mamá, ¿quién hizo esos pasteles?"

Ella le dijo:

"¡Yo los hice!"

"No, usted no fue. Tráigame a la que hizo los pasteles."

Ya la leoncita estaba vestida con el vestido color de las estrellas. Estaba preciosísima. Cuando llegó hasta donde Juanito estaba, él exclamó:

"Esta es la princesa que yo le decía."

Enseguida se alentó

Mandaron a buscar el cura y se casaron. Siguieron fiestas reales y bailes. Juanito fue rey y Rosa reina y se quedaron viviendo con la mamá.

~

The Three Dresses

Once upon a time, there was a man who had a wife. They had a daughter named Rosa.

The wife had a beautiful ring. One day she said to her husband:

"Take this ring. When I die, you will marry the woman that this ring fits."

Well, it happened that she died, and in a few days, the news spread far and wide that the widower would marry the woman whom the ring fit. Young ladies came from every direction to try on the ring, but it was too big for some of them and too small for others. That went on for many days.

The ring got lost and stayed lost about a year until Rosita, grown up now, found it while she was sweeping. She tried it on. It fit her quite well. The father came home from his vessel, and he was delighted to see that the ring fit Rosa. He said to her:

"You have to marry me because my wife told me so."

She said to him:

"Oh, Papa! How is it possible for me to marry my father?"

His answer did not change:

"Even so, you have to marry me."

"Yes, Papa, I am marrying you, but you must bring me a dress that is the color of the stars."

He said to her:

"Of course!"

And off he went to search for the dress.

Two or three days later, he came with the dress. Rosita became extremely sad.

"Well, Papa, I must have another dress; this one should be the color of the fish in the sea."

He left at once. Three days later, the father came with the dress. Upon seeing him, Rosita began to weep. She told him:

"Papa, I am not satisfied with the two dresses, since I must have three to get married. I need another dress; this one must be the color of all the flowers in the world."

Since he loved Rosita so much, her father went off to find it. The next day, he came with the dress the color of all the flowers in the world. He left at once for the town to buy things that were needed for the wedding.

As soon as he left, Rosita bundled up her clothes, took a magic wand that she had, and went deep into the wilderness. She had been on a mountain for two or three days when she came upon a little lioness. She killed it, removed its skin, and turned herself into a lioness. The magic wand kept the girl alive.

There was a prince, Juanito, who lived in a nearby kingdom, who had come to hunt deep in the wilderness. He saw a dove and shot it, but it kept flying from branch to branch, and he chased after it. He ran so much that he came to where the little lioness was. He said to himself:

"I am going to carry it with me so that Mama can entertain herself with it."

The prince grabbed the lioness and carried it home with him.

"Mama, look what I am bringing you—a little lioness to entertain you."

She took the lioness and chained her under the stove, where she fed her food.

The next Saturday, Juanito had a dance, and he dressed up and went out. As soon as night fell, the little lioness said to her lady queen:

"Let me go see the dance."

The queen told her:

"Look, if Juanito sees you there, he will kill you."

The lioness said to her:

"Let me go! He won't do anything to me."

"Well, go ahead, then."

At once the girl asked the magic wand for a horse with shining trappings of gold. She put on the dress that was the color of the stars. She mounted the horse and left.

When the beautiful girl got to the dance, all the people went out to receive her at the door. Everyone wanted to see that princess shining so much with gold. Juanito's girlfriend was there, although he had paid no attention to her. He too was excited about the princess.

Juanito and the gold princess started dancing. Soon he began to court the girl until she agreed to marry him. Suddenly, the princess said that dawn was coming. Juanito gave her a ring bearing his name. She gave him a ring in exchange, then mounted her horse and went home. The princess immediately got into her lioness skin.

Shortly afterward, Juanito arrived, telling his mother about a princess that he had just met. The little lioness responded:

"Maybe yes, maybe no, maybe it was I."

They stroked her. Juanito said to his mother:

"Mama, I am going to have another dance on Saturday."

The next week he did so. If that earlier ball was good, this one was even better. The little lioness asked the queen to let her go. The woman said:

"May God keep you from going!"

The lioness replied:

"I am going."

At once the girl said to her magic wand:

"Magic wand, by your own power and that which God has given you, if you made me pretty last time, make me prettier now. Give me the most gorgeous horse in the world."

She then put on the dress that was the color of the fish of the sea and mounted her magnificent horse. She left immediately.

The princess arrived at the ball, and soon people were dazzled by her looks. She began to dance with Prince Juanito, who was crazy about her. Again at dawn, she said to the prince:

"I am leaving because this is very late for me."

Juanito gave her a jeweled chain; in return, she gave him another piece of jewelry. She then mounted her horse and quickly disappeared.

By the time the people came to see her leave, she was already gone. Juanito was left feeling lonely, weeping from the pain of love.

The girl went home and put on the lioness skin. Soon afterward, Juanito came into the house. He said to his mother:

"Oh, Mama, I am dying! If the princess was pretty before, tonight she was even more beautiful."

The little lioness answered him:

"Maybe yes, maybe no, maybe it was I."

They hit her with a spoon. He announced to his mother:

"Without wasting any time, next Saturday I am going to have another dance."

Eight days later, Juanito had a dance. If the two earlier ones were good, this one promised to be better. That day the prince refused to eat. He left for the ballroom very early, so eager was he to meet the princess. At six o'clock that afternoon, the girl asked the lady for permission to go. To her whining, the queen told her to take to the road. She was hoping that the people would kill her. At once the girl dressed up, and if she was pretty the other two times, this time she was even prettier. She put on the dress that was the color of all the flowers in the world and mounted her horse, which was glittering with gold and silver. She left soon after.

Juanito dashed to his princess, took her arm, and led her to the ballroom. They began to dance. At once he put double guards on the doors to keep her from leaving, but none of that kept her from slipping away. Very soon the girl and Juanito exchanged tokens of love. She then, as usual, disappeared.

She went home and put on the lioness skin. When Juanito arrived, he took to his bed, so sick with love that he could not even drink water. The queen mother was exceedingly upset because he was her only son. After about two weeks, the little lioness asked the lady of the house whether Juanito would like to eat some pastries. He was asked, but he said he wanted nothing to eat.

The little lioness asked the lady for a favor; she wanted to make the pastries anyway. She was curious if Juanito would eat them. The old lady said no, claiming that if he knew she had made them, he would not want them. The little lioness replied that he would not suspect it.

The little lioness began to bake. She made three little pastries. In one she buried the jeweled chain; in another, the engagement band; and in the third, the ring.

"Even if he doesn't eat them, maybe he will cut them in two," she said to herself.

The mother took the pastries to Juanito. He cut the first one and found the chain; in the second, he found the band; and in the other one, he found the ring. Feeling stronger, he said:

"Mama, who made those pastries?"

She said:

"I made them!"

"No, it was not you. Bring me the woman who made the pastries."

The little lioness was already wearing the dress that was the color of the stars; she was extremely beautiful. When she appeared in front of the prince, Juanito said:

"This was the princess that I told you about."

At once he ate food.

A priest was sent for, and they got married, followed by large royal festivities and colorful dances.

Juanito became a king and Rosita, the lioness, his queen. They lived happily ever after with Juanito's mother.

Porto Rico, looking for a stray cocoanut [*sic*] among the hulls

CHAPTER 4

Juan Bobo

A DECEIVING TRICKSTER

Juan manda la cerda a misa[1]

Se dice que una vez había una señora muy rica quien solo tenía un hijo. Su nombre era Juan, pero como era bobo, le llamaban Juan Bobo.

Como su madre era rica, tenía muchas prendas finas y animales. Una vez la madre se fue para misa y dejó a Juan Bobo solo en la casa. Antes de salir para misa, la mujer dejó una cerda amarrada cerca de la casa. Cuando fue a salir, le dijo a Juan Bobo:

"Ten cuidado que no le dé sol a la cerda."

Se tardó mucho en la misa y la señora no pudo venir antes. El sol calentaba demasiado y la cerda empezaba a gruñir. Juan Bobo oyó que el animal gruñía, pero como bobo que era, pensó que la cerda estaba llorando por ir a misa también con su ama. Pensó un momento:

"Yo te voy a mandar a misa."

Luego cogió y desamarró el animal y lo llevó a una habitación donde la señora tenía todas sus prendas. Juan Bobo vistió la cerda con los mejores trajes de su mamá. Le puso pantallas en las orejas y pulseras en las patas. Después de prepararla, la mandó para misa.

Seguramente que, como la cerda lo que tenía era calor, el animal corrió apresuradamente hacia un bañadero que se encontraba en el camino de la casa. Se ensució y rompió la ropa que llevaba puesta y botó las prendas.

Cuando vino la madre, preguntó por la cerda. Juan Bobo respondió que ella había llorado por irse detrás de ella; él la había vestido y la había mandado para misa. Le preguntó a la madre si no la había visto en la iglesia.

La madre, llena de cólera por la torpeza del muchacho, le pegó muy fuerte para que así no fuera más bobo.

Pero Juan Bobo siempre siguió siendo bobo.

~

Juan Bobo Sends the Pig to Mass

They say that once upon a time, there was a lady who had only one son. His name was Juan, but because he was a dunce, everyone called him Juan Bobo.

Since his mother was rich, she had many jewels, pretty clothes and lots of farm animals. One day, the mother fixed herself up to go to Mass. She had a pig tied up near the house; before leaving for Mass, she said to Juan Bobo:

"Be careful that the sun doesn't hit the pig."

She left Juan Bobo alone in the house.

The Mass was long, and Juan Bobo's mother was late in getting home. The sun was getting too hot, and the pig was beginning to grunt. Juan Bobo heard the animal grunting. Fool that he was, he thought that the pig was crying to go to Mass with her mistress. He thought for a moment and said to the pig:

"I'm going to send you to Mass."

Immediately, Juan Bobo untied the animal. He took her into a room where his mother kept all her jewels. He dressed the pig in his mama's best dress; he put earrings on the sow's ears and bracelets on her hooves. After getting the pig ready, he sent her to Mass.

Of course, the only thing bothering the sow was the heat, so she ran in a hurry toward a water hole in the road to the house. She got filthy, she tore up the clothes that she was wearing, and she kicked off the jewelry.

When the mother came home, she asked Juan Bobo about the pig. He told her that the pig had cried to follow her. He had dressed the pig and had sent her to Mass; he asked his mother if she had not seen the pig in the church.

The mother, full of rage because of her son's stupidity, beat him very hard, hoping to keep him from being stupid again.

But Juan Bobo kept on being stupid.

Juan mata la vaca[2]

La casa en que la familia de Juan Bobo vivía estaba techada de paja. Como era ya un poco vieja, la paja se había podrido y había nacido una mata de berenjena. Bajo la mata de berenjena, había una yerba muy verde que se brindaba al animal que se la quisiera comer.

Una mañana en que Juan Bobo salió de su casa a llevar la vaca de su madre a pacer, no bien iba distante de la casa cuando su vista recorrió el techo de la casa. Entonces, vio las yerbas en la techada de la casa. Juan Bobo se detuvo un momento para pensar:

"Mamá ha sembrado esas yerbas para la vaca. Yo hoy no me voy al río. Yo voy a dejar la vaca aquí; se come las yerbas ésas."

Así lo hizo.

Cogió la vaca, volvió atrás con ella, la subió arriba de la casa. Cuando subió la vaca arriba de la casa, la ahorcó, pero la dejó porque pensó que la vaca estaba cansada con la jornada que había hecho. Se metió en la casa para decirle a su madre lo que había hecho. Cuando ella supo lo que había hecho, le echó tan gran regaño que Juan Bobo pensó abandonarla.

La madre fue entonces donde la vaca; la halló muerta y la bajó. Juan Bobo, viendo la vaca muerta, la cogió y le dijo a su madre:

"Mamá, no se apure; verá como vendo la carne de la vaca y nos hacemos ricos."

Cogió la vaca, le sacó el cuero, agarró la carne y se marchó a venderla a un pueblo cerca de donde ellos vivían.

Pero Juan Bobo no encontró venta para la carne y volvió a casa con ella. Cuando venía de la ciudad, vio un hato de moscas que venían zumbando detrás de la carne. Miró atrás, vio las moscas y les dijo:

"Ustedes son las señoritas del manto prieto?"

Mientras les hacía la pregunta, las moscas más zumbaban. Juan Bobo les dijo:

"Ustedes parece que quieren comprarme alguna carne. Yo puedo fiársela si es que en dos semanas me la pagan."

Al mismo tiempo arrojó dos pedazos a la orilla del camino; siguió caminando con la carne que le quedaba.

Más adelante, se encontró un perro que estaba muriéndose de hambre, el cual, viendo a Juan Bobo con la carne, se le fue detrás. Juan Bobo le dijo:

"Perro, ¿tú quieres alguna carne?"

Como el perro le seguía, al fin dijo:

"Yo te voy a fiar lo que me queda, pero me la pagas entre dos semanas."

El perro, que era tuerto, cuando oyó a Juan Bobo que hablaba, volteó la cabeza, y él creyó que le decía que sí. Le tiró la carne, igual que hizo con las moscas. Juan Bobo se fue para su casa.

Cuando llegó a su casa, la madre le preguntó si había vendido la carne. Juan Bobo le dijo que sí, pero la había fiado toda. La madre, indignada, no dijo nada y lo dejó porque sabía que su hijo era bobo.

Al cumplirse las dos semanas, Juan Bobo se marchó a cobrar su carne. Llevaba en las manos una pistola. Cuando miraba para ver si veía el perro tuerto, vio que en la casa del agricultor subía un perro tuerto. El amo de la casa también era tuerto, Juan Bobo pensó.

Juan se dirigió a la casa de este hombre. Al entrar dio cordialmente los buenos días. La familia lo saludó lo más amable. Juan Bobo, muy serio, dijo:

"Señores, échenme al tuerto abajo para que me pague mi dinero."

El dueño de la casa no estaba en la casa. Juan Bobo, ya impaciente, repitió dos veces que le echaran abajo al tuerto para que le pagara la carne. La señora del agricultor, creyendo que se refería a su marido, le dijo:

"Juan Bobo, yo te voy a dar una taleguita de dinero. Vete ahora mismo."

Juan Bobo cogió el dinero y se marchó para su casa. La madre lo recibió muy contenta porque ya era feliz.

El día siguiente Juan Bobo volvió a la misma casa; otra vez estaba pidiendo que le echaran al tuerto para abajo. La señora, temiendo que fuera a haber un compromiso, le ofreció diez talegas de dinero para que no volviera más. Juan Bobo las cogió y se fue muy satisfecho.

Su madre y él fueron ricos.

Juan Bobo se casó con una hija de un vecino y ahora viven muy felices.

~

Juan Kills the Cow

The house in which Juan Bobo's family lived had a straw roof. It was fairly old, and the straw had rotted where a sprig of eggplant had come up. Under that sprig, there was very green grass available to any animal that wanted to eat it, or so foolishly thought Juan Bobo.

One morning when Juan Bobo left the house to take his mother's cow to graze, not far from the house he looked at the house's roof. He saw the grass on it. He stopped for a moment and thought:

"Mama had planted this grass for the cow. Today I am not going to the river. I am going to leave the cow here to eat that delicious green grass."

And he did so.

Juan Bobo grabbed the cow, turned back with it, and took it up on top of the house. When the cow got on top of the house, it choked to death, but he left it on the roof. He thought that the cow was just tired out from walking. Juan Bobo went into the house to tell his mother what he had done. When she realized what he had done, she gave him a scolding that made Juan Bobo think of leaving home.

The mother found the cow dead. Juan Bobo, seeing that the cow was dead, took it and said to his mother:

"Mama, don't worry. You will see that I will sell the cow's meat, and we will get rich." He grabbed the cow, took the hide off, and packed the meat. Gladly, he went off to sell the meat in a nearby town.

But Juan Bobo found no buyers. He started to go home with the meat. On the way, he saw a swarm of flies coming buzzing after the meat. He said:

"Are you the young ladies of the black shawl?"

JUAN KILLS THE COW

While he was asking them, they buzzed more. He said to them:

"It seems that you want to buy some meat from me. I can let you have it on credit if you pay me in two weeks."

At the same time, he threw two pieces to the side of the road and kept going with the rest of the meat.

Later on, he met a dog who was starving to death. When the hungry dog saw Juan Bobo with the meat, it followed him. Juan said to it:

"Dog, do you want some meat?"

As the dog kept following him, he finally said:

"I will give you all of it on credit, but you must pay me in two weeks."

The dog, blind in one eye, tossed its head when it heard Juan Bobo, who believed that it was saying yes. He tossed the meat just as he had done with the flies. Juan Bobo left happily for home.

When he got home, his mother asked him if he had sold the meat; he told her yes, but all of it on credit. His angry mother said nothing to him; she turned away from him. She feared the worst knowing that her son was such a fool.

At the end of two weeks, Juan Bobo walked off to collect the money for his meat. This time he was carrying a pistol. While he was looking for the one-eyed dog, he saw that a one-eyed dog was going up to the house of a farmer. The owner of the house was also one-eyed.

Juan Bobo headed to that house and greeted the family politely. They welcomed him most cordially. Juan Bobo, very seriously, said to them:

"Ladies and gentlemen, hand over the one-eyed one to pay me my money."

But the owner of the house was not there. Twice Juan Bobo repeated that they should hand over the one-eyed one to pay him for the meat. The farmer's wife, believing that Juan Bobo meant her husband, said to him:

"Juan Bobo, I am going to give you a little sack of money. Please, go away now."

Juan Bobo took the money and left for home.

His mother was pleased to receive him. Now she was happy.

The following day, Juan Bobo went back to the same house, asking them to send down the one-eyed one. The lady, again fearing a dispute, offered him ten sacks of money if he would never come back. Juan Bobo took the money and happily went away. He and his mother became rich.

Juan Bobo married a daughter of his neighbor. They are now living happily.

Juan Bobo se muere cuando el burro se tire tres pedos[3]

Había una vez un muchacho que era lo más bobo. Su madre le puso el nombre de Juan Bobo.

Un día su madre lo mandó a buscar leña al bosque. Cuando Juan Bobo llegó se encaramó en un gancho seco que iba a picar. Pasaron dos caballeros, quienes le dijeron:

"Juan Bobo, ¿tú no ves que te vas a caer de ese palo?"

El les dijo que si ellos eran Dios.

Cuando ellos iban lejos se cayó Juan del gancho y echó a correr para alcanzarlos. Les gritaba:

"¡Eh, eh!"

Ellos se dijeron:

"¡Tú ves! Allí viene Juan Bobo. Se ha caído del gancho y viene a preguntarnos que si somos Dios."

Juan Bobo llegó. Les dijo:

"¡Ustedes sí que son Dios! Me caí del gancho. Díganme, ¿cuándo me muero yo?"

Ellos le dijeron:

"Cuando aquel burro se tire tres pedos."

Entonces, cuando Juan Bobo lo estaba cargando, el burro se tiró un pedo. Se dijo:

"¡Ay! Ya me faltan dos."

Cuando iba por mitad del camino el burro se tiró otro y dijo:

"Ya me falta uno."

Cuando llegó a la casa le dijo a la madre que se había encontrado con Dios:

"Yo le pregunté cuándo me moría; me dijo tan pronto cuando el burro se tirara tres pedos. Ya me faltaba uno solo."

Cuando fue a descargar el burro le dio un palo y se tiró el otro pedo que faltaba. Juan Bobo cayó muerto.

Por la noche fue el velorio de Juan Bobo. Aquel día había llovido mucho y los que lo llevaban tenían que pasar un río crecido. Ellos se decían:

"¿Por dónde pasaremos con este muerto?"

Cuando aquel río estaba crecido, Juan Bobo pasaba por unos palitos que él mismo había puesto. Estuvieron allí por mucho tiempo, tanto que Juan Bobo se sentó en la caja. Les dijo:

"Miren, cuando yo era vivo pasaba por aquellos palitos."

Ellos dijeron:

"¡Ay! Juan Bobo está vivo."

Lo arrojaron al agua.

Vinieron y le dijeron a la mamá de Juan Bobo que él estaba vivo y lo habían arrojado al agua.

~

Juan Bobo Dies When the Donkey Farts Three Times

Once upon a time, there was an extremely silly boy whose mother called him Juan Bobo.

One day his mother sent him out to look for firewood in the forest. When he arrived, he climbed to a dry branch that he was going to chop off. Two men passed by. They said to him:

"Juan Bobo, don't you see that you are going to fall from that branch?"

Juan Bobo wondered whether they were God.

When they had gone a good distance, Juan Bobo fell from the branch. He set out running to reach the men. He was shouting:

"Hey, hey!"

They said to each other:

"You'll see! Here comes Juan Bobo, who has fallen from the branch. He will ask us whether we are God."

Juan Bobo finally reached them. He said to the men:

"You really are God! I fell from the branch. So tell me, when am I going to die?"

They said:

"Whenever that donkey farts three times."

Then as he was loading a cart, the donkey farted once. Juan said to himself:

"Oh, that's one out of three."

When he was halfway home, the donkey farted again. Juan said to himself:

"That's two out of three."

When he got home, he told his mother that he had met God:

"I asked him when I am going to die. He told me when the donkey farted three times. Now there is only one to go."

Juan Bobo was about to unload the donkey, but it kicked him, farting the last of the three times. Juan Bobo immediately fell dead.

The wake for Juan Bobo was that night. That day it had rained a lot, and those carrying Juan Bobo's body had to cross the swollen waters of the river. They said:

"Where are we to cross with this corpse?"

When the river was very high, Juan Bobo used to cross it using some sticks that he had put into the river. As the men stalled for a long time, an impatient Juan Bobo sat up in his casket. He said to the men:

"Look, when I was alive, I crossed the river using those small sticks."

They said:

"Hey! Juan Bobo is alive!"

They threw him into the water.

They went to tell Juan Bobo's mother that her son was alive but they had thrown him into the river.

Juan y los objetos mágicos[4]

Un día salió Juan Bobo de su casa sin pedir permiso de sus padres para ir a casa de su padrino; quería pedirle el aguinaldo. Empezó a andar, anda que te anda, hasta que llegó a la casa de su padrino.

"Buen día, mi querido padrino. Yo he venido para que usted regale mi aguinaldo."

El padrino enseguida le dijo:

"Buenos días, querido ahijado, ¡cómo no! Tu aguinaldo está seguro."

Después convidó a Juan Bobo a sentarse.

Al poco rato trajo una cabrita.

"Toma, ahijado, esta cabrita. Cuando tú necesites dinero, dile 'Abre chivita' y después 'Cierra chivita.'"

Tomando Juan Bobo la chivita en la mano, le dijo:

"¡Ay! Padrino, ¿cómo va a ser esto?"

Juan Bobo se fue.

Como el camino era demasiado lejos, le cogió la noche y Juan Bobo tuvo que dormir en una casita que encontró en una montaña muy alta. Preguntó si le daban posada; le dijeron que sí. Antes de entrar Juan Bobo dijo que traía una cabrita. Si le decían "Ábrete," echaba dinero, y si le decían "Ciérrate," no echaba nada. Las personas que estaban en la casa, contentas al oír esta maravilla, dijeron que entrara. Enseguida se acostaron a dormir. Juan Bobo, como era poco sabio de verdad, inmediatamente empezó a roncar. Los de la casa, entonces, le escondieron la chivita.

Al otro día, cuando se levantó, procuró su chiva, pero no la encontró. Juan Bobo volvió otra vez a la casa de su padrino.

"Padrino, deme mi aguinaldo que el otro me lo cogieron."

Su padrino le dio una potranquita. Le dio estas instrucciones:

"Si necesitas dinero, dile 'Abre potranquita.'"

Entonces, Juan Bobo empezó a andar hasta que llegó a aquella casa otra vez.

Pidió posada y, enseguida, muy contentos le dijeron sí. Se acostaron. El Bobo empezó a roncar; le cogieron la potranquita y la escondieron. Al otro día no encontró su aguinaldo, pero comprendió que en la misma casa ya le habían robado.

Salió otra vez en busca del aguinaldo, pues hacía tres días que no iba a su casa y no quería llegar sin nada.

"Padrino, deme otro aguinaldo. Me cogieron el que me dio en la casa donde quedé durmiendo."

El padrino no pudo mucho ya. Le dijo con coraje:

"Caramba contigo, ahijado. Toma este garrote; cuando quieras que dé palos, dile 'Ábrete garrote'; cuando no quieras, 'Ciérrate.'"

Llegó a la casa donde él ya había dormido. Juan Bobo pidió posada. Subió con el garrote, advirtiendo que no dijeran "Ábrete garrote," pues le daría palos. Ellos no le creyeron. Inmediatamente, dijeron "Abre garrote"; el garrote empezó a dar palos a las viejas, a las mozas y a las niñas.

Llamaron a Juan Bobo, quien dijo que hasta que no le dieran sus intereses no decía "Ciérrate." Se los dieron. El garrote no dio más palos.

~

Juan and the Magical Objects

One day, Juan Bobo left his home without his parents' permission in order to visit his godfather. He wanted to ask his godfather for a gift. Juan Bobo started walking and walking and walking until he arrived at his godfather's house.

"Good day, dear godfather. I have come to ask you for my gift."

The godfather said at once:

"Good day, dear godson, certainly. Your gift is a sure thing."

He invited Juan Bobo to sit down.

Shortly afterward, he brought Juan a little goat.

"Godson, take this little goat. When you need money, say to it 'Open up, little goat' and then, 'Close, little goat.'"

Juan Bobo took hold of the little goat. He said:

"Come on, godfather, how can this be?"

Juan Bobo left at once.

As the trip was too long, night overtook him. Juan Bobo had to sleep in a little house that he found on a very high mountain. He asked for shelter and they agreed. Before entering the house, Juan Bobo said that he was bringing with him a little goat that spat out money when he said "Open up." It threw out nothing when he said "Close." Pleased to hear about this enchanted animal, the people in the house told him to come in; they were getting ready to go to bed. At once they went to bed. Juan Bobo, who really wasn't very smart, soon began to snore. The people in the house took Juan's little goat and hid it away.

When Juan got up the next day, he looked for his goat, but he could not find it. His cunning hosts managed to fool him.

Juan Bobo went back to his godfather's.

"Godfather, give me another present, since some mean people took mine away."

Juan Bobo's godfather gave him a little filly. He told him:

"If you need money, say to it 'Open up, little filly.'"

Juan Bobo began to walk until he arrived at the same house as before.

He asked for shelter; of course, very pleased, the evil people agreed. Everyone went to bed; soon the dummy began to snore loudly. They took Juan Bobo's filly and hid her. The next day, Juan Bobo could not find his gift. He then remembered that they had stolen from him in this very same house.

Again, Juan Bobo went in search of a gift, since for three days he had been away from home. He did not want to return without anything.

"Godfather, give me another present. At the house where I was sleeping, those mean people took from me the ones that you had given me."

The godfather, who was already fed up, said to Juan Bobo:

"What on earth is the matter with you, godson? Take this stick. When you want it to beat somebody, tell it 'Open up, stick,' and when you don't, say 'Close.'"

Juan Bobo arrived at the house where he had slept before. He asked again for shelter. He went in with the stick, telling them that they should not say "Open up, stick," since the stick would then strike blows. They did not believe him.

They said, "Open up, stick," and it began to beat the old women, young women, and girls.

They called Juan Bobo. He said that he was not going to say "Close" until they gave him back his other belongings. They gave the goat and the filly back to him. The stick struck no more people.

La olla que calienta el agua sin fuego[5]

Juan Bobo estaba en su casa cuando vio venir al compadre. Inmediatamente, le dijo a la madre que si la comida estaba hecha, le sacara toda la candela y las cenizas. La madre fue y le sacó todas las cenizas y la candela. Cuando el compadre llegó, Juan Bobo preguntó a su madre cómo podía cocinar sin candela. La madre le dijo que ella había puesto la olla que cocinaba sola. El le contestó

"Pues, deme mi almuerzo y el de mi compadre."

La madre les sacó el almuerzo a los dos. El compadre, como tenía hambre, encontró la comida buenísima. Le pidió a Juan Bobo que le vendiera la olla. Juan Bobo le contestó que era imposible que él la vendiera; su olla le ahorraba el carbón y la cocinera. El hombre le ofreció tres talegos de dinero por la olla. Juan Bobo le dijo:

"¡Chú! ¡Ya a usted se la he dado!"

El hombre se fue. Cuando llegó a la casa le dijo a la mujer que botara a la cocinera. El traía una olla que se ahorraba el carbón y que no necesitaba cocinera. Enseguida le arreglaron la cuenta a la cocinera y la botaron. El hombre se fue para su oficina.

La señora puso su olla en un rincón con los granos y la tapó. Cuando se llegó la hora de que estuvieran las habichuelas cocidas, fue a ver y estaban lo mismo. Tapó su olla otra vez y la dejó allí. Cuando el marido llegó y vio que no estaba el almuerzo, se tiró abajo y se fue en perseguimiento de Juan Bobo.

~

The Pot That Heats Water without Fire

Juan Bobo was at home when he saw his buddy coming. At once he told his mother that if the meal was cooked, she should remove all the fire and the ashes. As instructed, the mother took away all the fire and the ashes. When the buddy arrived, Juan Bobo asked his mother whether she was going to cook without fire. The mother replied that she was using just the pan that was cooking on its own. Juan Bobo told her:

"So give my buddy and me our lunch."

The mother put out lunch for the two. The buddy was hungry and found the food delicious. He asked Juan Bobo to sell him the pot. Juan Bobo said that he could not possibly sell it. His pot had saved him a lot of money on coal, and so he had no need for a cook. The man offered Juan Bobo three bags of money for the pot. Juan Bobo said to him:

"Well, it's yours! Take it!"

The man left. Once at home, he told his wife to fire the cook. He had brought home a pot that saves on coal and needs no cook. At once they paid off the cook and fired her. The man went off to his office.

His wife put the pot with uncooked beans in a corner and covered it. When the time came for the stewed beans to have cooked, she went to check, but nothing had happened. Again, she covered the pot and left it there. When the husband arrived and saw that lunch was not cooked, he headed out for the street and went off in pursuit of Juan Bobo.

El conejo que llama a su amo[6]

Juan Bobo tenía un compadre, a quien convidó a que fuera a su casa al otro día al medio día. El compadre le dijo que iba a las once en punto. Juan Bobo tenía que ir a trabajar todos los días y también venía a su casa a las once.

Juan Bobo tenía dos conejitos blancos que no se distinguían uno del otro. Le dejó un reloj a su madre y se llevó otro, pero los puso a los dos a andar iguales para que cuando diera el reloj las once, que soltara el conejito que él había dejado acá. Como él tenía el otro allá, pues cuando el reloj diera las once, él se venía a la casa.

Al otro día, Juan Bobo cogió un conejito y un reloj y se fue para su trabajo. Le dejó a su madre un reloj y un conejito. Cuando llegó el compadre a la casa de Juan Bobo, ya eran las once. La madre de Juan Bobo sacó el conejito de un cajón y le dijo:

"Vete a buscar a Juan Bobo que aquí lo procuran."

El conejito se fue por el camino por donde habría de venir Juan Bobo. Desapareció y no lo vieron más.

Juan Bobo, como el reloj de él había dado las once también, se vino con su conejito en el hombro, pasándole la mano y acariciándolo decía:

"¡El pobrecito, tan fatigado de tanto correr para irme a encontrar!"

El compadre era un hombre muy codicioso, que todo lo que veía a otro lo quería, enseguida, se le antojó el conejo. Juan Bobo le decía:

"¡Chu! ¡Yo vender mi conejito que me va a buscar donde quiera que voy!"

"¡Ay, compadre, véndamelo, yo le doy dos talegos de dinero!"

"Mire, compadre, yo le voy a vender el conejo porque está muy empeñado; si no, no se lo vendía."

El compadre le dio los dos talegos de dinero y se llevó el conejo.

Cuando llegó a su casa le dijo a su señora que botara al peón; él traía uno mejor. Enseguida arreglaron las cuentas del peón y lo botaron. El hombre le dijo a su señora que él se iba para su oficina; cuando estuviera el almuerzo debía soltar el conejito para que lo fuera a buscar. El hombre se fue para la oficina.

Cuando el almuerzo estuvo listo la señora soltó el conejo, que se desapareció y no se volvió a ver más. El hombre ya estaba cansado de esperar que el conejo llegara y no llegaba. Muerto de hambre se tuvo que ir a su casa. Cuando llegó le dijo a su mujer que por qué no había soltado el conejo. Ella le dijo que lo había soltado y se había ido.

El hombre se fue a matar a Juan Bobo.

~

The Rabbit That Calls His Master

Juan Bobo had a good buddy. One day Juan Bobo invited his friend to his house to eat lunch at midday. His friend said that he would arrive at exactly eleven o'clock. Juan Bobo had to work every day, but he too came back home at eleven o'clock.

Juan Bobo had two white rabbits that looked just alike. He left his mother a clock and he took another, but he set the two to run at the same time so that when the clock struck eleven, the rabbit left at home would leap up. Since he had the other one with him at work, when the clock struck eleven, he would come home carrying it.

The next day, Juan Bobo picked up one rabbit and one clock and went off to work. He left his mother a clock and a rabbit. When the friend arrived, it was eleven o'clock. Juan Bobo's mother took the rabbit from a box. She said to the rabbit:

"Go get Juan Bobo. His buddy is here waiting for him."

The little rabbit left by the path where Juan Bobo was to come. It soon disappeared; they never saw him again.

Juan Bobo, since his clock had also struck eleven, left work. He came down with his rabbit on his shoulder, patting it and caressing it. He was saying:

"Poor little one, so tired from so much running to find me!"

The buddy was a very greedy man who wanted everything that other people had, and at once, he took a fancy to Juan Bobo's rabbit. Juan Bobo told his friend:

"Hey! Why should I sell my little rabbit? He fetches me wherever I am!"

"Come, come, friend. If you sell it to me, I'll give you two bags of money."

"Look, buddy, I agree to sell you the rabbit—but only because you are so insistent."

The friend gave him two sacks of money. He happily carried away the rabbit.

When he got home, he told his wife to get rid of the ranch hand; he had brought a better one. At once they settled the money due to the ranch hand and threw him out. The man told his wife that he was going to the office; when lunchtime came, she should release the rabbit to fetch him at work. The man left for the office.

When lunch was ready, the wife released the rabbit; it disappeared, of course, never to be seen again. The man got tired of waiting for the rabbit to arrive, but it didn't arrive. Half dead from hunger, he had to go home. He asked his wife why she had not released the rabbit. She told him that she had released it and it had gone off.

The man left to kill Juan Bobo.

El pito que resucita[7]

Juan Bobo le había advertido a la madre que cuando su compadre fuera a la casa, cogiera en la cocina y matara un puerquito. Tenía que sacarle la vejiga y la soplara. Cuando estuviera bien hinchada, la llenara de sangre y se la metiera debajo del brazo derecho.

Juan Bobo tenía siempre la costumbre de traer un puñal. Cuando vio venir al compadre fue y se lo dijo a la madre. La madre cogió un puñal; mató el puerquito, le sacó la vejiga, la llenó de sangre y se la metió debajo del brazo derecho.

Cuando el compadre llegó, el hombre se puso a quejarse de lo que le había pasado con Juan Bobo. El Bobo llamó a la madre y la madre fue. Juan Bobo se puso a decir:

"¡Esta ma'i[8] es quien tiene la culpa!"

Sacó el puñal y la mató.

El compadre estaba lo más apurado. Le dijo a Juan Bobo que lo había metido en un compromiso; no debía haber hecho eso cuando él estaba allí.

Juan Bobo le dijo:

"¡Chú! Si yo quiero, ¡la resucito!"

"¡Ay! Juan Bobo, ¡resucítala!"

Juan Bobo sacó un pito que siempre cargaba y empezó:

"¡Fififio, menea un dedito."

Lo meneó hasta que le dijo que meneara la mano entera y la meneó; ahora los pies, hasta que los meneó también. Después le ordenó:

"Menea la cabeza."

La meneó. Después le gritó:

"Abre la boca."

La abrió. Después le exhortó:

"Abre los ojos."

Los abrió. Después le mandó:

"Párate."

Se paró.

Entonces, el hombre le dijo que le vendiera el pito. Juan Bobo le dijo que el pito no lo vendía por ningún dinero. Tanto lo hostigó hasta que le ofreció cinco talegos de dinero. Juan Bobo se lo vendió.

El hombre se fue a su casa y se puso a organizar un proyecto de una gira; convidó a todas las gentes del vecindario. Cuando estaban todos reunidos, se sentó al lado de su señora a comer y a conversar. Al poco rato, sin que la pobre señora hiciera nada, sacó un puñal y la mató.

Las gentes de la gira estaban lo más asustadas; decían en qué compromiso el señor los había venido a meter. Entonces, el señor dijo:

"Si yo quiero la resucito."

Las gentes le dijeron que la resucitara.

El hombre sacó el pito y dijo:

"¡Fififio, menea un dedito."

Mierda era lo que se meneaba.

"¡Fififio, menea la mano; fififio, menea un pie; fififio, menea la cabeza, fififio . . . !"

Y de allí llegó la justicia, lo cogió prisionero y todavía está cumpliendo. Juan Bobo se hizo rico.

~

The Whistle That Brings People Back to Life

Juan Bobo had advised his mother that his buddy was coming over for a visit. She should catch a piglet and take it into the kitchen and kill it. She was to remove the bladder and blow it up. When it was well inflated, she should fill it with blood and place it under her right arm.

Juan Bobo had a habit of carrying a dagger. When he saw his buddy coming, he went and told his mother. She grabbed a kitchen knife and killed a piglet, took out its bladder, filled it with blood, and put it under her right arm.

When the friend arrived, he began to complain to Juan Bobo about everything the rascal had done to him. The dunce called his mother to come. He began by saying:

"Ma is the one to blame."

He took out the dagger and killed her.

The buddy was extremely upset. He told Juan Bobo that his criminal action had put him in an extremely awkward position. Juan Bobo should not have done that when his buddy was there. Juan Bobo said:

"I can revive her if I want to!"

"Yeah, Juan Bobo, do resuscitate her."

Juan Bobo took out a whistle that he always carried and began:

"Fififio, wiggle a finger!"

She wiggled it. She wiggled the fingers one by one. Next Juan Bobo told her to wiggle the whole hand, and she wiggled it. Then he said to wiggle her feet, and she wiggled them.

Next Juan Bobo said to his dead mother:

"Open your mouth."

She opened it.

Next he commanded:

"Open your eyes."

She opened them.

Next he demanded:

"Stand up."

She stood up.

Right then the man implored Juan Bobo to sell him that whistle. Juan Bobo told his buddy that he would not sell the whistle for any amount of money. His friend pestered Juan Bobo so much, but Juan kept resisting until the man offered him five bags of money. Juan Bobo immediately sold the whistle to him.

The man went home and set up a day trip; he had invited the whole neighborhood to go along. Once they arrived, he sat down beside his wife to eat and to talk. Shortly afterward, without the poor woman's doing anything at all, he took out the knife and killed her.

The people on the trip were extremely frightened. They screamed at the man that he had put them on the spot. The man said to them:

"I can resuscitate her if I wish."

The people told him to resuscitate her.

The man took out the whistle and said:

"Fififio! Move a little finger!"

Not even a shitty finger moved.

"Fififio, wave your hand; fififio, wave a foot; fififio, wiggle your head; fififio . . . !"

At once the police arrived. They arrested the desperate man, and he is still in jail.

Juan Bobo became a rich man.

Juan y los ladrones[9]

Era una vez que había un hombre que se llamaba Juan Bobo, quien habitaba en el centro de una montaña. Juan Bobo no tenía familia ninguna, y bien podríamos decir, él había sido la causa de la muerte de su querida madre por todos los bochornos que la hacía pasar.

Juan Bobo había conseguido una gran riqueza. Supiéronlo unos bandidos que trataban de vivir como ratones, robando nada más. A Juan Bobo le gustaba labrar la tierra, por lo tanto, hacía abundantes cosechas. Sucedió que hizo una cosecha de melones y cada melón pesaba una arroba. Siendo tan dulces que algunas gentes tenían con un melón para no comprar azúcar durante veinticinco días.

Una mañana fue Juan Bobo a la plaza. Era día de carnaval, por cierto, y había un muerto que iban a enterrar. El cadáver era de un policía que aquella misma noche habían matado en un motín, por causa de la fiesta y, como siempre, hay tunantes en todas partes. Juan Bobo se dio con uno de estos títeres.

Ya el cadáver habíase colocado en una caja con estas iniciales: "M y B." Juan Bobo sabía leer un poquito. Se dijo:

"Esto quiere decir 'Muerto Bueno.'"

Se quedó con la boca abierta frente a ellos. Uno de los cuatro que cargaban al muerto preguntó a Juan Bobo:

"¿Qué vendes?"

Juan Bobo le contestó:

"¡Melones buenos! Y ustedes, ¿qué venden?"

"¡Muertos buenos!"

Juan Bobo les preguntó que si querían algunos melones; todos le contestaron:

"¡Sí, sí, sí!"

Y, poniendo el muerto en el suelo, le comieron todos los melones que llevaba; entonces, fueron desapareciendo uno a uno, dejando solo a Juan Bobo con el muerto.

"¡Dios mío!" exclamó Juan Bobo. "Me han robado y se han ido, pero en pago de mis melones me llevaré este muerto bueno."

Y, poniéndolo sobre la espalda de su caballo, regresaba a su casa cuando se encontró a un niño, a quien le preguntó:

"¿Quién compra muerto por aquí?"

"Yo no sé, pero Papá salió a enterrar uno hace poco y entró en estos momentos con un melón más grande que yo."

"¡Caramba! Los muertos se venden bien, pero yo no vendo éste para que me acompañe."

Tan pronto como llegó a su casa se apeó de su jaca, y tomando al muerto por el medio, le decía:

"¡Apéate, pendejo! ¿En tu casa no hay yegua?"

El muerto no le contestó.

"¡Maldito si sé lo que me dices!"

El muerto permanecía atravesado sobre la bestia.

Juan Bobo, incomodado, le dijo:

"Si no te apeas te apeo, pero eres mío."

Y tomándolo por el medio, le decía:

"Por la razón y la fuerza
por la fuerza y mi razón,
dirá alguno que es torpeza
cambiar muerto por melón."

Así lo apeó de la yegua y lo puso en el suelo.

Después que Juan Bobo cenó, cogió el muerto y lo guardó en una chillera donde guardaba sus viandas; rendido de cansancio se iba a dormir cuando oyó un fuerte golpe en la puerta.

"¡Buenas noches!"

"Buenas sean," contestó Juan Bobo. "¿Qué desean?"

"Señor, nosotros hemos perdido el camino. Nos ha cogido la noche y, no teniendo donde hacer posada, venimos para que nos deje pasar la noche, si es su gusto."

"No tengo inconveniente," dijo Juan Bobo. "¡Adelante, pasen!"

Subieron los recién llegados, unos ladrones que venían a robar a Juan Bobo el dinero que había adquirido con sus cosechas. Los ladrones tenían el propósito de matar a Juan Bobo tan pronto como se quedara dormido para llevarle el dinero.

Los ladrones traían tres talegos de dinero que habían robado a un rico comerciante. Juan Bobo les preguntó:

"¿No han comido?"

"¡No, señor!" le contestaron.

Inmediatamente les fue preparada la comida. Después que hubieron comido y conversado, dijo uno de los bandidos:

"Vamos a dormir."

"Sí," dijo Juan Bobo. "Pero antes entréguenme lo que porten; es una costumbre mía."

Los bandidos entregaron a Juan Bobo tres talegas de dinero y tres carabinas que llevaban. Ya iban a preparar las camas cuando Juan Bobo les dijo:

"Voy a decirles una cosa."

"¿Qué es?" dijo uno de los bandidos.

"Lo que es no tiene importancia. Tengan mucho cuidado en no cagarse. Antes de tomar café serán registrados; quien se haya cagado será ahorcado sin tardanza."

"Si es por eso, pierda cuidado, Don Juan," le contestaron.

Juan Bobo les entregó una escupidera a cada uno para que se cagaran en ellas.

"Estas escupideras," dijo Juan Bobo, "son para que si les dan ganas lo hagan en ellas, pues pagará con la vida el que lo haga en la cama."

Diciendo esto, los bandidos se acostaron refunfuñando:

"¡No dará el reloj las once, sin que Juan Bobo haya dejado de existir!"

Los bandidos no querían quedarse dormidos para lograr su criminal intención, pero rendidos de cansancio, no tardaron en quedarse dormidos como muertos. Juan Bobo se dijo:

"Esta noche no duermo yo."

Habiéndose satisfecho de que estaban dormidos, tomó una calabaza muy grande, la sancochó y, después que estuvo bien blandita, la molió como para cataplasmas y la dejó enfriar. Se dirigió con mucha sutileza a donde estaban los bandidos y, bajándoles los pantalones a cada uno, les colocó una buena pila de la calabaza molida. Les puso los pantalones en su lugar y se dirigió a su cuarto. Apagó la luz y se quedó en vela. A las cuatro de la mañana abrió la puerta de su cuarto, observando que los ladrones dormían a pata suelta y, condenando las puertas, dijo:

"¡Ahora sí que están bien seguros!"

Juan Bobo se recogió en su cuarto y, a las cinco y media, se puso a preparar café. Después que estuvo hecho, les llamó. Ellos se despertaron muy sorprendidos, diciendo:

"¿Qué pasa?"

Estaban muy azorados. A lo que Juan Bobo contestó:

"Lo que pasa es que no he podido dormir mientras ustedes duermen tranquilos como cerdos."

"¡Duerma, duerma tranquilo, Don Juan!" dijeron ellos.

"¿Quién diablos puede dormir tranquilo? ¡Más bien esto parece una letrina que una casa de personas decentes!"

"No entendemos lo que quiere usted decir, Don Juan."

"Lo que quiero decir es que se levanten, que aquí hay mierda. ¡Y mucha! ¡Apéense, cantos de canallas!"

Los tres volaron como rayos al ver a Juan Bobo tan incomodado.

"¡Hay que hacer un registro!" dijo Juan Bobo, tomando una carabina.

"¡En fila todos! ¡Apea tú el pantalón, cara de yegua!" dijo al mayor.

"¡Pero, señor, cree usted que soy tan . . . !"

"¡Nada!" No dejándole terminar. "¡Apea, apea el pantalón!"

El bandido se apeó el pantalón. ¡Cata! Tenía tanta mierda para fregar un piso.

"¡Vaya, vaya, yo me engaño!"

Y, tomando una soga, dijo:

"Esta es para ti. ¡Vamos!"

"Tú, cara de perro, ¿qué haces que no has pelado el pantalón?"

"Yo no tengo . . ."

"¡Qué no ni qué no! Apea ligero. Mi padre me dijo 'Ver para creer.'"

El segundo bandido se bajó el pantalón.

"¡Fo! ¡Qué plasta! ¡No se puede aguantar!" decía Juan Bobo, manejando la carabina como si supiera.

Todos tenían ante Juan Bobo el temblor de la muerte. Separó la soga del segundo, diciendo:

"Tú, ¿qué haces cambiando tanto de colores? ¡Vamos, vamos! No perdemos tiempo, apea el pantalón que si no te has cagado, serás el único que se salvará."

Los demás ladrones ayudaron a bajar el pantalón al tercero que, medio muerto de miedo, no podía. Juan Bobo, fastidiándolo, le dijo:

"¡Uf! ¡Qué plastita! Habían comido más los otros manganzones."

Juan Bobo, haciendo puntería a uno de los bandidos, le dio orden para que amarrara al compañero por el cuello, lo que fue hecho al instante. Iba a dar orden cuando uno de los ladrones le ofreció un talego para que los dejara en libertad. Juan Bobo le contestó:

"¡No puedo, no puedo! ¡A la horca!"

Entonces, cabeza de perro gritó:

"¡Dos talegas le damos; nosotros no somos malos; tenga piedad de nosotros!"

Juan Bobo le contestó:

"Tengo más dinero del que me ofrecen."

"¡Coja los tres talegos!" gritó el tercero. "¡Déjenos ir en paz a nuestras casas!"

"¡Fíjense en éste que tengo ahorcado!" Señalándoles el muerto. "Éste me daba más dinero que ustedes. Voy a coger los tres talegos y los dejaré ir en paz, ofreciéndome no volver más por estos lares."

Y, abriendo la puerta, Juan Bobo disparó un tiro. Los bandidos desaparecieron como rayos, diciendo:

"¡Fuimos por lana y salimos trasquilados!"

~

Juan and the Thieves

Once upon a time, there was a man called Juan Bobo who lived on a mountain. He had no family. One can truly say that Juan Bobo had been the cause of his beloved mother's death because of the embarrassment that he had made her suffer.

Juan Bobo had earned great riches, and some bandits found that out. They were living like rats—by stealing, no less. Juan Bobo liked to work the soil, so he grew abundant harvests. It so happened that he produced a harvest of melons; each melon weighed about thirty pounds. They were so sweet that people used only one melon and bought no sugar for twenty-five days.

One morning Juan Bobo went to the town square. It was a day during carnival season, by the way, and there was also a procession of a corpse that the townspeople were about to bury. It was the body of a policeman who had been killed that night in a riot because of the celebrations; as always, there were scoundrels everywhere. Juan Bobo ran into one of those.

The body had already been placed in a wooden box with the defunct man's initials carved: "G. D." Juan Bobo, who could barely read, said to himself:

"That must mean 'Good Dead.'"

He stood there with his mouth wide open facing the letters. One of the four men loading the corpse asked Juan Bobo:

"What are you selling there?"

Juan Bobo answered him:

"Good melons! And you, what are you selling?"

"Good dead people!"

Juan Bobo asked the men whether they wanted some melons. They all replied:

"Yes, yes, yes!"

They set the corpse on the ground and ate all the melons that Juan Bobo was carrying. One by one the men disappeared, leaving Juan Bobo with the corpse.

"My God!" exclaimed Juan Bobo. "They have robbed me and gone away, but I will carry away this good dead man as payment for my melons."

And putting the corpse on his horse, he started heading back home when he met a boy, whom he asked:

"Who around here buys corpses?"

"I don't know, but Papa left to bury one a while back. He just came back with a melon bigger than I am."

"God heavens! The dead sell well, but I won't sell this one; he will keep me company."

As soon as Juan Bobo got home, he got down from the horse. Grabbing the corpse by the waist, he said to it:

"Come on, get down, you jerk! Were there no horses at your house?"

The dead man did not answer him.

"Damn if I know what you are saying to me!"

The corpse was still hanging from the horse. Juan Bobo, uncomfortable, said to him:

"If you don't get down, I'll put you down; you belong to me."

And grabbing him by the waist, he said to him:

"By reason and by force,
by force and by my reason,
somebody will say that it is stupid
to exchange a melon for a dead man."

So he took the corpse down from the horse and placed it on the ground.

After eating his dinner, Juan Bobo seized the corpse and put it away in the vegetable shed. Exhausted, he was about to get ready for bed when he heard a heavy blow on the door.

"Good evening!"

"Good evening to you," Juan Bobo replied. "What do you want?"

"Sir, we have lost our way, and the night has caught us without any shelter. We come for you to let us spend the night here, if you do not mind."

"I don't mind," said Juan Bobo. "Come right in!"

The newcomers came in. They were thieves who were coming to rob Juan Bobo of the money earned from his harvests. The thieves intended to kill Juan Bobo as soon as he went to sleep and to carry off his money.

The thieves were carrying three bags of coins stolen from a rich merchant. Juan Bobo asked them:

"Have you had dinner?"

"No, sir," they answered.

At once the meal was prepared. After they had eaten and talked, one of the bandits said:

"Let's go to sleep!"

"Yes," said Juan Bobo. "But first, hand over what you are carrying; it's a custom of mine."

The bandits handed over the three bags of coins and the three rifles that they were carrying. They were about to go to bed when Juan Bobo said to them:

"I'm going to tell you something."

"What's that?" said one of the thieves.

"What it is isn't that important. Be very careful not to soil yourselves. Before you drink your morning coffee, you will be searched. Anyone who has crapped himself will be hanged at once."

"Don't worry about that, Don Juan," the thieves answered.

Juan Bobo handed each one a chamber pot for his use.

"These chamber pots," said Juan Bobo, "are for your use as you feel the need to poop, since you will pay for your life for what you do in the bed."

Grumbling, the thieves went to bed, saying:

"Before the clock strikes eleven, Juan Bobo will stop living!"

The bandits wanted to stay awake in order to carry out their criminal intentions, but exhausted, they lost no time in going to sleep like the dead. Juan Bobo said to himself:

"Tonight, I will not sleep."

Satisfied that they were asleep, Juan Bobo took a very big pumpkin and cooked it. When it was quite soft, he mashed it as if for a spread and let it cool. Very cleverly, he slipped into the room where the bandits were sleeping, and lowering each one's pants, he put in place a sizeable mound of mashed pumpkin. After pulling up their pants, he went to his room, put out the light, and stayed on guard. At four in the morning, he opened the door of his room. Observing that they were still sound asleep, he closed the doors tightly. He said to himself:

"Now they are really secured!"

Juan Bobo went to bed. At five thirty, he began to brew the coffee; after it was ready, he called the thieves. They woke up, very surprised, saying:

"What's going on?"

They were astonished.

Juan Bobo answered:

"What's happening is that I haven't been able to sleep while you slept as calm as pigs."

"Sleep, sleep, sleep in peace, Don Juan!" they said.

"Who the hell can sleep in peace if this looks more like a latrine than a house of decent people?"

"We don't understand what you mean, Don Juan."

"What I mean is that you must get up—that there is shit and a lot of it! Get up, you nasty bums!"

The three men rushed like lightning upon seeing Juan Bobo so upset.

"I have to do a search!" said Juan Bobo, picking up a rifle. "All of you in a line! You, drop your pants, bonehead!" he said to the largest man.

"But, sir, you believe that I am so . . . !"

"Shut up!" Juan Bobo said, not letting him finish. "Drop your pants now!"

The bandit lowered his pants.

"Look! Behold!"

There was enough crap to soil a whole floor.

"Come, come, I am not fooled!"

And taking a rope, Juan Bobo said:

"This is for you! Let's go! And you, horse face, what are you waiting for? How come you have not dropped your pants?"

"I got no . . ."

"No, no, no, drop your pants now! My father told me 'Seeing is believing'!"

The second thief dropped his pants and . . .

"Whew! What a pile! That is unbearable," said Juan Bobo, handling the rifle as if he knew how to shoot.

All three were trembling from fear of death before Juan Bobo. He put out the rope for the second man, saying:

"And you, what are you doing changing colors so much? Come, come, let's not waste my time; drop your pants. If you haven't soiled them, you will be the only one who will be saved!" The other bandits helped lower the third man's pants, since, half dead from fear, the thief could not do it himself. Juan Bobo, taunting him, said:

"Wow, what a little pile! The other fatsos must have eaten more."

Juan Bobo, aiming at one of the bandits, ordered him to tie up his companion by the neck, which was done instantly. He was going to give the order when one of the thieves offered him a bag of coins if he let them go free, but Juan Bobo answered:

"I can't accept it! I can't! To the gallows!"

Then the horse-faced one shouted:

"We'll give you two bags of coins! We are not evil. Have pity on us!"

Juan Bobo answered:

"I got more money than you are offering me."

"Take the three bags of coins," shouted the third bandit, "and let us go home in peace!"

"Take a good look at this dead man here that I've already hanged," Juan Bobo said, pointing to the corpse. "This one offered me more money than you. I am going to take your three bags of coins, and I will let you go in peace—only if you swear never to come back around here."

And opening the door, Juan Bobo shot one bullet. The bandits disappeared like lightning, saying:

"We came to get wool and we leave scalped!"

Porto Rico, coffee berries

CHAPTER 5

Beware of Strangers

Los niños perdidos[1]

Una vez había un viejito que tenía dos niñitos. A uno de ellos le decía Mariquita y, al otro, Juanito.

Un día les dijo el viejo:

"Mariquita y Juanito, vayan a buscar agua."

Se fueron los dos niños y se pusieron a llenar las vasijas. Mariquita se fue a buscar flores. Juanito le dijo a Mariquita:

"Mira, vámonos a casa."

Echaron a andar y se encontraron a una vieja que venía a buscar agua; ellos se escondieron en una cueva. Dejaron que pasara la vieja, pero después que había pasado, ella dijo:

"Aquí parece que hay gente."

Y se fue.

Los niños se echaron a reír. Mariquita se reía más. Juanito le decía:

"Nos come la vieja."

Dejaron que la vieja se fuera y ellos caminaron detrás de ella.

Llegó la vieja a su casa y se puso a freír carne; también hizo arroz blanco y habichuelas guisadas. Mariquita se metió debajo de la cocina. Había tres perros y la vieja les echaba comida a los perros. Los perros cogían la comida en la boca y se la daban a Mariquita. La vieja decía:

"¡Ea! ¡Condenados, tanta hambre tienen hoy! ¡Miren, condenados, hártense!"

Los perros hacían que comían.

Mariquita llevó la comida en la falda para su hermano. A él le gustó y se vino con ella. Entonces, cuando se metieron en la cocina se rieron duro al ver a la vieja. Miró la vieja y les dijo:

"¡Ay! Mira, mis hijitos. Entren para arriba."

Los dos niños se metieron en la casa y se pusieron a comer de lo que la vieja les daba. La vieja, al ver que ellos comían, les dijo:

"Mira, mis nenes desmayados de hambre. Los voy a poner en un cuarto para que engruesen, porque están muy flacos."

Los puso a cebar.

En el cuarto se encontraron los niños un rabo de ratón y, por un roto, se lo enseñaban los muchachos a la vieja, quien les decía:

"Enséñenme sus deditos para ver si ya están gruesos."

Ellos le enseñaban el rabo de ratón.

Un día se fue por un roto del cuarto el rabo. La vieja vino a ver si ya estaban gruesos; le enseñó Mariquita un dedo y Juanito el suyo. La vieja exclamó:

"¡Gracias a Dios! Mis hijitos están gruesos."

Les mandó a buscar leña para que le llenaran una hoguera.

Los niños se pusieron a llorar, pero se fueron. Se encontraron a un viejo, quien les dijo:

"¡Ay! Ustedes van a buscar leña para la vieja. Les va a decir que ella quiere que ustedes le bailen un son en una tabla, entonces, les vira la tabla para que se quemen. Ella quiere comérselos. Pero ustedes le dicen que baile ella primero para que les enseñe cómo lo han de hacer. Entonces, ustedes le viran la tabla."

Volvieron los niños y la vieja les dijo lo mismo que les había dicho el viejo. Ellos le dijeron a la vieja:

"Ma'i, baile usted para que nos enseñe cómo lo hemos de hacer."

Ella bailó y, en el último paso, le viraron la tabla. La vieja cayó dentro de la hoguera y se quemó.

Entonces, los muchachos fueron alegres. Cogieron los perros y todo lo que tenía la vieja. Los dos hermanos se quedaron allí en la casa.

~

The Lost Children

Once upon a time, there was an old man who had two children. The old man called them Mariquita and Juanito.

One day the old man said to them:

"Mariquita and Juanito, go to fetch water."

They left and at once started filling jars with water. Mariquita started picking flowers. Juanito said to her:

"Look, we better get going."

As they began to walk, they saw an old woman who was coming to fetch water. They hid in a cave. They let the old woman go by. As she passed, she said:

"It seems that there are people here."

And she left.

The children started laughing. Mariquita was laughing louder. Juanito warned her:

"The old woman will eat us."

They followed the old woman.

The old woman arrived at her house, and at once, she began to cook. She fried meat and cooked white rice and stewed kidney beans. Mariquita hid under the stove. Nearby there were three hungry dogs; the old woman kept throwing food at them. But the dogs caught the food in their mouths and gave it to Mariquita. The old woman kept wondering:

"Ah, little devils, you are very hungry today! Here, damn you, get your grub!"

The dogs pretended to eat.

Mariquita carried the food in her skirt to her brother. He too liked it; they went back into the house. As the children got into the kitchen, they laughed very hard upon seeing the old woman. She saw them and said to them:

"Oh, look, my little children! Come in here."

The two children began to eat what the old woman was giving them. Once the old woman saw that they were eating so much, she said to them:

"Look, my little ones, you are starving to death. I am going to lock you up so that I can fatten you up. You are way too lean."

She locked them in a room to continue feeding them up.

In the locked room, the children found a rat's tail; through the keyhole, the children would show it to the old woman. She would say:

"Show me your fingers so that I can see if they are plump."

The children would show her the rat's tail.

One day the rat's tail dropped down a hole. The old woman inquired if the children were fat enough. Mariquita had to show her a finger, and Juanito showed his as well. The old woman said:

"Thank goodness! My little children are fattened up!"

She sent them to get wood to fuel a bonfire.

The children began to cry, but they left for the forest, where they met an old man. He told them:

"Oh, you are going to get wood for the old woman. Be aware that she is going to tell you that she wants you to dance to a song on a board for her; know that the board is over the fire. She intends to turn the board so that you burn up; she will then eat you up. But you tell her to dance first to show you how to do it, and you turn the board!"

The children went back to the house. The old woman told them the very thing that the old man had predicted. They said to the old woman:

"Ma, dance to show us how to do it."

She started dancing, but at her last step, the children turned the board. The old lady fell into the fire and burned up.

Right away the children happily gathered the dogs and the old woman's possessions. The two children stayed living in the old woman's house.

Los niños huérfanos (1)[2]

Había una vez un padre que tenía dos hijos. Eran huérfanos de madre, pero tenían una madrastra que era muy mala con ellos.

Una noche le dijo a su esposo:

"Mañana iremos a buscar leña con los niñitos al bosque."

Los niños dormían sobre un banco. El nene estaba despierto, y por lo tanto, oyó lo que hablaban.

"Los dejaremos en el bosque perdidos," decía la mujer.

El padre no quería, pero al fin, tuvo que acceder.

Por la mañana llamaron a los niñitos. Les dieron un pedacito de pan viejo y se fueron. El niño cogió un poco de cenizas en las manos e hizo un camino, pero cayeron unas lloviznas y se borró el camino. Ellos se quedaron en el bosque perdidos.

Los niños siguieron andando hasta que llegaron a la choza de una vieja bruja. Ella los tomó en los brazos muy contenta, pensando:

"Mañana me como al muchachito."

Por la mañana temprano llamó al niñito y le dijo:

"Párate en frente de ese horno."

Pero él no quiso y le dijo:

"Póngase, usted, primero."

Ella lo hizo así. El nene le dio un tremendo empujón que fue ella a caer dentro del horno. La vieja bruja se quemó.

Los niños cogieron todo lo que había en la casa. Se fueron para su hogar muy felices. Su madrastra había muerto.

Los niñitos vivieron muy felices con su padre hasta el fin de su vida.

~

The Orphaned Children (1)

Once upon a time, there was a father who had two children. Their mother was dead, but they had a stepmother who treated them very badly.

One night she said to her husband:

"Tomorrow we will go to gather wood with the children in the forest."

The children were sleeping on a bench. The boy was awake, so he heard what they were chatting about.

"We will leave them lost in the forest," the woman finished saying. The father did not want to, but finally, he had to agree.

In the morning, they called the children and gave them a piece of old bread. Then they left. The boy gathered a handful of ashes, and with them he made a path, but showers came and erased the ashes. The children were left lost in the forest.

The children kept walking until they came to the hut of an old witch. She took them into her arms, happily thinking:

"Tomorrow I'll eat the little boy."

Early in the morning, the witch called the boy and said to him:

"Stand in front of that oven."

But he refused, saying to her:

"You stand there first."

She did so, and he gave her a tremendous push so that she fell into the oven. She was burned up.

The children collected the old woman's possessions in the hut. They went home very happy. Their stepmother had died.

The children lived happily with their father until the end of his life.

Los niños huérfanos (2)[3]

Había un leñador que tenía dos hijos. El mayor era una hembrita que se llamaba Anita; el otro, un varoncito que se llamaba Pepito. El padre pasaba grandes apuros para mantener a sus hijos. Un día le dijo la madrastra de los niños al marido que era necesario llevar a los hijos a las selvas más lejanas del mundo. El le dijo que eso no lo podía hacer con sus hijos de su corazón.

"Lo mejor sería dárselos a cualquiera persona caritativa," dijo el marido.

Ella le contestó que ninguna persona los recogería.

Los hermanos habían oído la conversación. Anita se echó a llorar. Pepito le dijo que no llorara.

A la mañana siguiente, la madrastra llamó a los niños bien temprano. Les dijo:

"Vamos a las selvas a buscar leña."

Y, como los hermanos habían oído la conversación, Pepito le dijo a Anita que no se apurara.

Cuando ya iban a salir, Pepito se llenó los bolsillos de piedrecitas blancas. Mientras caminaban con la madrastra, Pepito siempre se quedaba atrás y, por todo el camino, iba echando piedrecitas.

Después que llegaron les dijo la madrastra que se quedaran allí recogiendo leña seca; por la tarde los vendría a recoger. Llegó la tarde. Ni la madrastra ni el padre vinieron a buscar a los niños.

Al anochecer Anita sintió ruido y le dio miedo. Se echó a llorar. Pepito le dijo que no llorara; cuando saliera la luna se irían a ver si daban con la casa.

Salió la luna. Anita y Pepito se fueron a ver si daban con la casa. Las piedrecitas que Pepito había echado por el camino brillaban como monedas de oro. Pudieron llegar a su casa, donde fueron recibidos por su padre con gran alegría.

~

The Orphaned Children (2)

Once upon a time, there was a woodcutter who had two children. The older was a girl called Anita, and the other was a boy named Pepito. The father endured great difficulties in order to support his children. One day the children's stepmother told their father that it was necessary to ~~lose the children into the world a most remote place. He said her that he~~ could not do that to his beloved children.

"It will be better to give them to any charitable person," the husband replied.

She said that nobody would take them in.

The children heard the conversation. Anita began to cry. Pepito told her not to cry about that.

The next morning, the stepmother called the children quite early. She told them:

"Let's go to the forest to find wood."

The children remembered the conversation, but Pepito told Anita not to worry.

When they were ready to leave, Pepito went outside and filled his pockets with little white pebbles. They left with the stepmother. Pepito always walked in the rear, and along the way, he kept dropping little stones.

As soon as they arrived, the stepmother told them to stay there gathering dry wood; in the afternoon she would come to get them. The afternoon came. Neither the stepmother nor the father came to look for the children.

At twilight Anita heard a noise that scared her. She began to cry. Pepito told her not to cry—that when the moon came up, they would be able to find the way home.

The moon finally came up. Anita and Pepito went to see whether they could find their way home. The little stones that Pepito had thrown along the way shone like gold coins. They managed to get home, where their father received them with great joy.

La mata de ají[4]

Una vez había un matrimonio que tenía cuatro hijos: una Josefa, otro Juan, otro Fernando y, el tercero, Francisco.

Un día salió el padre a trabajar y la madre a lavar en el río. La madre le dijo a su hija:

"Mira, en la mesa quedan tres higos. Si me falta alguno cuando regrese te mataré."

La muchacha se quedó muy triste.

Al poco tiempo de haberse ido la madre, llegó una viejita y le dijo:

"Niña, deme una poquita de sal."

La niña contestó:

"Cójala usted misma."

La vieja le volvió a decir:

"Hágame el favor de dármela usted."

Tanto estuvo la vieja insistiendo hasta que la muchacha tuvo que ir a buscarle la sal. Cuando regresó la muchacha de buscar la sal, ya se había ido la vieja. Se había llevado consigo un higo. La muchacha se puso muy triste.

Vino otra vieja a pedirle también sal. Ella le dijo que la fuera a buscar a la cocina y la vieja le insistió que se la fuera a buscar. La muchacha, como su mamá le había enseñado a que obedeciera a todas las personas más viejas, le fue a buscar la sal. Cuando vino ya se había ido la vieja. Se había llevado otro higo. La muchacha se encontraba completamente triste cuando volvió otra vieja y le hizo lo mismo. La muchacha, entonces, se apuró muchísimo y lloró amargamente.

Unos minutos después llegó la madre. Le dijo:

"¿Dónde están los tres higos?"

La muchacha llorando le contó lo sucedido.

Se fue la madre al patio e hizo un hoyo, donde tiró una sortija. Le dijo a la hija:

"¡Métete ahí! Sácame esa sortija."

La muchacha se metió, y cuando estaba bien adentro, la mamá tapó el hoyo con tierra. La enterró. Pocos minutos habían pasado cuando apareció una mata de ají donde se había enterrado a la muchacha.

Vino la tarde y llegó el padre de los muchachos a comer. Preguntó por su hija porque no la había visto. La madre le dijo que andaba paseando. El señor empezó a comer, miró para el patio; grande fue su asombro al ver una frondosa mata de ají que cuando salió no estaba allí. Mandó a uno de sus hijos que le fuera a buscar un ají de aquella mata.

El muchacho se sorprendió al escuchar una voz que le decía:

"Hermano, si eres mi hermano, no me hales los cabellos, que mi madre me ha enterrado por tres higos que han faltado."

Se fue a donde estaba el padre y le dijo:

"¡Ay, Papá! ¡Si allí canta una cosa!"

El papá le contestó que esas eran cosas de él. Mandó a otro de los hijos y le pasó igual.

Mandó al último y también le pasó lo mismo. El padre para desengañarse fue él mismo y le dijo igual cosa. El hombre llamó a su esposa y le dijo:

"Agarra un ají de aquella mata."

Cuando la señora lo haló, la voz le dijo:

"Madre, por ser mi madre, no me arranques mis cabellos, que tú misma me has enterrado por tres higos que han faltado."

El padre empezó a cavar y resultó que la muchacha, por casualidad, no se había muerto. El padre la sacó y ella le contó todo lo que le había pasado.

Entonces, el padre montó a la señora en cuatro mulas, les pegó para que se fueran. Todavía no se sabe su paradero.

~

The Pepper Plant

Once upon a time, there was a married couple who had four children: a daughter, Josefa; a son, Juan; another son, Fernando; and a third son, Francisco.

One day the father went to work, and the mother went off to the river to wash clothes. She said to her daughter:

"Look here, there are three figs left on the table. If I find any missing when I get back, I'll kill you."

The girl was left very sad.

Shortly after the mother had left, an old woman came and said to her:

"Girl, give me a little bit of salt."

The girl answered:

"Take some for yourself."

The old woman repeated:

"Will you go get it for me?"

The old woman kept insisting until the girl had to go to fetch the salt. When the girl came back with the salt, the woman had already left. She had carried off a fig. The girl became very sad.

Another old woman came to ask her for salt. She told the old woman to go into the kitchen to get it, but the old woman told Josefa to get it for her. The girl, since her mother had taught her to obey all older people, went to fetch the salt. When she got back, the old woman had already left; she had carried off another of the figs.

The girl was overwhelmed with sadness when still another old woman came. She did the same thing to her. It was then that the girl became extremely worried and wept bitterly.

A few minutes later, the mother arrived. She said to Josefa:

"Where are the three figs?"

The weeping child told her what had happened.

The mother went to the patio and dug a hole, then threw a ring into it. She ordered Josefa:

"Get in there! Get me that ring!"

The girl did so, and when she was deep inside in the hole, her mother filled it with soil. She buried her daughter. Only a few minutes had passed when on the spot where the girl had been buried, a pepper plant appeared.

Afternoon came, and the children's father came to eat dinner. He asked for his daughter, since he had not seen her. The mother said that she was out walking. The man began to eat. He looked toward the patio; his astonishment was great when he saw a lush pepper plant that had not been there when he had left. He sent one of his sons to get a pepper from that plant.

Great was the boy's surprise upon hearing a voice that said to him:

"Brother, if you call yourself my brother, don't pull on my hair. My mother has buried me because of three missing figs."

The boy ran to where his father was and told him:

"Oh, Papa, something is singing out there!"

The father answered that the boy was imagining things. He sent another of the sons. Again, the same happened to him.

He sent the last son, and it happened to him as well. The father went out to see for himself, and he too experienced the same thing. He called his wife and told her:

"Pluck a pepper from that plant."

When the woman pulled it, the voice said to her:

"Mother, because you are my mother, don't pull out my hair. You yourself have buried me because of three missing figs."

The father began to dig, and it turned out that by chance, the girl had not died.

Her father dug her out. Josefa told him what had happened to her.

Then he mounted his wife on four mules that he beat to make them run away. Even today nobody knows their whereabouts.

A chicken peddler, Porto Rico

CHAPTER 6

El Pirata Cofresí

A NATIONAL HERO AND OTHER NOTABLE BANDITS

El niño Cofresí[1]

Cuando Cofresí era un niño, que solamente contaba la edad de diez años, le gusta andar y acompañar siempre a su padre. Este último se ocupaba de vender café a todos los buques mercantes que a Guánica iban.

Un día en que tuvo que ir a vender café a un gran buque iba con su hijo. El capitán le compró su cargamento de café; luego, sin haberle dado nada por él, le dieron una gran paliza. Amarraron al padre de Cofresí y lo echaron en el mismo bote en que había ido.

Cofresí, que como hemos dicho, iba con él, se indignó con esto. Como era tan pequeño no pudo defender a su padre, pero se juró vengarse algún día. Constantemente recordaba las facciones del capitán del buque y siempre le perseguía la idea de vengarse.

Pasaron muchos años y su padre murió. El cumplió los veintiún años, y por consiguiente, heredó de su padre lo que le pertenecía.

Mandó a construir un buque todo lo más fuerte posible, y después de tenerlo, dio a unos veinticuatro amigos un banquete. Todos se fijaban en que Cofresí no hablaba ni se reía, sino que permanecía triste y pensativo.

Uno de ellos le preguntó qué le pasaba, y entonces, les contó lo que tantos años hacía le había sucedido a su padre. Todos los amigos se ofrecieron a ayudarle. Cofresí aceptó. Mandó equipar el buque con todo lo necesario, y una semana después, los piratas se hacían a la mar.

Después de navegar sin encontrar buque alguno, por último encontraron un barco. Dio la casualidad que en él navegaba el capitán del buque que Cofresí buscaba.

Ellos como fieras se arrojaron sobre el buque; saltaron a bordo, y cogiendo al capitán, lo amarraron del palo mayor. Cofresí lo golpeó hasta matarlo. Robaron todo el dinero que llevaban, luego hundieron el buque.

Este fue su primer impulso a la piratería. Regresó a Guánica, donde dicen que enterró el tesoro que había robado. El pirata Cofresí siguió siendo la fiera de los mares hasta que murió.

~

The Boy Cofresí

When Cofresí was a boy of only ten years old, he liked to wander around and accompany his father on his errands. His father's business was to sell coffee to all the merchant ships that came into Guanica.

One day when the father had to go to sell coffee to a large ship, he was accompanied by his son. The captain bought a load of coffee from him, and then, without having paid him anything for it, they gave him a great beating. They tied him up, and then they threw him into the boat in which he had gone out to the ship.

Cofresí, who, as we have said, was with him, became outraged by this. Since he was so little, he could not defend his father, but he swore to avenge him someday. He constantly recalled the features of the boat captain's face. The idea of vengeance always pursued him.

Many years passed, and Cofresí's father died. Cofresí, who had reached the age of twenty-one, consequently inherited all his father's belongings.

He ordered a boat to be built—the strongest one possible. The day he took possession of it, Cofresí had a banquet for twenty-four of his best friends. All of them noticed that Cofresí did not speak or laugh; he stayed looking sad and extremely pensive.

One of his pals asked what was wrong with him. Only then did Cofresí start telling his friends what had happened to his father so many years ago. All of these brave men offered to help him. Cofresí accepted at once.

Cofresí ordered his ship to be equipped with all the necessary equipment. One week later, the pirates went to sea. After sailing without encountering any ships at all, they finally met a ship. Luckily, the captain sailing that ship was the same coward that Cofresí was looking for.

Like wild beasts, Cofresí and his friends fell upon the ship. They jumped on board, and seizing the captain, they bound him to the mainmast. Cofresí beat the man to death. His men stole all the money that was on board. They finally sank the ship.

This was Cofresí's first venture into piracy. He returned to Guanica, where they say he buried the treasure that he had stolen. Cofresí the pirate was the wild animal of the seas until his death.

Cofresí defiende su honor[2]

Allá por el cuarto primero del pasado siglo, imperaba como el mayor rey, el valeroso pirata Cofresí, hijo de este pueblo.

El tal pirata era muy perseguido por sus hechos censurables que lo ponían fuera del amparo de la ley, pero como por aquel entonces había en Cabo Rojo muy pocas fuerzas públicas para echarle el guante a personaje de aquella naturaleza, se daba el caso que, algunas veces, esto es claro, no con mucha frecuencia, Cofresí le daba la humorada de dar sus paseítos por tierra. Se corría, como quien no quiere la cosa, hasta el mismo casco de la población.

Para que esto sucediera era necesario que el señor pirata tuviera confidencias muy seguras de que en la población no estuviera de paso ningún piquete de soldados, ni que el domingo que destinaba a su visita, hubiera formación o revista de los chenches. Cofresí, aparte de ser pirata, que es cosa muy mala, era también un hombre muy generoso con sus amigos y compinches, y de esta clase de personas tenía muchas en tierra.

Regaba a manos llenas el oro por donde pasaba, porque como "lo que poco cuesta hagámoslo fiesta," según se dice, aunque bien pensado, no muy poco le costaba. Nada menos que su cabeza exponía, y la de otros muchos, pero así era el hombre por el sino que lo trajo a la vida y por las circunstancias que después le rodearon.

Un domingo de aquellos años que digo, los informes le serían satisfactorios, se presentó Cofresí en Cabo Rojo. Esto era un suceso extraordinario; los que no estaban en el complot de la visita les causaba verdadero asombro y dignos de ver eran los corillos que se formaban. La noticia circulaba por toda la población con rapidez; todo el mundo quería ver al hombre tan temido, a quien se le consideraba como de insuperable valor.

"¡Allí está Cofresí!"

Iban diciendo al oído, muy bajito; poco a poco, a distancia, sin que él se apercibiera, se le iba formando una escolta de curiosos y admiradores.

Cuando llegó Cofresí al pueblo eran horas muy tempranas de la mañana. Todavía casi no había llegado la aglomeración de gente que, entonces como ahora, concurre los domingos al poblado. Nuestro hombre dio su vuelta por la playa, y al oír que las campanas tocaban a misa, dirigió sus pasos al Santo Templo.

"¡Cofresí en misa!" se decía por todas partes. Y aquel día hubo mayor concurrencia en los Santos Oficios.

A la sazón llegaba también al pueblo, por el camino de la parte llana de la jurisdicción, un señor de apellido Torres, cuyo primer nombre no recuerdo bien, que montaba hermoso y brioso alazán, ensillado con banastillas, que era lo que entonces se usaba.

Apeóse en la casa de un amigo, dio a cuidar su montura, sacó de debajo de la almohada que le servía de asiento su espada Coco y Cruz y se la puso debajo del brazo. Fuese como de costumbre a la plaza pública para después ir también a oír la correspondiente misa. Porque han de saber ustedes que, en aquellos tiempos de que estoy hablando, toda persona de alguna representación llevaba espada de bien acerado temple, y antes de olvidar su compañera inseparable, podían hacerlo de cualquier otra cosa que fuera para ellos de menos importancia. No la llevaban como objeto de lujo ni como jactancioso alarde; la llevaban para la propia defensa y para defender su honra de caballero intachable, que como tales se consideraban y, como a tales se les exigían, que se les tratasen. Para ese entonces, entre la gente de fuste no había disputas ni malas expresiones, sino estocadas de punta y filo que, a lo mejor, marcaban un soberbio chirlo en el cuerpo del adversario.

El señor Torres era conceptuado como un hombre a carta cabal, enérgico hasta la temeridad y de un valor reconocido en más de un caso en que supo demostrarlo a toda prueba. Integro y franco, con una franqueza a veces ruda, pero que estaba patrocinada por su brazo y su corazón, Torres era altivo e intransigente con los fulleros y malandrines, también decidor y chancero. Era alto, robusto y de un vigor que imponía respeto al más decidido.

No bien llegó a la plaza, aun antes de llegar a ella, oyó decir la consabida frase:

"Cofresí está en la iglesia."

Esto le llamó la atención. El conocía las hazañas del pirata por los relatos que por todas partes corrían; a él, parece no le hacían ninguna gracia, por el fondo inmoral que revestían. Las oía y comentaba con cierto desenfado.

Sólo admiraba en el pirata su valor temerario, pero como él se creía dueño de otro, por nadie sobrepujado, tampoco aun esa condición le subyugaba como a los demás. Sabía que siempre fue generoso y que jamás ultrajó al débil, pero no se recataba para censurar que aquellas apreciables condiciones debían emplearse en mejor servicio, fueran cuales fuesen los accidentes que a tan peligrosa senda lo llevaran.

"Oye," le dijo a un amigo que encontró al paso, "he oído decir a varios que el Cofresí ese está allí en la iglesia."

"Sí, está," le contestó el otro. "No hace mucho le vi entrar."

"Bueno, pues tú que lo conoces, vente conmigo para que me lo enseñes."

"Tengo ganas de verle cerca y sentir el efecto que me produce su vista."

Los dos amigos se dirigieron al templo y, por la puerta mayor, entraron. Tomaron agua bendita, se hincaron, como buenos devotos para hacer las oraciones del ritual. Después de un rato de fervorosa devoción, se levantaron. Torres le dijo a su acompañante:

"Vamos, enséñame al hombre."

La casualidad hizo que solo a dos pasos de los dos amigos estaba, en actitud muy contrita, el héroe de nuestra narración.

Cofresí era un hombre bajito, aunque fornido, se conocía que sus músculos eran de acero, muy ágil y de temperamento nervioso y exaltado. Claro, al lado de Torres, de estatura colosal y de una robustez muy proporcionada a su cuerpo, el pirata resultaba un medio hombre. Así que Torres, quien se había forjado en su imaginación, algo andaluza como su abolengo, otro tipo de merodeador de nuestras costas, por lo tanto, sufrió un desencanto al verle. Lo cierto es que al contemplarle un breve rato y, dirigiéndose a su amigo, con su vozarrón de costumbre, porque tenía la voz en armonía con su cuerpo que, aunque quisiera, no podía bajarla de diapasón bastante para decir un secreto, le dijo:

"¿Ese hombrecillo es Cofresí? Valiente muñeco."

Tal exabrupto fue oído por nuestro héroe, y al oír su nombre unido al calificativo hombrecillo, volvió rápidamente como una centella sus ojos hacia quien lo pronunciaba, a tiempo que oía el otro mote de muñeco.

Sus nervios de pantera vibraron; si no dio un salto para caer encima del que de tal modo le ofendía, fue por recordar a tiempo que en la casa de Dios estaba. Pero se le acercó temblando de furor, y después de medir de pies a cabeza a su adversario, con una mirada centellante y de hacer un mohín de olímpico desprecio, como desquite al insulto recibido, le dijo:

"Mire, don, debajo de su brazo tiene lo necesario para que se divierta con este muñeco. Ahí afuera lo espero."

"Mi intención no fue esa," contestó Torres, "pero si tanto te empeñas, vamos allá, hombre."

Y los dos contendientes, sin una palabra más, salieron al atrio, midieron con la vista la distancia, y cada uno tomó el sitio conveniente desenvainando sus tizonas.

Ya en guardia los dos campeones, Torres dijo a Cofresí:

"Espérate, muchacho, que voy a encender un cigarro."

Y, uniendo la acción con la palabra, sacó de su bolsillo cigarro, pedernal y mecha; como lo dijo lo hizo, sin cuidarse gran cosa de su adversario.

Cruzaron los aceros y emprendieron el combate. Por demás está decir, plaza e iglesia quedaron desiertas; las mujeres se fueron chillando para las casas y los hombres a contemplar la contienda. Muchas personas respetables trataron de poner la paz entre los combatientes, pero nada consiguieron.

"Al que se meta lo rajo," gritaba Torres con su vocerrón de trueno.

"Al que intervenga lo mato," rugía Cofresí.

A tales anuncios, ¿quién iba a meter la cabeza?

Llegó el teniente, jefe de la población, presentando su vara de autoridad, acompañado de los cuatro urbanos, pero como nada. Los urbanos temblaban de miedo y tenían por conveniente tomar alguna distancia.

"¡Plaza, plaza!" gritaban los combatientes, y a su alrededor, no se oía más que el zic, zac de los aceros y el retintín al tocar. Cofresí daba saltos de tigre y acometía con furor terrible, con toda la regla del arte que le convenía y acosaba a su adversario como un rayo a su adversario. Torres era un muro inexpugnable; a la estocada más bien tirada oponía un quite magistral con una calma insufrible, tesón indomable y siempre seguía fumando su cigarro. A veces, soltaba una bocanada de humo para encima de su adversario, y tomando el cigarro con la mano derecha, atendía a su defensa. Le gritaba a Cofresí:

"Compa'i,[3] ¿quieres candela?" mientras daba a su voz unas modulaciones de burla y su rostro una muestra de ironía.

A tales chanzonetas, el furor de Cofresí no tenía límites y su empuje llegaba hasta la temeridad. Se comprendía que Torres no abusaba de aquella exasperación y no quería herirle.

Cuando a tal estado llegaban las cosas, ya se habían formado dos bandos: unos partidarios de Cofresí y otros de Torres. Ya empezaban a mirarse con miradas toscas y agresivas. Hubo quien vaticinaba que aquello terminaría en una batalla campal, pero cuando más se iban enardeciendo los ánimos, se abrió una parte del redondel que formaban los expectantes y apareció el Señor Cura, quien venía revestido con todos sus ornamentos y la custodia en la mano. Se dirigió a los combatientes, gritándoles:

"¡Abajo los aceros ante el Cuerpo Sagrado de Dios Nuestro Señor!"

Y aquellos dos hombres, que ya llegaban a límite de las fieras, rápidamente obedecieron el mandato del cura, bajaron sus aceros y doblaron la cabeza ante la Sagrada Forma.

"Ahora señores," dijo el cura, "ustedes" (dirigiéndose a los partidarios de Cofresí), "lleváoslo hacia ese lado; ustedes" (a los de Torres), "sacad por este otro lado a nuestro amigo. Os ordeno en nombre de Dios que no volváis a reñir."

Así pudo terminar aquella contienda que es tradición en Cabo Rojo.

~

Cofresí Defends His Honor

Back in the first quarter of the past century, a son of this town reigned like the greatest king, the courageous pirate Cofresí. This said pirate was much pursued because of his reprehensible deeds that put him beyond the shelter of the law. Because at that time there were very few police in Cabo Rojo who could get a hand on a personage of that nature, sometimes, perhaps not with great frequency, Cofresí had a silly whim to take strolls on land. He would parade around into the very heart of the colony.

In order for his walks to happen, Mr. Pirate had to be completely sure that he would not encounter any squads of soldiers; nor would there be a formation or review of the local militia on the Sunday that he assigned for his visit. Cofresí, besides being a pirate, which is a very bad thing, was also a very generous man with his friends and henchmen. There were many such people on land.

He showered people with money with full hands as he passed by because, as he said, "Let's party on what does not cost you much"— although, on second thought, the cost for him was not low. It was nothing less than his head that he was risking, and that of many others, but this was the kind of man he was. He was well aware that fate had brought him into life, and he understood the circumstances that surrounded him later.

One Sunday, in those years that I have spoken about, when reports on shore were satisfactory for him, Cofresí showed up in Cabo Rojo. This was an extraordinary happening; it caused real astonishment among those who were not in the know about the visit and among the gossiping crowds. The news rapidly circulated. Everybody wanted to see the man so feared that he was considered to be of insurmountable valor.

"There is Cofresí!" they whispered into one another's ears. Little by little, at a distance, and without his perceiving it, he gathered an escort of the curious and the admiring.

He arrived in the town very early in the morning. As yet, there were no crowds of people who, then as now, gathered there on Sundays.

Our man strolled through the plaza, and when he heard the bells calling to Mass, he walked toward the Holly Temple.

"Cofresí at Mass!" was repeated everywhere. And that day, there was a greater gathering for the Divine Offices.

At that time, on the road in the lower part of the jurisdiction, a gentleman named Torres, whose first name I don't recall, was entering the town on a handsome, spirited sorrel, saddled with little baskets, which was what they used then to carry things.

He dismounted at a friend's house and handed his horse off for care. He took from under the pillow that served as his saddle his sword, Coco y Cruz, and put it under his arm. He went off to the public square, as was his custom, in order to attend Mass afterward too. Because you must know that in those days of which I am speaking, all persons of some importance wore a sword of well-tempered steel, and rather than forget their inseparable companion, they could forget anything else as less important to them. They did not wear the sword as an ornament or in a boastful display; they wore it for personal protection and to defend their impeccable knightly honor, since they considered themselves to be so, and they required everyone else to treat them as such. At that time among prominent people, there were no verbal disputes or harsh language but instead sword thrusts and cuts that left their profound marks on the bodies of their adversaries.

Mr. Torres was well regarded as completely and utterly manly; energetic, even audacious; and of great valor, which he had displayed in more than one situation in which he managed to prove it beyond doubt. Upright and outspoken, with a frankness that sometimes was even rude but that was proven by his arm and his heart, he was arrogant and intransigent with cheaters and scoundrels. He was witty and a joker. He was tall, robust, and of a vigor that demanded respect from those most determined.

Just as he arrived at the plaza, even before arriving there, he heard the usual statement:

"Cofresí is in the church."

This drew his attention. He knew about the exploits of the pirate through the tales that spread everywhere. For him, it seems, these stories were offensive because of the element of immorality beneath them. He heard them and commented with a certain self-assurance.

The only thing that he admired in the pirate was his audacity, but Torres believed that he himself possessed more courage than anyone else, so it did not restrain him as it did others. The gentleman knew that Cofresí was always generous and that he never offended the weak, but Torres openly declared that those substantial qualities in the pirate should be used in better services, no matter to what actions such a dangerous path might lead.

"Listen," Torres said to a friend that he met in passing, "I have heard several people say that Cofresí is in the church."

"Yes, he is," answered the other man. "I saw him go in not long ago."

"Good. Since you know him, come with me and show him to me. I want to see him up close and feel the effect that the sight of him produces in me."

The two friends headed to the temple and went in through the great doors. They took holy water, and they knelt, as do good worshipers, to offer ritual prayers. After a period of fervent devotion, they stood up. Torres said to his companion:

"Come, show me the man."

By chance, only two steps away from the friends was, in a very contrite attitude, the hero of our story.

Cofresí was a short man, although hefty. It was known that his muscles were of steel; he was also extremely agile and of a nervous and hot-headed temperament. Of course, next to Torres, a man of colossal stature and of robustness in proportion to his body, the pirate came out looking like half a man. Torres had imagined someone as huge as his own Andalusian ancestry, a different kind of prowler type of our coasts, so he suffered disillusionment upon actually seeing Cofresí. The fact is that upon contemplating him a short while and speaking directly to his friend with his usual booming voice, because his voice was in harmony with his body, so even if he had wanted to, he could not lower the volume in order to tell a secret, he said:

"That little guy is Cofresí? A brave puppet!"

That sharp remark was heard by our hero. Upon hearing his name spoken with ridicule, Cofresí turned his eyes as quickly as a flash of lightning toward the person speaking. At that very same instant, Torres uttered the other the insult about the pirate being a puppet.

Cofresí's nerves vibrated; if he did not leap like a panther on top of the one who was offending him this way, it was because he remembered that he was in a house of God. But he approached Torres trembling with fury, and after measuring his adversary from head to toe with a glittering glance and making a face of fantastic scorn as revenge for the insult received, Cofresí said to Torres:

"Look, mister, under your arm you have all you need in order to have fun with this puppet. Outside I will wait for you."

"That was not my intention," answered Torres, "but if you insist, let's go out, man."

Without another word, the two adversaries went out of the church and visually measured the distance. Then each took a suitable place and drew his sword.

Now with the two champions on guard, Torres said to Cofresí:

"Wait a minute, boy, I am going to light a cigar."

And linking action and word, he took a cigar, flint, and wick out from his pocket. He did as he had said, paying little attention to his adversary.

They crossed their swords and began the duel. Needless to say, plaza and church were deserted; women had gone home screaming, and men gathered to watch the fight. Many respectable persons tried to make peace between the combatants, but they all failed.

"If anybody meddles, I'll slice him," shouted Torres in his thunderous, booming voice.

"If anybody intervenes, I'll kill him," roared Cofresí.

After such announcements, who would dare to risk his neck?

The lieutenant, the chief of the colony, arrived holding his official baton shaft of office, accompanied by four soldiers, but nothing happened. The soldiers were trembling with fear, and they found it advisable to stand at a distance.

"To the square, to the square!" the combatants were shouting. Around them the only sound heard was the zigzag of the steel swords and the ringing as they clashed. Cofresí was leaping like a tiger; he was attacking Torres with terrible fury, using every rule of the art of sword fighting. He was pounding his adversary like lightning. But Torres was like an unassailable wall; he dodged the best-thrown sword thrust like a master with insufferable calm and with indomitable determination, and always he kept smoking his cigar. Often, he puffed a mouthful of smoke up over his adversary. Taking his cigar with his right hand, Torres tended to his defense, shouting to Cofresí:

"Buddy, do you want a light?" He spoke mockingly and grimaced ironically.

For such jibes, Cofresí's anger had no limits; his spirit rose in temerity.

It was obvious that Torres did not want to take advantage of that exasperation, and he did not want to wound the pirate.

When things came to a certain point, two bands had already formed: some supporters of Cofresí and others of Torres. They were beginning to look at each other with solemn, aggressive glances. There were predictions in the crowd that this situation would end in a riot, but when spirits were becoming most heated, there was a break in one part of the ring of people waiting to see what happened. The priest appeared, wearing all his vestments and with the Host in his hands. He addressed the combatants, shouting to them:

"Down with the swords in the presence of the Sacred Body of our Lord God!"

And those two men, who were now on the verge of acting like wild beasts, rapidly obeyed the priest's orders. They lowered their swords before the Sacred Form.

"Now, gentlemen," said the priest, "you" (pointing to Cofresí's supporters) "bring him to this side; and you" (pointing to Torres's supporters) "bring our friend to this other side. I order you in God's name not to continue fighting."

And that was the end of that fight, which is now part of the oral tradition of Cabo Rojo.

Cofresí en el palacio misterioso[4]

Cofresí era un ladrón que robaba para enterrar.

Cierta vez cogió él sus siete mulas, que según me han contado, tenía, y se fue a robar. Llegó a una hermosa casa, cuyo balcón era dorado y muy bonito.

Rompió una puerta tan fácilmente que nadie lo oyó. Cofresí entró, buscó y solo vio allí cuatro hermosas doncellas.

Se acercó a ellas. Cofresí vio que se habían hecho nada, pues cuando las iba a tocar, no encontraba nada. Era que esa hermosa casa estaba gobernada por el demonio.

Después de esa visión no vio nada más. Cofresí salió atemorizado y con mucho coraje. Cuando fue a salir oyó una voz ronca, triste a momentos y alegre a instantes, pero no entendió lo que la voz decía.

Cofresí se fue a otra casa que parecía un palacio, donde cargó de dinero sus siete mulas. Atravesó el monte con ellas, pero tenía dudas porque distinguía a lo lejos la misma casa que había dejado tras de sí, allá donde no había entendido la voz que le hablaba.

Se acercó a la misteriosa casa, llamó a la puerta y salió a responder una hermosa joven con un vestido verde muy bonito, adornado de seda y llenos de sortijas los dedos.

Se le quedó mirando y se transformó en una figura extraordinaria que había tendido su mano. Al saludarla, Cofresí notó que las manos de la mujer eran blandas y se iban endureciendo, pero él era valiente.

La joven le dijo que muy bien podía, si tenía confianza, dejar su dinero allí. Esa casa se conducía donde quisiera y, debajo de ella, iba quedando un subterráneo con agua, donde podía siempre guardar su dinero.

Por eso se dice que en Puerto Rico hay mucho dinero enterrado. Cofresí estaba enterrando lo que robaba.

~

Cofresí in the Mysterious Palace

Cofresí was a robber who buried what he stole.

One day, he gathered together his seven mules that, as I heard, he owned, and he left to rob people. He arrived at a gorgeous house with a beautiful golden balcony.

At once, Cofresí broke the door so easily that no one heard a peep. He went into the house, looked around, and came upon four beautiful maidens.

As he came near them, he noticed that they became nothing. As Cofresí reached out to touch them, he found nothing. This beautiful house was governed by the devil.

Once the vision of the maidens stopped, unable to see anything else, Cofresí started to leave, feeling fearful and angry. As he was leaving the house, he heard a hoarse voice, at moments sounding sad and happy, but he could not make out what the voice was saying.

Cofresí went into another house that looked much like a palace. There he loaded his seven mules with money. He set out into the wilderness, but he became utterly confused. Far in the distance, he saw the same odd house he had left behind, the one where he had heard the strange voice that he could not understand.

Cofresí approached the mysterious house and knocked at the door. A beautiful maiden came to meet him. She was wearing a very beautiful green dress adorned in silk, and her fingers were covered with rings.

While Cofresí was staring at her, she transformed herself into an extraordinary figure whose soft hand hardened as he reached out to greet her. He was brave, though.

The maiden spoke. She told him that if Cofresí trusted her, he could leave all his money there. The house could move anywhere he so desired. Underneath it, there was a subterranean cave filled with water where he could bury his money.

That is why it is said that there is a lot of money buried in Puerto Rico. Cofresí always went around burying everything he stole.

Recordando a Cofresí[5]

Se contaba que había en Guánica un hombre llamado Ricardo, a quien le gustaba muchísimo que le contasen cuentos de Cofresí.

Un día este Ricardo en una reunión oyó contar un cuento de Cofresí, aquél que se trataba del viaje que el pirata hizo a América para vengar a su padre. Desde ese día nuestro hombre, Ricardo, se quedó con la idea de que si él hubiese sido hombre entonces se hubiera ido con Cofresí. Siempre que se encontraba solo le pedía a Dios que le dejase ver a Cofresí.

Una vez Ricardo iba por un camino cargado con muchísimas gallinas e iba pensando en que si Cofresí viviera, él no estaría pasando tantos trabajos. Por el camino no había casas y solamente tres o cuatro árboles. Cuando él ve que de entre los árboles sale un hombre, que se le acerca, diciéndole:

"¿Qué piensa, buen hombre?"

Ricardo miró por todas partes. No vio a nadie, pero contestó:

"Yo venía pensando en ese hombre tan renombrado, que se llamaba Cofresí, porque creo que si él estuviera vivo yo no sería tan pobre como soy."

"¿Y qué? ¿Tú tienes deseos de conocer a ese monstruo?"

"¡Va! ¿Qué si tengo deseos? Si sueño todas las noches con él sin conocerlo."

"Pues bien, mira hacia aquel cerro. Tú verás quién viene allí."

Ricardo miró asustado, pero no vio a nadie, y entonces, el hombre le llamó la atención, diciéndole:

"No creo que tengas tantos deseos de conocerlo, porque lo tienes delante y ni siquiera le das la mano para saludarlo."

Ricardo se echó a temblar, cayendo de rodillas a los pies de aquel hombre, le dijo:

"Bienvenido y bendito seas, gran señor."

"¡Cómo es eso! Tú que tantos deseos tenías de conocerme, ¿ahora tiemblas? No temas; levántate. Pon atención a lo que voy a decirte:

"Vete a tu pueblo y reparte todas esas gallinas; si acaso te dicen que estás loco, no hagas caso. Después te vas a tu casa y te preparas un pico y una azada, sin decírselo a nadie. A las doce de la noche te vas a la posesión del señor Méndez y hacia la izquierda del jardín encontrarás un piedra grandísima. Quítala de allí; debajo hay cinco millones que pertenecieron al capitán del buque que maltrató a mi padre. Coge todo el dinero que te quepa en cuatro talegas. Deja el otro allí, cuidando de volver a poner la piedra según estaba. Haz obras de caridad y sé bueno."

Al decir esta palabra, se desapareció.

Ricardo hizo todo según se lo había dicho Cofresí. Ahora es un rico hacendado que se conoce por sus obras de caridad.

~

Remembering Cofresí

The story is that there was a man in Guanica named Ricardo who very much liked to hear stories about Cofresí.

One day when Ricardo was at a small gathering, he heard a story told about Cofresí, which was about the trip that Cofresí took to America to avenge his father. From that day forward, this man believed that if he had been a grown man at that time, he would have gone off with Cofresí. Whenever Ricardo found himself alone, he asked God to let him see Cofresí.

Once, Ricardo was walking down a road with a load of many, many chickens. He was, of course, thinking that if Cofresí were alive, he himself would not be working so hard. There were no houses and only three or four trees along the road he was traveling. Right then Ricardo saw a man come out from among the trees. The stranger approached him, saying:

"What are you thinking, my good man?"

Ricardo looked everywhere and saw nobody else. He answered:

"I am thinking about that most famous man named Cofresí. I strongly believe that if he were alive, I would not be so poor as I am."

"And why do you want to meet that monster?"

"Well! You bet I want to meet him! Why, every night I dream about him without knowing him!"

"Then look toward that hill. You will see who is coming there."

Alarmed, Ricardo looked, but he could not see anybody. The man called his attention by telling him:

"I don't believe you want to know Cofresí that much because you have him in front of you and you don't even put out your hand to greet him."

Ricardo started shaking and fell to his knees at the feet of that man, saying:

"Welcome, great sir, and blessings upon you."

"What is this? You were saying how much you wanted to know me, and now you are trembling? Don't be afraid. Stand up and pay close attention to what I am going to say to you:

"Go to town and give away all those chickens. If by chance they say that you are crazy, pay no attention. Afterward, go home and get a pickax and a hoe without saying anything to anybody. At midnight, you should head to Mr. Mendez's property; at the left of the garden, you will find a huge stone. Remove it; under it there are five million dollars that belonged to a ship's captain who treated my father poorly. Fill four sacks to the brim with coins. Leave the rest there, and take care to put the stone back where it was. Do acts of charity and be a good man."

After saying this, Cofresí disappeared.

Ricardo did everything just as Cofresí had told him. Now he is a rich landowner known for his acts of charity.

Contreras[6]

Existió en Puerto Rico cierta vez una cabalgata de bandidos, entre los cuales se distinguieron por sus fechorías los ladrones Silvio Alere, Cofresí y Contreras.

De este último, que aún no ha dejado de existir, es del que voy a relatar una anécdota.

Este Contreras, aún en su muy temprana edad, se dedicó, en unión de dos compañeros suyos, a ejecutar toda clase de daños. Estos otros dos compañeros cometían grandes crímenes por doquier. Contreras, que según he sabido, no le agradaba cometer crímenes, procuró salirse de la sociedad que los tres habían formado.

A él solamente le gustaba hacer grandes robos en cuanto establecimiento de alto rango podía. Después de estas ejecuciones, la mayor parte de lo que había robado distribuía a los pobres infelices que a su paso hallaba. Por fin, tanto lo perseguían a él como a sus compañeros hasta que lograron los guardias civiles ponerlos en prisión.

Después de haber permanecido por espacio de cuarenta años en prisión, hará como dos años que Contreras logró fugarse de la cárcel. A consecuencia de lo muy viejo que está y de lo agotadas que están ya sus fuerzas, no se ocupó nadie de perseguirlo.

Tan pronto como Contreras estuvo fuera de su prisión, se fue enseguida a sacar varios de sus entierros de lo que le habían dado. Todos eran prendas muy bonitas y de mucho valor. Después que hizo esta operación, la mayor parte de estas prendas se las distribuyó entre varios infelices que a su paso se iba encontrando; solamente dejó para sí un magnífico reloj de oro.

Contreras ahora últimamente habita una casa de un hombre muy caritativo en un barrio de Aguadiela. Todos los pobrecitos lo aman mucho, y como está algo viejo, cuando ven que algún peligro lo amenaza, todos los pobrecitos son los primeros en protegerlo.

~

Contreras

At one time, there was a succession of bandits in Puerto Rico, among whom those most distinguished for their crimes were Silvio Alere, Cofresí, and Contreras.

The last of these, who is still alive, is the one about whom I am going to relate this anecdote.

This famous Contreras, even in his youth, dedicated himself, along with two of his companions, to perform all kinds of misdeeds. These two other companions of his were committing serious crimes everywhere. Contreras, according to what I have learned, did not like to commit crimes; he tried to get out of the society that the three of them had formed.

What Contreras really liked was to carry out grand robberies in whatever luxurious establishments he could find. Afterward, he distributed most of what he had stolen to the poor wretches that he found in his path. Finally, Contreras and his companions were pursued so much that the police succeeded in putting all three of them in prison.

After remaining in prison for forty years, about two years ago, Contreras managed to escape. Because of his advanced age and his feebleness, nobody even bothered to pursue him.

As soon as Contreras was outside the prison, he went at once to dig up some of the buried items to which he had helped himself. The jewels were still very pretty and still very valuable. After he had carried out this operation, he scattered most of these items among various unfortunate people whom he encountered in his path. He kept only a magnificent gold watch for himself.

Contreras now secretly lives in a house of a very charitable man in a neighborhood of Aguadiela. All the poor people love him dearly, and since he has become rather old, when they see some danger threatening him, the poor are the first to protect him.

In the mountains of Porto Rico on the Military Road between Cayry [*sic*] (Cayey) and Aibonita [*sic*] (Aibonito)

Brief Stories and Anecdotes

Dios, el rico y el pobre[1]

Me contaba mi papá que había una vez un hombre muy rico, quien tenía un castillo muy grande, pero era muy miserable. En aquel tiempo, decía la gente antigua, Dios todavía andaba por el mundo.

Sucedió que un día se apareció un viejo a pedirle posada, porque ya era tarde. El señor le respondió con mal modo:

"Aquí no se le da posada a nadie."

El viejo se fue. Llegó a la chocita de un hombre muy pobre a quien pidió posada por aquella noche. El hombre le contestó:

"Yo con mucho gusto le daría posada, pero aquí no hay comodidades para ello."

El viejo simplemente dijo que él se conformaba con lo que hubiera.

Sucedió que al otro día, cuando amaneció, el viejo tomó café y se preparó para seguir su camino. Antes de salir de la casa, le dijo a los dueños:

"Pidan ustedes una dicha. Yo se la concederé."

El hombre pidió salud y buena suerte para él y toda su familia.

Al otro día, cuando se levantaron se encontraron en un hermoso castillo mucho mejor que el castillo del hombre rico que le había negado hospitalidad al anciano peregrino.

Cuando las gentes ricas se levantaron, vieron aquel hermoso castillo. Se dijeron inmediatamente:

"Vamos allá a ver cómo ha sido esto posible; ayer tarde no estaba ese castillo en ese sitio y hoy amaneció ahí."

Allá se fueron y preguntaron a los dueños. Ellos les contestaron que había estado un viejo, quien les pidió posada, luego les concedió una gracia. Ellos pidieron salud y buena suerte, al otro día, amanecieron dueños de este castillo.

"Yo me voy detrás de él," dijo el hombre rico.

Pronto dio con el viejo y le enfrentó:

"¿Por qué ha sido que le ha dado un castillo al hombre pobre y no me concedió otro a mí?"

El mendigo le dijo:

"Ahora no puedo."

"Pues, concédame una gracia."

"¿Cuál?"

"Deseo que cuando regrese a mi castillo sea un palacio."

El anciano siguió su camino. El hombre rico se fue corriendo a su casa. Al llegar, se encontró su castillo convertido en cenizas.

~

God, the Rich Man, and the Poor Man

Once upon a time, a long time ago, my father spoke to me about a very rich man who had an enormous castle, but he was very greedy. Back then, ancient people said that God was still wandering around the world.

It happened that one day, an old man appeared at the rich man's house asking for shelter because it was late at night. The rich man rudely replied:

"There is no shelter for anybody here."

The old man left. He arrived at a small hut that belonged to a very poor man. The old man asked for shelter to spend the night. The poor man replied:

"I would kindly shelter you, but there are no amenities here."

The old man replied that he would be appreciative of whatever was given to him.

The next morning at dawn, the old man drank coffee and got ready to walk away. Before leaving the house, he told the owners, "Ask for a bliss, and it will be granted."

The man asked for health and good luck for him and his family.

The next day when they woke up, they found themselves in a beautiful castle, much better than that of the rich man who had denied hospitality to the old pilgrim.

When the wealthy people woke up, they saw a beautiful castle standing next to theirs. They said to themselves:

"Let's go there to find out how this has happened, since yesterday afternoon there was no castle and at dawn there is one."

They left at once and asked the owners. The poor man explained that an old man had asked for shelter in their house, and later he gave them a blessing. They had asked for health and good luck; the following morning, they found themselves the owners of this castle.

"I'll chase him down," the rich man said at once. He started walking. Soon he reached the old man. He challenged him:

"How come you gave a castle to that poor man and you did not give me one?"

The beggar replied:

"I am unable to give you a palace now."

"Well, then, grant me a wish."

"Which one?"

"I wish for a palace to replace my castle as soon as I get back."

The old man kept on his way. The rich man ran back to his house. Upon arriving, his castle had been turned into ashes.

El carbonero[2]

Había una vez un hombre muy pobre, quien era carbonero. Todos los días pedía a Dios que hubiese un día que le sobraran cincuenta centavos para comprar una gallina para comérsela él solo. Llegó el día en que le sobraron cincuenta centavos y compró la gallina.

Enseguida se puso a guisarla. Cuando estaba guisándola, llegó un hom-bre muy bien vestido y le pidió comida.

El carbonero le preguntó:

"¿Quién es usted?"

El hombre le contestó:

"Yo soy la suerte. Vengo a ayudarte a comer tu gallina."

El carbonero le respondió:

"No, señor, váyase ahora mismo. ¡Yo no le doy mi gallina! La suerte protege solamente al rico."

La suerte se fue. Al momento, llegó otro hombre también mal puesto. El carbonero le preguntó:

"¿Quién es usted?"

El misterioso hombre contestó:

"Yo soy la muerte. Vengo a ayudarte a comer tu gallina."

El carbonero le dijo inmediatamente:

"Suba usted para que nos la comamos. A usted sí le doy mi gallina porque la muerte no escoge; cuando usted viene, lo mismo se lleva al rico que se lleva al pobre. No como la suerte que no es perro que sigue a su amo."

~

The Charcoal Maker

Once upon a time, there was a very poor man who was a charcoal maker. Every day he prayed to God for a fifty-cent surplus to buy a hen to eat all by himself. One day, he had fifty cents in savings and bought a hen.

Immediately he began to cook the hen. In the meantime, a well-dressed man appeared in front of him. He asked the charcoal maker for food.

The charcoal burner asked him:

"Who are you?"

The man replied:

"I am Luck. I have come to help you eat your hen."

The charcoal man answered him:

"No, sir, go away. I will not give you my hen! Luck only protects wealthy people."

Luck went away. At once a poorly dressed man arrived. The charcoal burner asked him:

"Who are you?"

The mysterious man answered:

"I am Death. I have come to help you eat your hen."

The charcoal burner immediately replied:

"Come in, sir, and eat the hen with me. I will indeed give my hen to you; Death does not choose. Whenever you come, rich and poor alike are taken away—unlike Luck, who is a dog that does not follow its master."

La mala esposa[3]

En cierta época había un matrimonio que vivía en el campo. El marido era un hombre trabajador y bueno, pero su esposa era egoísta. Todo lo quería para sí misma.

Por las mañanas, todos los días el buen hombre cogía el hacha o la azada y se iba a labrar la tierra, de la cual sacaba el alimento para él y su esposa. Tenían también una gallinita y una vaquita, pero antes que el esposo llegaba a almorzar, la esposa se había preparado para ella una buena tortilla con los huevos que se comía sin su esposo. Cuando el hambriento hombre llegaba a almorzar, la esposa le presentaba un plato repleto de coles.

Todos los días la esposa hacía lo mismo, hasta que un día el esposo le dijo:

"Esposa, ¿por qué todos los días me pones un plato repleto de coles sancochadas?"

Ella le contestó:

"Ay, marido, el diario que tú me das no me alcanza para nada."

El pobre hombre le dijo:

"Bueno, está bien."

El marido se quedó pensativo.

Al otro día, el marido decidió no ir a trabajar, pero no le dijo nada a su esposa. Detrás de la casa había un árbol en dirección a la estufa, en el seto de la cocina había un agujero por el cual, subiéndose al árbol, se veía la cocina en el interior. El hombre se subió rápidamente al árbol y esperó algún tiempo. Como a las diez, vino la mujer con un cacharro de leche y una pasta de chocolate; se preparó chocolate caliente y se lo tomó sola. El hombre lleno de coraje pensó en apearse, pero no lo hizo; esperó que la mujer hiciera el almuerzo. Poco rato después, la mujer llegó a la cocina cargada con un par de huevos, una mano de guineos y un pollo listo para cocerlo. Hizo una buena tortilla, una deliciosa sopa de pollo con arroz y bolitas de guineo y se las comió.

El hombre, no bien había ella acabado de comerse aquel sabroso almuerzo, se bajó del árbol. Una vez en la casa, la mujer le dijo:

"Hoy hay que ir a coger las coles para comer."

Su esposo ya se estaba preparando para lo que le iba a decir. Poco tiempo después la esposa lo llamó para que fuese a almorzar.

El le dijo:

"Ay, mujer, hoy no quiero coles; yo estoy medio malo. Me cayeron unas lloviznas tan finas como la sopa que te comiste, y si no me meto en una cueva tan grande como la tortilla que te comiste, hubiera saltado como el pollo que te almorzaste cuando cayó el aguacero tan espeso como el chocolate que te tomaste."

"Ay, marido, ¿quién te dijo eso? ¡No puede ser!"

Pero desde ese día, y todos los días, la esposa siempre le daba a su marido todo de lo que ella preparaba.

~

The Bad Wife

Once upon a time, a couple lived in the countryside. The husband was a hardworking man. His wife was selfish. She wanted everything for herself.

Every day, early in the morning, the man grabbed his ax or his hoe and left to work in the fields. He harvested food for himself and his wife. They also owned a hen and a cow, but whenever the man came back to the house to eat lunch, the cruel woman had cooked a hearty omelet with the eggs that she ate by herself. Then hurriedly she boiled cabbages and fixed a salad for her husband. When the hungry man came to eat lunch, his wife only served him a plate full of boiled cabbages.

The woman kept serving the same dish every day until one day, the man asked his wife:

"Wife, why do you always serve me a plate full of boiled cabbages for lunch?"

The wife replied:

"Oh, my husband, the allowance you give me barely pays for anything."

The man replied:

"All right. Everything is fine."

The husband remained pensive.

The following day, he decided not to leave for work, but he kept this secret from his wife.

Behind the house there was a tree facing the kitchen, and through a hole in the kitchen's wall, the man could see the inside from the tree. At once he climbed the tree and waited quietly. Around ten in the morning, his wife entered the kitchen carrying a tin cup full of milk and a chocolate stick; she fixed a hot chocolate beverage just for herself. The man, angry at her, thought for a moment about getting down from the tree, but he decided against it, instead staying up there until lunchtime. A short while later, his wife entered the kitchen carrying two eggs, some bananas, and a chicken ready to be cooked. She fixed herself a good-sized omelet and a delicious chicken soup with rice and banana dumplings. The woman ate it all.

The man got down from the tree and walked into his house. The wife told him:

"You need to bring cabbages for lunch."

The man plotted what to say to his wife. Minutes later, the wife called her husband for lunch.

The man said:

"Hey, wife, I don't feel like eating cabbage today. I am feeling sick. Rain-drops as thin as the soup that you ate got me wet. If I had not found refuge in a cave as big as the omelet you ate, I would have jumped around as high as the chicken you ate as soon as the downpour came with drops as thick as the chocolate you drank."

The woman said:

"My husband, who told you that? It cannot be."

But afterward, and every day ever since, the wife always shared every-thing she cooked with her husband.

La vieja miserable[4]

Una vez había una vieja que era muy miserable. Un día se trepó a un palo de china y se fue por un camino comiéndose las chinas. Quería las pepas para semillas y las cáscaras para hacer guarapos. Se encontró con una muchacha que tenía hambre y le pidió una china, pero la vieja no se la dio. La muchacha le pidió una pepa, pero tampoco se la dio; entonces, le pidió una cáscara, pero ni caso le hizo. La vieja se fue y la muchacha se quedó parada mirándola. Dio la casualidad que se le cayó una pepita a la vieja. La muchacha la vio; muy calladita se fue, la cogió y la sembró en un barranco.

La muchacha, que tenía una virtud, dijo:

"¡Perolar, perolar, crecer, crecer!"

El palo de chinas creció. Después dijo:

"¡Perolar, perolar, echar chinas!"

Y echó chinas.

Después dijo:

"¡Perolar, perolar, madurar, madurar!"

Y maduraron las chinas.

La muchacha se escondió detrás del palo de chinas, la vieja vino exclamando:

"¡Mira, mi árbol de chinas!"

Se trepó para coger todas las chinas; no quería darle ninguna a la muchacha. Entonces, la muchacha dijo:

"¡Perolar, perolar, caer, caer!"

Y el palo cayó. La vieja se estropeó muchísimo.

Esto quiere decir que quien todo lo quiere, todo lo pierde.

~

The Miserable Old Woman

Once, long ago, there was an old woman who was very miserable. One day she climbed an orange tree and walked away eating oranges. She wanted to plant the seeds and fix an infusion with the peels. The old lady came across a young girl who was hungry. The girl asked for an orange, but the old lady did not give it to her. The girl asked for a seed, but the old lady did not give that to her either. The girl then asked for a piece of the peel, but the old lady also ignored that request. The old woman walked away while the girl kept looking at her. Just by chance, the old woman dropped a seed. The young girl noticed it, quietly picked it up, and planted it by a precipice.

The young girl, who had magical powers, started chanting:

"Power, power, grow, grow now!"

An orange tree grew. Then she chanted:

"Power, power, give me oranges."

The tree produced bountiful oranges.

She chanted again:

"Power, power, ripe, ripe."

And the oranges turned bright yellow.

The young girl hid behind the orange tree. The old woman came and said:

"Look, it's my orange tree."

She climbed the tree to get all of the oranges, not wanting to share any fruit with the girl.

The girl started chanting:

"Power, power, may you fall now."

The tree fell down. The old woman got badly hurt.

This lesson means that whoever wishes to grab anything their heart desires may lose everything.

Juan sabe más que el rey[5]

Pues señor, ésta era una vez que había un hombre muy sabio, que se llamaba Juan. Como vivía cerca del palacio del rey, sus vecinos le pusieron el sobrenombre de Juan sabe más que el rey. Juan adivinaba toditas las adivinanzas que le echaban.

Un día supo el rey que había por el palacio, o mejor dicho, alrededor del palacio, un hombre que le apodaban Juan sabe más que el rey. Tuvo miedo que sus cortesanos lo podían traicionar, colocar en el trono al dichoso Juan y, por lo tanto, matarlo. Pero el rey quiso saber si era cierto que Juan era tan inteligente, y un día lo mandó a buscar a su casa. El rey esperaba ver a un hombre cualquiera, pero cuando se le presentó, quedó asombrado al ver un hombre tan buen mozo, tan bello y tan gallardo como un príncipe. Se enojó aún más porque creyó que sus vasallos podrían volver al joven Juan en rey y quitarle la corona.

Entonces, el rey le dijo a Juan:

"Quiero que me traiga el hay y no hay. Si no lo hace, por mi corona real, lo mando a matar."

Juan se fue enseguida, pero tan pacífico como había llegado, llegó a su casa. Allí cogió una hoja de salvia, la mondó por un lado; por el otro le dejó la cáscara. Se la llevó al rey diciendo:

"Aquí tiene, mi Majestad, el hay y no hay. Verá usted que por un lado tiene cáscara, por el otro no la tiene; por lo tanto, esto es el haber y no haber."

El rey vio que, en realidad, le había traído el hay y no hay, pero le dijo que viniera al otro día para que le hiciera otro trabajito.

Al otro día el rey ordenó a sus vasallos que le trajeran un buey; tenía la intención de mandar a Juan que lo ordeñara. Cuando Juan venía vio el buey amarrado, inmediatamente reconoció la intención para lo que lo habían mandado. Se marchó de vuelta y se puso a cortar un árbol de moralón con una hacha sin filo.[6] Viendo el rey que Juan se tardaba mucho en venir, mandó a un criado a buscarlo. Cuando el criado llegó a donde

Juan estaba, le dio la razón del rey. Juan le mandó a decir al rey que iría después de haber partido unas astillitas de leña para hacerle sopas de fideo a su padre que estaba de parto.

El rey le mandó a decir a Juan:

"¿Cuándo era que los hombres parían?"

Juan le contestó:

"Cuando un buey se pudiera ordeñar."

Viendo el rey que, en realidad, Juan era un hombre listo, quiso matarlo de cualquier manera. Mandó a sus peones a hacer un hoyo muy grande y muy profundo.

Juan lo supo, y con doble cantidad de peones que los que tenía el rey, se puso a hacer otro en su casa. Pronto tuvo un hoyo muy profundo con un túnel en el fondo de la tierra que comunicaba con el del rey.

El rey ordenó tapar su hoyo con un piso, pero muy débil, con muchas rocas alrededor. Su intención era, cuando Juan cayera, taparlo con todas aquellas piedras allí reunidas. Juan había dejado una escalera en el hoyo que había hecho.

Así que todo estuvo arreglado, el rey mandó a buscar a Juan para que lo divirtiera un poco. Juan tocaba la guitarra. El rey tenía la intención de sentar a Juan en una silla, mientras tocaba la guitarra remover el piso falso. Juan se hundiría en el hoyo con guitarra, silla y todo. Después, el rey se daría se un gustazo con las piedras, tirándoselas encima del pobre Juan.

Pero Juan no era tonto; tenía arreglado el camino por debajo de la tierra. Agarró bien la guitarra y la silla en la que estaba sentado cuando cayó al suelo. Así medio aturdido y sin luz, cogió por el camino que había preparado con la silla y la guitarra, como a los quince minutos llegó a su casa. Después cogió la guitarra y la silla, caminando al palacio iba cantándole al rey.

El rey, finalmente, viendo que Juan merecía su atención como una persona prudente, quiso que fuera un amigo de mucha confianza del palacio. Le pidió que le perdonara los atentados que había hecho contra su vida. Juan le dijo que todas eran insignificancias de hombres ignorantes y de poca capacidad.

Sucedió que el rey tenía una hija muy bonita, su más querida hija. Comprobado que Juan era un hombre sabio y de valor, quiso casarla con él. Así se hizo.

Juan llegó a ser el rey de más prudencia del mundo. Vivieron todos muy felices.

Este cuento se ha acabado con arroz de melado.

~

Juan Knows More Than the King

Listen, all, it happened that once upon a time, there was a very wise man named Juan. Since he lived near the king's palace, his neighbors gave him the nickname Juan Knows More Than the King. Juan knew the answers to all kinds of riddles with which people often challenged him.

One day, the king heard that at the palace—rather, near the palace—lived a man known as Juan Knows More Than the King. His majesty was afraid that his servants would betray him and give the throne to the so-called Juan, who would later kill him. So the king, wanting to know if Juan was really a smart man, sent servants to bring him to the palace. The king expected to see an ordinary man, but he was impressed when Juan came before him. He was astonished to look at a very handsome man, as gallant and as good looking as a prince. The king became even more furious at the thought that his servants would make Juan the king, taking away his own crown.

So the king ordered Juan:

"I want you to bring me the object known as There Is and There Is Not. Upon my regal power, I will order your death if you fail."

Juan left for his house as quietly as he came in. There he grabbed a salve leaf, peeling only one side. He brought it to the king, saying to him:

"Your Majesty, I present to you the object known as There Is and There Is Not. As you can see, one side has the peel and the other does not; therefore, this is There Is and There Is Not."

The king saw that indeed Juan had brought him the object known as There Is and There Is Not. He asked Juan to come back the next day. He would have another small task for him.

The king sent his servants to bring him an ox; he intended to order Juan to milk the animal. When Juan was approaching the king's palace, he saw the ox tied up and immediately figured out the king's intentions. Juan turned around back toward his house and began to cut a moralón tree with an unsharpened ax.¹ As soon as the king noticed that Juan was taking a long time to come over, he sent a servant to fetch him. Once the servant found Juan, Juan told him to tell the king that he would make an appearance as soon as he was done cutting moralón wood for the fireplace. He was about to fix a soup for his father, who was in labor.

The king sent another servant to inquire:

"How is it possible that this man can give birth to a child?"

Juan answered:

"It only happens whenever you milk an ox."

The king right then knew that Juan was in fact an intelligent man, but he still wanted to kill him. For that purpose, he ordered his servants to dig a wide and deep hole. Someone informed Juan about it. With double the number of peons working for him than were working for the king, Juan started digging a bigger hole in his house. Afterward, he built an underground tunnel connecting the hole in his house to the one at the king's palace.

The king ordered the servants to cover the hole in his palace with a plank, but a thin one, with lots of stones surrounding it. As soon as everything was ready, the king ordered his servants to bring Juan to the palace; he wanted to be entertained with music, and Juan was a good guitar player. The king planned to have a chair stationed near the hole so he could push Juan in while he played the guitar. He would fall into the hole with the chair and everything else. The king would then enjoy covering poor Juan's body with a bunch of stones.

Juan, who was smart, fell down the hole as intended, tightly holding his guitar and his chair. Once at the bottom, although stunned, Juan found his way in the darkness, following the path he had dug. Fifteen minutes later, Juan had reached his house. Immediately, Juan took his guitar and his chair and started walking toward the palace while singing.

The king finally acknowledged that Juan was a wise man. He wanted Juan to become his trusted friend and begged for his forgiveness for his attempts against his life. Juan said those were insignificant actions coming from ignorant men and incapable people.

The king had a very beautiful daughter, his dearest daughter. Since the king considered Juan to be a wise and courageous man, he decided to marry them. And so it happened.

Juan became the most prudent king in the world.

They lived happily ever after, and this story is finished with them eating sweetened rice.

Juanito, el Hijo de la Burra[8]

Se dice que una vez un pobre niñito quedó huérfano a la edad de seis meses. Dos viejos, ya muy viejos, se hicieron cargo de él. Estos viejitos tenían una burra. El sostén del niño era la leche de la burra. El niño se crió tan fuerte y tan robusto que todo el mundo le decía el Hijo de la Burra.

Cuando este joven fue grande, le empezó a molestar el dichoso sobre-nombre, el Hijo de la Burra, entonces, decidió mudarse de su lugar a tierras donde nadie supiera sino su verdadero nombre. El se llamaba Juanito.

Una mañana, el buen joven se levantó temprano y cogió en dirección del sur. Había escuchado decir que allá solo podían ir los valientes, porque en esas tierras había muchos gigantes y apariciones extrañas. Llegó a un lugar donde no podía vivir nadie a consecuencias de un gigante que estaba atacando a la gente. Todo lo que se poseía en aquel lugar era quitado por el gigante.

El Hijo de la Burra se hospedó en una finquita donde parecía vivir gente. Como a las doce del día, cuando el joven estaba preparando almuerzo, se le presentó un hermoso gigante, quien le dijo:

"A buena comida me huele aquí; si no me la das te llevo a ti."

El Hijo de la Burra no le dio la comida, inmediatamente emprendió la lucha con el terrible gigante. En la lucha, el gigante perdió la cabeza.

Después de haberse muerto el gigante, el joven se fue en la dirección donde el gigante había venido hasta que encontró una gran cueva. El Hijo de la Burra buscó muchas sogas, se amarró por la cintura y se tiró a ver lo que había allí. Cuando iba llegando al fondo, oyó una voz que le dijo:

"Éste me lo como yo; éste es mío."

El Hijo de la Burra le respondió:

"Me comerán solo si pueden."

Después de haber llegado al fondo de la cueva el Hijo de la Burra descubrió que había millares de personas presas sin poder salir, entonces, las fue sacando por la misma soga que él bajó. Las liberó a todas, quienes vieron a formar una de las más importantes ciudades de Puerto Rico. Esta ciudad se llama Ponce.

~

Juanito, the Son of the Donkey

Once, a while ago, a poor boy became an orphan at six months old. An old couple took care of him, but they were very old. The couple had a donkey. They fed the boy with the donkey's milk. The boy grew to become an extremely strong and robust young man that everyone called the Son of the Donkey.

When he grew up, this young man began to dislike that people called him the Son of the Donkey. He decided to move away to a city where nobody knew his nickname. His real name was Juanito.

One morning, Juanito got up and headed south. People used to say that only courageous people should go there; many giants and strange spirits lived in that direction. Juanito reached a place where nobody could live because a giant was killing the population. Everything that people owned, the giant took away. The Son of the Donkey stayed at a little ranch that seemed to be uninhabited. Around noon, as Juanito was fixing lunch, a handsome giant appeared and said to him:

"I can smell good food here. Unless you give it to me, I will take you away with me."

The Son of the Donkey did not give any food to the giant; instead, he immediately began to fight the terrible giant. In the fight, the giant lost his head.

After the giant's death, Juanito walked in the direction the giant had come until he came upon a big cave. The Son of the Donkey gathered many ropes and tied them around his waist. He jumped inside the cave, eager to find out what was there. Juanito was about to reach the ground when he heard:

"I will eat this one; this one is mine."

The Son of the Donkey replied:

"You will eat me only if you can get me."

When Juanito reached the floor of the cave, he discovered thousands of people who had been kept as prisoners; at once, he brought them out with the same rope he had used. He freed them all. They founded an important city in Puerto Rico named Ponce.

La Cucarachita Martina[9]

Una vez y dos son tres que había una cucarachita llamada Martina. La cucarachita estaba barriendo la puerta de su casa cuando se encontró un centavo. Se dijo:

"Si lo compro de cebolla, se me acaba."

Se fue a la tienda. Martina compró un centavo de harina de pan; se metió en la bolsa de papel y cuando se salió se asomó a la ventana. Pasó un caballo y le dijo:

"Caballo, ¿te quieres casar conmigo?"

El le dijo:

"¡Sí!"

"¿Cómo tú haces?"

"¡Gí, gí, gí!"

"¡No, señor! Me asustas."

Pasó un gato. Martina le dijo:

"Gato, ¿te quieres casar conmigo?"

El le dijo:

"¡Sí!"

"¿Cómo tú haces?"

"¡Miau, miau!"

"¡No, señor! Me asustas."

Pasó un perro. Martina le dijo:

"Perro, ¿te quieres casar conmigo?"

El le dijo:

"¡Sí!"

"¿Cómo tú haces?"

"¡Jau, jau, jau!"

"¡No, señor! Me asustas."

Pasó un ratón. Martina le dijo:

"Ratón, ¿te quieres casar conmigo?"

El le dijo:

"¡Sí!"

"¿Cómo tú haces?"

"Juí, juí, juí."

Cucarachita Martina y Ratoncito Pérez se casaron.

La mañana era domingo. Martina se fue a misa, dejando a Ratoncito Pérez al cuidado de una sopa, pero le advirtió que no la meneara con la cuchara chiquita sino con la grande. Ratoncito Pérez la desobedeció. Meneó la sopa con la chiquita y se cayó dentro de la sopa.

Nadie contestaba cuando Cucarachita Martina vino a tocar a la puerta. Empujó, abrió la puerta y entró a la casa cuando vio que Ratoncito Pérez había caído en la sopa.

Se puso a cantar:

"Ratoncito Pérez cayó en la olla, Cucarachita Martina lo canta y lo llora."

Cucarachita Martina convidó al caballo, al gato y al perro. Entre todos se comieron la sopa.

~

Martina, the Charming Cockroach

Once upon a time, there was a little cockroach named Martina who found a penny while sweeping her porch. She said to herself:

"If I buy an onion, it will not last me long."

She left for the store and bought a pennyworth of bread flour. She got home, after getting in and of out the package, and immediately sat by the window. A horse went by. Martina said to him:

"Horse, would you marry me?"

He replied:

"Yes!"

"Let me hear more of your voice."

"¡Gi, gi, gi!"

"Dear, no. That sound scares me."

A cat went by. Martina said to him:

"Cat, would you marry me?"

He replied:

"Yes!"

"Let me hear more of your voice."

"¡Miau, miau, miau!"

"Dear, no! That sound scares me."

A dog went by. Martina said to him:

"Dog, would you marry me?"

He replied:

"Yes!"

"Let me hear more of your voice."

"¡Jau, jau, jau!"

"Dear, no! That sound scares me."

A mouse went by. Martina said to him:

"Mouse, would you marry me?"

He replied:

"Yes!"

"Let me hear more of your voice."

"Juí, juí, juí."

Cucarachita Martina married Ratoncito Pérez at once.

The following morning was Sunday. Martina got ready to leave for Mass. Before leaving, she asked Ratoncito Pérez to keep stirring a pot of soup, warning him not to stir it with a small spoon; he should use a large one. Ratoncito Pérez disobeyed her instructions. When he stirred the soup with a small spoon, he stumbled and fell inside the pot.

No one answered Cucarachita Martina when she knocked at the door. She opened it and came into the house. She saw that Ratoncito Pérez had fallen into the pot.

She started singing:

"Ratoncito Pérez fell into the pot. Cucarachita Martina sings to him and cries for him."

Cucarachita Martina invited the horse, the cat, and the dog to come over. All of them ate the soup.

Arañita Martina y Ratoncito Pérez[10]

Había una vez una arañita que vivía con Ratoncito Pérez. Un día en que la Arañita Martina estaba barriendo se encontró un centavo.

"¿Qué compraré con este centavo?" se puso a pensar. "¿Carne?"

"No, se me acabará muy pronto."

"¿Pan? ¡Tampoco! También se me acabará pronto."

"¿Azúcar? ¡No, se me acabará pronto!"

Después de mucho pensar, se dijo:

"¡Ya sé! Me compraré un pedazo de cinta y me la pondré en el cuello."

La Arañita Martina se fue a comprar la cinta, dejando a Ratoncito Pérez cuidando una caliente olla de sopa. Ratoncito Pérez fue a menear la olla y cayó adentro. Al poco rato la arañita Martina llegó a la casa, pero no encontró a su ratoncito. Se puso a buscarlo detrás de la puerta, en el ropero, en el baúl, en el tocador. Nada, no había ni rastro de Ratoncito Pérez.

Arañita Martina se dijo de repente:

"¡Ay, Dios, no! Quizás adentro de la olla."

Y se fue a ver si estaba dentro de la olla. Allí lo encontró.

La arañita se puso a cantar y a llorar:

"Ratoncito Pérez cayó en la olla; Arañita Martina lo canta y lo llora."

Después cogió la cinta, se la amarró en el cuello y se sentó pensativa en el balcón de su casita. Al poco rato pasó por allí un buey quien le preguntó:

"Arañita, ¿te quieres casar conmigo?"

"¿Cómo haces tú?" le respondió Arañita Martina.

"Moo, moo."

"¡Ay, no! Me asustas."

Después pasó un perro, quien le preguntó:

"Arañita, ¿te quieres casar conmigo?"

"¿Cómo haces tú?" le respondió Arañita Martina.

El perro le ladró fuerte.

"¡Ay, no! Me asustas."

Pronto llegó un lobo.

"Arañita, ¿te quieres casar conmigo?"

"¿Cómo haces tú?"

El lobo aulló con mucha más fuerza que el perro.

"¡Ay, no! Me asustas."

Por fin pasó un ratoncito, quien le dijo:

"Arañita, ¿te quieres casar conmigo?"

"¿Cómo haces tú?"

"Chui, chui, chui."

"¡Ay, sí, sí, sí! Me haces recordar a mi maridito Ratoncito Pérez."

Arañita Martina y el ratoncito se casaron. La noche de bodas el ratoncito llevó pan, azúcar, queso y arroz.

Este ratoncito no se quema.

~

Arañita Martina and Ratoncito Pérez

Once upon a time, there was a little spider that lived with Ratoncito Pérez. One day Arañita Martina was sweeping the floor when she found a penny.

"What could I buy with this penny?" she said to herself. "Perhaps meat?"

"Not meat, because it would run out fast."

"How about some bread?"

"Not bread, because it too would run out fast."

"Some sugar?"

"No, it too would go fast."

After thinking about her dilemma for a long time, she exclaimed:

"I know! I will buy myself some ribbon to wear around my neck."

Arañita Martina left at once to buy some ribbon, telling Ratoncito Pérez to keep an eye on a boiling pot of soup.

As soon as Arañita Martina left the house, Ratoncito Pérez started stirring the soup and fell into the boiling pot. A bit later, the little spider came back to the house, but she could not find Ratoncito Pérez anywhere. She looked behind the door, inside the closet, and in the chest of drawers. Nothing at all. There were no signs of Ratoncito Pérez.

All of a sudden, Arañita Martina said to herself:

"Dear Lord, no! Maybe he is inside the pot!"

At once she headed into the kitchen and looked inside the pot. There he was.

Arañita Martina started singing and crying.

"Ratoncito Pérez fell inside the pot; Arañita Martina sings to him and cries for him."

Afterward, she grabbed the ribbon, tied it around her neck, and sat on the porch of her homey house, looking very pensive. After a while, an ox wandered by, and he asked her:

"Little spider, would you marry me?"

"Let me hear more of your voice," the little spider said to him.

The ox brayed:

"Moo, moo."

"Dear, no! That sound scares me."

A dog followed. He said:

"Would you marry me?"

"Let me hear more of your voice," the little spider said to him.

The dog barked loudly:

"Jau, jau."

"Dear, no! That sound scares me."

Soon afterward, a wolf dropped by.

"Little spider, would you marry me?"

"Let me hear more of your voice."

He howled at once, even louder than the dog's barking.

"Dear, no! That sound scares me."

Finally, a mouse went by, who said to the little spider:

"Would you marry me?"

"Let me hear more of your voice," she said.

"Chuí, chuí, chuí."

"Oh, dear, yes, yes, yes! You remind me of my darling husband, Ratoncito Pérez."

On the wedding night, Arañita Martina's new husband, Ratoncito, brought over bread, sugar, cheese, and rice.

This little mouse never got burned either.

Acknowledgments

Many thanks to Debbie Adams, former interlibrary loan coordinator, and Stephany Atkins Kurth, access services and interlibrary loan coordinator at Agnes Scott College, for their indefatigable help in locating many obscure titles.

Muchas gracias to former student and rising poet Paige Sullivan, who effectively cleaned up my grammar.

I am indebted to my sister, Edna Ocasio Medina, whose guidance in putting together this anthology helped me in the selection and translation of many of the stories. It was fun to read some of these stories that we still remember from our school days.

Special thanks to Kimberly Guinta, editorial director at Rutgers University Press, who kindly oversaw the production of this anthology. I am thankful for her careful editing of the English translations.

Notes

INTRODUCTION

1. Available at the American Philosophical Society in Philadelphia, the correspondence between Mason and Boas describes Mason's preparation prior to his trip to Puerto Rico, his busy whereabouts on the island before Boas's arrival, and his tedious dealings with governmental and public figures while performing fieldwork. Unless otherwise indicated, all my references to administrative details pertaining to the Survey of Porto Rico come from this collection.

2. For a study of Espinosa's rather marked preference for native Spanish Peninsular models in his documentation of early New Mexican oral folklore, see Carlos G. Vélez-Ibáñez, Phillip B. (Felipe) Gonzales, Luis F. B. Plascencia, and Jesús Rosales, "Interrogating the Ethnogenesis of the Spanish and Mexican 'Other': The Literary Work of Aurelio M. Espinosa."

3. All references to Mason's field notes are from surviving notebooks, part of the "J. Alden Mason Puerto Rican Survey Records" at the University of Pennsylvania, Penn Museum Archives.

4. See, for instance, Arí Acevedo-Feliciano and Tom Wrenn, *Juan Bobo Sends the Pig to Mass*; Bernice Chardiet, *Juan Bobo and the Pig: A Puerto Rican Folktale Retold*; Carmen T. Bernier-Grand, *Juan Bobo: Four Folktales from Puerto Rico*; and Virginia Schomp, *Juan Bobo and the Bag of Gold*.

5. The appeal to document local versions of Cinderella endured after Mason's documentation of the oral folklore collection. In 1929, American folklorist Ralph S. Boggs published six folk stories, which he described as "a humble supplement to the grand collection of Porto Rican folktales gathered by Espinosa and Mason" (157). Two of the stories were versions of Cenizosa and Juan Bobo, identified by the name, age, and occupation of the cultural informants.

6. For an extensive comparative study of Puerto Rican Cenizosa's versions contrasted against Peninsular Spanish oral folk renderings, see Julia Cristina Ortiz Lugo, "La cenicienta criolla."

7. To the best of my knowledge, only one of Mason's stories has appeared published in an English translation—McCarthy's "Juan Bobo and the Riddling Princess: A Puerto Rican Folktale"—and none of the folk collection has been published in book format in the United States. Likewise, except the documented conundrums, published as *Folklore puertorriqueño: Adivinanzas*, the collection also remains unpublished.

8. At the time of her death, Judith Ortiz Cofer (1952–2016) was working on her versions of popular Puerto Rican oral folktales, including various adaptations of Cenizosa. She had explored another iconic female character, María Sabida, well known in Puerto Rico as the "know-it-all" female version of Juan Bobo. Ortiz Cofer's story "The Woman Who Slept with One Eye Open" highlights how the smart young woman manages to tame a bloodthirsty assassin by faking her death during their honeymoon. María Sabida resembles yet another such popular Italian brave-woman character: Sorfarina, who, as Jack Zipes describes her, "serves as the model of the 'emancipated woman'" (xxiii). A notable plot coincidence is the way in which both of them use a honey-filled doll to sweeten up their recently married husbands and thus avoid a certain death. As was the case with Mason's informants, Ortiz Cofer had heard anecdotes about María Sabida and other popular folk stories from her maternal grandmother, who had a reputation as an outstanding storyteller in the small town of Hormigueros on the western coast of the island.

CHAPTER 1 — JÍBARO READAPTATIONS OF FAIRY TALES

1. Published as "Blanca Nieves," *Journal of American Folklore* 38, no. 150 (1925): 517–519.

2. Published as "Blanca Nieves," *Journal of American Folklore* 38, no. 150 (1925): 520–521.

3. Published as "Blanca Flor," *Journal of American Folklore* 38, no. 150 (1925): 522–524.

4. Published as "La Cenicienta," *Journal of American Folklore* 38, no. 150 (1925): 511–512.

5. Published as "La Cenizosa," *Journal of American Folklore* 38, no. 150 (1925): 512–513.

6. Published as "La Cenizosa," *Journal of American Folklore* 38, no. 150 (1925): 513–515.

CHAPTER 2 — RESCUING ENCANTADOS

1. Published as "El príncipe clavel," *Journal of American Folklore* 38, no. 150 (1925): 610–611.

2. Forma coloquial de *sudado*.

3. Published as "El Príncipe Becerro," *Journal of American Folklore* 38, no. 150 (1925): 607–608.

4. Published as "El príncipe encantado," *Journal of American Folklore* 38, no. 150 (1925): 608–610.

5. Published as "Los siete cuervos," *Journal of American Folklore* 38, no. 150 (1925):565–566.

6. Published as "El caballo misterioso," *Journal of American Folklore* 38, no. 150 (1925): 591–592.

7. Published as "El caballito," *Journal of American Folklore* 38, no. 150 (1925): 593–594.

8. Published as "El padre y los tres hijos," *Journal of American Folklore* 38, no. 150 (1925): 588–591.

9. Published as "El caballo de los siete colores," *Journal of American Folklore* 38, no. 150 (1925): 582–583.

CHAPTER 3 — FANTASTIC AND IMPOSSIBLE QUESTS

1. Published as "La flor del olivar," *Journal of American Folklore* 38, no. 150 (1925): 548–550.

2. Published as "La joven y la serpiente," *Journal of American Folklore* 38, no. 150 (1925): 538–539.

3. Published as "Los tres trajes," *Journal of American Folklore* 38, no. 150 (1925): 572–574.

CHAPTER 4 — JUAN BOBO

1. Published as "Juan manda la cerda a misa (c)," *Journal of American Folklore* 34, no. 132 (April–June 1921): 148.

2. Published as "Juan mata la vaca (4)," *Journal of American Folklore* 34, no. 132 (April–June 1921): 150–152.

3. Published as "Juan se muere cuando el burro menea la cola (versión b)," *Journal of American Folklore* 34, no. 132 (April–June 1921): 176.

4. Published as "Juan y los objetos mágicos (versión a)," *Journal of American Folklore* 35, no. 135 (January–March 1922): 3.

5. Published as "La olla que calienta el agua sin fuego (39)," *Journal of American Folklore* 34, no. 132 (April–June 1921): 177–178.

6. Published as "El conejo que llama a su amo (38)," *Journal of American Folklore* 34, no. 132 (April–June 1921): 176–177.

7. Published as "El pito que resucita (40)," *Journal of American Folklore* 34, no. 132 (April–June 1921): 178.

8. Una palabra cariñosa para las madres común en los jíbaros.

9. Published as "Juan y los ladrones (56)," *Journal of American Folklore* 34, no. 132 (April–June 1921): 198–201.

CHAPTER 5 — BEWARE OF STRANGERS

1. Published as "Los niños perdidos," *Journal of American Folklore* 38, no. 150 (October–December 1925): 594–595.

2. Published as "Los niños huérfanos," *Journal of American Folklore* 38, no. 150 (October–December 1925): 599.

3. Published as "Los niños huérfanos," *Journal of American Folklore* 38, no. 150 (October–December 1925): 598.

4. Published as "La mata de ají," *Journal of American Folklore* 38, no. 150 (October–December 1925): 557–558.

CHAPTER 6 — EL PIRATA COFRESÍ

1. Published as "51. Cofresí," *Journal of American Folklore* 42, no. 164 (April–June 1929): 93–94.

2. Published as "44. Cofresí," *Journal of American Folklore* 42, no. 164 (April–June 1929): 85–89.

3. Expresión coloquial entre los jíbaros para compadre.

4. Published as "46. Cofresí," *Journal of American Folklore* 42, no. 164 (April–June 1929): 90.

5. Published as "50. Cofresí," *Journal of American Folklore* 42, no. 164 (April–June 1929): 92–93.

6. Published as "56. Contreras," *Journal of American Folklore* 42, no. 164 (April–June 1929): 96–97.

CHAPTER 7 — BRIEF STORIES AND ANECDOTES

1. Published as "Dios, el rico y el pobre," *Journal of American Folklore* 37: 145–146 (July–December 1924): 270.

2. Published as "El carbonero," *Journal of American Folklore* 37: 145–146 (July–December 1924): 325.

3. Published as "La mala esposa," *Journal of American Folklore* 37: 145–146 (July–December 1924): 306.

4. Published as "La vieja miserable," *Journal of American Folklore* 37: 145–146 (July–December 1924): 307.

5. Published as "Juan sabe más que el rey," *Journal of American Folklore* 37: 145–146 (July–December 1924): 288–289.

6. El moralón es un árbol de gran crecimiento que llega a medir hasta setenta pies, de madera dura, utilizada en las construcción de muebles ("Moralón," Árboles Nativos para la Naturaleza, consultado el 24 de noviembre de 2020, http://arbolesnativos.paralanaturaleza.org/arbol/moralon/).

7. The moralón is a tall hardwood tree, capable of reaching a height of seventy feet, used for making furniture ("Moralón," Árboles Nativos para la Naturaleza, accessed November 24, 2020, http://arbolesnativos.paralanaturaleza.org/arbol/moralon/).

8. Published as "Juanito," *Journal of American Folklore* 37: 145–146 (July–December 1924): 261–262.

9. Published as "La Cucarachita Martina," *Journal of American Folklore* 40, no. 158 (October–December 1927): 340.

10. Published as "La arañita y el Ratoncito Pérez," *Journal of American Folklore* 40, no. 158 (October–December 1927): 339.

Works Cited

Acevedo-Feliciano, Arí, and Tom Wrenn. *Juan Bobo Sends the Pig to Mass*. Atlanta: August House Story Cove, 2008.

Alicea Ortega, Luz Milagros. *La formación de la clase obrera en Puerto Rico: Aproximación teórica-metodológica (1815–1910)*. Puerto Rico: First Book Publishing of Puerto Rico, 2002.

Baatz, Simon. *Knowledge, Culture, and Science in the Metropolis: The New York Academy of Sciences 1817–1970*. New York: New York Academy of Sciences, 1990.

Bernier-Grand, Carmen T. *Juan Bobo: Four Folktales from Puerto Rico*. New York: HarperCollins, 1994.

Boas, Franz. "The Anthropometry of Porto Rico." *American Journal of Physical Anthropology* 3, no. 2 (1920): 247–253.

———. "The Development of Folk-Tales and Myths." In *Race, Language, and Culture*. New York: MacMillan, 1940. 397–406.

Boggs, Ralph S. "Seven Folktales from Porto Rico." *Journal of American Folklore* 42, no. 164 (1929): 157–166.

Chardiet, Bernice. *Juan Bobo and the Pig: A Puerto Rican Folktale Retold*. New York: Walker, 1973.

Elswit, Sharon Barcan. *The Latin American Story Finder: A Guide to 470 Tales from Mexico, Central America and South America, Listing Subjects and Sources*. Jefferson, N.C.: McFarland, 2015.

Espinosa, Aurelio M. "La ciencia del folklore." *Archivos del Folklore* 3, no. 4 (1929): 3–16.

———. *Cuentos populares españoles recogidos de la tradición oral de España y publicados con una introducción y notas comparativas*. New York: AMS Press, 1967.

Fermín Pérez, Juan J. "Prólogo a esta edición." In *Saturnino Calleja: Cuentos de Calleja*, by Saturnino Calleja. Madrid: Ediciones Negras, 2018. 9–15.

Fernández de Córdoba y Calleja, Enrique. *Saturnino Calleja y su editorial: Los cuentos de Calleja*. Madrid: Ediciones de la Torre, 2006.

Figueroa Colón, Julio C. "Introduction." In *The Scientific Survey of Puerto Rico and the Virgin Islands: An Eighty-Year Reassessment of the Island's Natural History*, edited by Julio Figueroa Colón. New York: New York Academy of Sciences, 1996. vii–viii.

Jacobson, Matthew Frye. *Whiteness of a Different Color: European Immigrants and the Alchemy of Race*. Cambridge, Mass.: Harvard University Press, 1998.

Mason, John Alden. *Folklore puertorriqueño: Adivinanzas*. San Juan: Instituto de Cultura Puertorriqueña, 1960.

Mason, John Alden, and Aurelio M. Espinosa. "Introductory Remarks." *Journal of American Folklore* 34, no. 132 (April–June 1921): 143–144.

McCarthy, William Bernard. "Juan Bobo and the Riddling Princess: A Puerto Rican Folktale." *Marvels & Tales* 19, no. 2 (2005): 295–302.

Miyares González, Fernando. *Noticias particulares de la Isla y Plaza de San Juan Bautista de Puerto Rico*. Río Piedras: Ediciones de la Universidad de Puerto Rico, 1957.

Ortiz Lugo, Julia Cristina. "La cenicienta criolla." *Miradero* 2 (January–June 2010): 1–9.

Schomp, Virginia. *Juan Bobo and the Bag of Gold*. New York: Cavendish Square, 2014.

Stocking, George W., Jr. "Introduction." In *The Shaping of American Anthropology, 1883–1911: A Franz Boas Reader*, edited by George W. Stocking Jr. New York: Basic Books, 1974. 1–20.

Vélez-Ibáñez, Carlos G., Phillip B. (Felipe) Gonzales, Luis F. B. Plascencia, and Jesús Rosales. "Interrogating the Ethnogenesis of the Spanish and Mexican 'Other': The Literary Work of Aurelio M. Espinosa." *Aztlán: A Journal of Chicano Studies* 44, no. 2 (Fall 2019): 41–76.

Zipes, Jack. *Beautiful Angiola: The Great Treasury of Sicilian Folk and Fairy Tales Collected by Laura Gozenbach*. New York: Routledge, 2004.

Zumwalt, Rosemary Lévy. *American Folklore Scholarship: A Dialogue of Dissent*. Bloomington: Indiana University Press, 1988.

Index to the Introduction

About the Author

RAFAEL OCASIO is the Charles A. Dana Professor of Spanish at Agnes Scott College, Decatur, Georgia, near Atlanta. He teaches upper-level courses on Latin American literature and film as well as Spanish-language courses, and he is the author of two books on dissident writer Reinaldo Arenas: *Cuba's Political and Sexual Outlaw* (2003) and *A Gay Cuban Activist in Exile* (2007). His other books include *Literature of Latin America* (2004), *Afro-Cuban Costumbrismo: From Plantations to the Slums* (2012), *A Bristol, Rhode Island, and Matanzas, Cuba, Slavery Connection: The Diary of George Howe* (2019), and *Race and Nation in Puerto Rican Folklore: Franz Boas and John Alden Mason in Porto Rico* (2020).

Available titles in the Critical Caribbean Studies series:

Printed and bound by CPI Group (UK) Ltd, Croydon, CR0 4YY

13/04/2025

14656547-0004